Edition

VOLUME 1

# North

AND

# South

CRIMSON
ROMANCE

F+W Media, Inc.

This edition published by
Crimson Romance
an imprint of F+W Media, Inc.
10151 Carver Road, Suite 200
Blue Ash, Ohio 45242
*www.crimsonromance.com*

ISBN 10: 1-4405-7016-7
ISBN 13: 978-1-4405-7016-2
eISBN 10: 1-4405-7017-5
eISBN 13: 978-1-4405-7017-9

*Dedicated to my wonderful husband and daughters, with thanks for your love and support. Many thanks to my dear friends, to Marga, for your patient reading and encouragement, and to Tonianne, for urging me to watch the movie.*

*I would also like to thank Jennifer Lawler and Crimson Romance for giving me the opportunity to adapt this wonderful, passionate novel for this line.*

# CHAPTER I—"HASTE TO THE WEDDING"

"Wooed and married and a'."

"Edith!" said Margaret, gently, "Edith!"

But, as Margaret half suspected, Edith had fallen asleep. She lay curled up on the sofa in the back drawing-room in Harley Street, looking very lovely in her white muslin and blue ribbons. If Titania had ever been dressed in white muslin and blue ribbons, and had fallen asleep on a crimson damask sofa in a back drawing-room, Edith might have been taken for her. Margaret was struck afresh by her cousin's beauty. They had grown up together from childhood, and all along Edith had been remarked upon by every one, except Margaret, for her prettiness; but Margaret had never thought about it until the last few days, when the prospect of soon losing her companion seemed to give force to every sweet quality and charm which Edith possessed. They had been talking about wedding dresses, and wedding ceremonies; and Captain Lennox, and what he had told Edith about her future life at Corfu, where his regiment was stationed; and the difficulty of keeping a piano in good tune (a difficulty which Edith seemed to consider as one of the most formidable that could befall her in her married life), and what gowns she should want in the visits to Scotland, which would immediately succeed her marriage; but the whispered tone had latterly become more drowsy; and Margaret, after a pause of a few minutes, found, as she fancied, that in spite of the buzz in the next room, Edith had rolled herself up into a soft ball of muslin and ribbon, and silken curls, and gone off into a peaceful little after-dinner nap.

Margaret had been on the point of telling her cousin of some of the plans and visions which she entertained as to her future life in the country parsonage, where her father and mother lived; and where her bright holidays had always been passed, though for the last ten years her Aunt Shaw's house had been considered as her home. But in default of a listener, she had to brood over the change in her life silently as heretofore. It was a happy brooding, although tinged with regret at being separated for an indefinite time from her gentle aunt and dear cousin. As she thought of the delight of filling the important post of only daughter in Helstone parsonage, pieces of the conversation out of the next room came upon her ears. Her Aunt Shaw was talking to the five or six ladies who had been dining there, and whose husbands were still in the dining-room. They were the familiar acquaintances of the house; neighbours whom Mrs. Shaw called friends, because she happened to dine with them more frequently than with any other people, and because if she or Edith wanted anything from them, or they from her, they did not scruple to make a call at each other's houses before luncheon. These ladies and their husbands were invited, in their capacity of friends, to eat a farewell dinner in honour of Edith's approaching marriage. Edith had rather objected to this arrangement, for Captain Lennox was expected to arrive by a late train this very evening; but, although she was a spoiled child, she was too careless and idle to have a very strong will of her own, and gave way when she found that her mother had absolutely ordered those extra delicacies of the season which are always supposed to be efficacious against immoderate grief at farewell dinners. She contented herself by leaning back in her chair, merely playing with the food on her plate, and looking grave and absent; while all around her were enjoying the mots of Mr. Grey, the gentleman who always took the bottom of the table at Mrs. Shaw's dinner parties, and asked Edith to give them some music in the drawing-room. Mr. Grey was particularly agreeable over this farewell dinner, and the gentlemen staid down stairs longer than usual. It was very well they did—to judge from the fragments of conversation, which Margaret overheard.

"I suffered too much myself; not that I was not extremely happy with the poor dear General, but still disparity of age is a drawback; one that I was resolved Edith should not have to encounter. Of course, without any maternal partiality, I foresaw that the dear child was likely to marry early; indeed, I had often said that I was sure she would be married before she was nineteen. I had quite a prophetic feeling when Captain Lennox"—and here the voice dropped into a whisper, but Margaret could easily supply the blank. The course of true love in Edith's case had run remarkably smooth. Mrs. Shaw had given way to the presentiment, as she expressed it; and had rather urged on the marriage, although it was below the expectations, which many of Edith's acquaintances had formed for her, a young and pretty heiress. But Mrs. Shaw said that her only child should marry for love,—and sighed emphatically, as if love had not been her motive for marrying the General. She had encouraged Margaret to do the same: to marry for love. Margaret remembered the conversation well:

"Marry a man you can love as well as respect and admire. Money alone cannot fill the cold places in your heart." Then to both Margaret and Edith's surprise, she had added, "And when you do find someone, do not wait for your wedding nights. Remember: one does not purchase a pair of gloves without trying it on."

And as if that had not been enough to make both girls blush, she had described in a matter-of-fact way what went on in the bedroom between husband and wife, so that they should not be surprised, as she had been on her own wedding night. Edith had recently confessed to Margaret that she had taken her mother's advice. In fact, what Margaret did not know was that Edith was not actually sleeping, but enjoying the rather delightful memory of that event.

They had gone to the Blanchard's one evening for a ball, and Edith had danced several times, mostly with Captain Lennox, to whom she was newly affianced. She whirled round in his arms during one of the waltzes played, thankful that she knew the steps by heart, for his nearness had its usual unsettling effect upon her. The touch of his hands, even through gloves, made her pulse race. This led her to imagine how his hands would feel on her skin, and caused her to miss a beat. Then she wondered how his body looked out of his clothes, and how it would feel to run her hands over his tall, lean form. It did not help matters much that she had been thinking of doing as her mamma had suggested. She wondered what he would think of that if she told him.

"I'm going out for a bit of fresh air," Captain Lennox murmured, his mouth close to her ear, causing little goose bumps to work their way down Edith's spine. "Would you care to join me?"

Edith glanced around. The dance had ended. "I'd love to."

He led her out onto one of the balconies on the back of the house. The moon drifted behind a cloud, casting them in shadow. Edith breathed in the cool air and slowly regained her composure. She looked at Captain Lennox, who stood beside her, his hand on the rail next to hers.

"Thank you. It's lovely out here."

"I had an ulterior motive," he admitted, as the strains of another waltz drifted out to them. He held out his hand. "Dance with me."

"Delighted, Captain Lennox," Edith said, taking on the coquettish voice of several of her contemporaries inside.

He took her hand and drew her flush against his body and all thoughts of light flirtation fled. Edith stiffened in shock at first, but relaxed into him as if he had held her thusly many times before. He was lean and hard, and her pulse began to race faster than before as they moved in time to the music. If she had been unable to concentrate earlier, this was worse. And better. How good he felt! But she could barely breathe, and she trembled and tingled from head to foot. Her breasts ached and between her thighs she felt dampness form. Edith looked up at Captain Lennox as she felt something rigid between them. He smiled, but it was strained, and she wondered what was wrong.

Before she could ask, Captain Lennox danced them over next to the side of the house. He bent his head, his mouth claiming hers with soft, gentle brushes of lips. Edith's hands moved over his shoulders, at last touching him as she had longed to do. Her hands slipped up next to the back of his neck, where she caressed the taut muscles. Captain Lennox groaned and increased the pressure of his mouth on hers, his tongue darting against the seam of her lips. Edith parted them on a gasp and it swept in to stroke her palate, slide over her teeth, twine with and suckle her own.

He jerked away from her at the sound of her mother calling her name. She watched his throat work up and down and his hands tighten into fists.

"I'm not angry, Edith," he assured her. "I nearly lost control. If it weren't for your mother I don't know what I'd have done."

"Lost control?"

Captain Lennox stepped closer. "I want to make love with you, dearest."

"So do I. I mean I want to make love with you, as well," she whispered. Edith's mind raced. She wanted to be with him, now, this instant. "Come to my house later on. I'll let you inside."

They had parted reluctantly, but a few hours later, Captain Lennox followed Edith as she let him in the house, a finger over her lips, unnecessarily warning him to be as quiet as possible, and led him up to her room. She locked the door and moved back around to face him. With shaky fingers, she unfastened and let her nightgown slide to the floor. Captain Lennox let his gaze travel over her body as he removed his own clothing.

"You're beautiful, Edith."

"I was going to say the same of you," she whispered.

He reached for her, and Edith eagerly pulled him close. His kiss was more insistent than before, hot and ravaging, his tongue plunging in and out of her mouth while his hands roamed over her bare skin, setting trails of fire across her skin. One squeezed in between them and found a breast. He palmed it, brushed the tight bud of her nipple until she whimpered. Each thrust of his tongue, each caress, made Edith's core ache, and soon she was drenched with need, longing to feel his rigid length inside her.

Captain Lennox manoeuvred her back to the bed and soon she was sprawled upon it, her legs hanging off the side. He knelt between them, his hands and fingers tickling her as he spread her nether lips apart. But her soft laughter died as she felt his tongue slowly swipe over her flesh again and again until she could do little more than mewl in pleasure. And just when she thought she could not feel anything more wonderful, heat exploded inside her.

Limp and replete, she moved further onto the bed, Captain Lennox following. He settled between her thighs and she felt the press of him against her wet and still sensitive opening before he pushed into her. Edith stiffened in pain and clutched at him, gasping as she tried not to cry out. But when he kissed her and began to move, Edith wound her arms around him as the wonderful friction wiped away all traces of discomfort. Her body followed his lead, and soon she raised her hips and wrapped her legs around him, drawing him farther inside.

Captain Lennox leaned back on his heels and his fingers caressed the spot his tongue had moments before, the one that had driven her wild. Edith tumbled over the edge, moaning, her hands fisting her bed sheets, her hips rising frantically to meet him. Abruptly he withdrew and spilled his seed on her belly, only to collapse over her. He smiled and kissed her tenderly, whispering words of love. At last when he raised his head, Edith said, "That was wonderful! Can we do it again soon?"

He brushed her lips with another kiss. "As often as you like."

He had stayed a while after that, but dressed and let Edith lead him from her room and out the door before the servants stirred.

She had told Margaret all of that, as much as she dared, at least. Her cousin had not seemed scandalised, which Edith was glad of, for she hoped one day Margaret would know such rapture in a man's arms. And with that happy thought, Edith did indeed fall asleep.

But Margaret had no plans to "try on" any man. She had never met anyone to whom she could give her heart, let alone her body. Still, she was happy for her cousin, for her coming marriage. Her aunt was even more ecstatic. Mrs. Shaw enjoyed the romance of the present engagement rather more than her daughter. Not but that Edith was very thoroughly and properly in love; still she would certainly have preferred a good house in Belgravia, to all the picturesqueness of the life, which Captain Lennox described at Corfu. The very parts which made Margaret glow as she listened, Edith pretended to shiver and shudder at; partly for the pleasure she had in being coaxed out of her dislike by her fond lover, and partly because anything of a gipsy or make-shift life was really distasteful to her. Yet had any one come with a fine house, and a fine estate, and a fine title to boot, Edith would still have clung to Captain Lennox while the temptation lasted; when it was over, it is possible she might have had little qualms of ill-concealed regret that Captain Lennox could not have united in his person everything that was desirable. In this she was but her mother's child; who, after deliberately marrying General Shaw with no warmer feeling than respect for his character and establishment, was constantly, though quietly, bemoaning her hard lot in being united to one whom she could not love.

"I have spared no expense in her trousseau," were the next words Margaret heard.

"She has all the beautiful Indian shawls and scarfs the General gave to me, but which I shall never wear again."

"She is a lucky girl," replied another voice, which Margaret knew to be that of Mrs. Gibson, a lady who was taking a double interest in the conversation, from the fact of one of her daughters having been married within the last few weeks.

"Helen had set her heart upon an Indian shawl, but really when I found what an extravagant price was asked, I was obliged to refuse her. She will be quite envious when she hears of Edith having Indian shawls. What kind are they? Delhi? With the lovely little borders?"

Margaret heard her aunt's voice again, but this time it was as if she had raised herself up from her half-recumbent position, and were looking into the more dimly lighted back drawing-room. "Edith! Edith!" cried she; and then she sank as if wearied by the exertion. Margaret stepped forward.

"Edith is asleep, Aunt Shaw. Is it anything I can do?"

All the ladies said "Poor child!" on receiving this distressing intelligence about Edith; and the minute lap-dog in Mrs. Shaw's arms began to bark, as if excited by the burst of pity.

"Hush, Tiny! You naughty little girl! You will waken your mistress. It was only to ask Edith if she would tell Newton to bring down her shawls: perhaps you would go, Margaret dear?"

Margaret went up into the old nursery at the very top of the house, where Newton was busy getting up some laces, which were required for the wedding. While Newton went (not without a muttered grumbling) to undo the shawls, which had already been exhibited four or five times that day, Margaret looked round upon the nursery; the first room in that house with which she had become familiar nine years ago, when she was brought, all untamed from the forest, to share the home, the play, and the lessons of her cousin Edith. She remembered the dark, dim look of the London nursery, presided over by an austere and ceremonious nurse, who was terribly particular about clean hands and torn frocks. She recollected the first tea up there—separate from her father and aunt, who were dining somewhere down below an infinite depth of stairs; for unless she were up in the sky (the child thought), they must be deep down in the bowels of the earth. At home—before she came to live in Harley Street—her mother's dressing-room had been her nursery; and, as they kept early hours in the country parsonage, Margaret had always had her meals with her father and mother. Oh! Well did the tall stately girl of eighteen remember the tears shed with such wild passion of grief by the little girl of nine, as she hid her face under the bed-clothes, in that first night; and how she was bidden not to cry by the nurse, because it would disturb Miss Edith; and how she had cried as bitterly, but more quietly, till her newly-seen, grand, pretty aunt had come softly upstairs with Mr. Hale to show him his little sleeping daughter. Then the little Margaret had hushed her sobs, and tried to lie quiet as if asleep, for fear of making her father unhappy by her grief, which she dared not express before her aunt, and which she rather thought it was wrong to feel at all after the long hoping, and planning, and contriving they had gone through at home, before her wardrobe could be arranged so as to suit her grander circumstances, and before papa could leave his parish to come up to London, even for a few days.

Now she had got to love the old nursery, though it was but a dismantled place; and she looked all round, with a kind of cat-like regret, at the idea of leaving it for ever in three days.

"Ah Newton!" said she, "I think we shall all be sorry to leave this dear old room."

"Indeed, miss, I shan't for one. My eyes are not so good as they were, and the light here is so bad that I can't see to mend laces except just at the window, where there's always a shocking draught—enough to give one one's death of cold."

"Well, I dare say you will have both good light and plenty of warmth at Naples. You must keep as much of your darning as you can till then. Thank you, Newton, I can take them down—you're busy."

So Margaret went down laden with shawls, and snuffing up their spicy Eastern smell. Her aunt asked her to stand as a sort of lay figure on which to display them, as Edith was still asleep. No one thought about it; but Margaret's tall, finely made figure, in the black silk dress which she was wearing as mourning for some distant relative of her father's, set off the long beautiful folds of the gorgeous shawls that would have half-smothered Edith. Margaret stood right under the chandelier, quite silent and passive, while her aunt adjusted the draperies. Occasionally, as she was turned round, she caught a glimpse of herself in the mirror over the chimney-piece, and smiled at her own appearance there—the familiar features in the usual garb of a princess. She touched the shawls gently as they hung around her, and took a pleasure in their soft feel and their brilliant colours, and rather liked to be dressed in such splendour—enjoying it much as a child would do, with a quiet pleased smile on her lips. Just then the door opened, and Mr. Henry Lennox was suddenly announced. Some of the ladies started back, as if half-ashamed of their feminine interest in dress. Mrs. Shaw held out her hand to the new-comer; Margaret stood perfectly still, thinking she might be yet wanted as a sort of block for the shawls; but looking at Mr. Lennox with a bright, amused face, as if sure of his sympathy in her sense of the ludicrousness at being thus surprised.

Her aunt was so much absorbed in asking Mr. Henry Lennox—who had not been able to come to dinner—all sorts of questions about his brother the bridegroom, his sister the bridesmaid (coming with the Captain from Scotland for the occasion), and various other members of the Lennox family, that Margaret saw she was no more wanted as shawl-bearer, and devoted herself to the amusement of the other visitors, whom her aunt had for the moment forgotten. Almost immediately, Edith came in from the back drawing-room, winking and blinking her eyes at the stronger light, shaking back her slightly-ruffled curls, and altogether looking like the Sleeping Beauty just startled from her dreams. Even in her slumber she had instinctively felt that a Lennox was worth rousing herself for; and she had a multitude of questions to ask about dear Janet, the future, unseen sister-in-law, for whom she professed so much affection, that if Margaret had not been very proud she might have almost felt jealous of the mushroom rival. As Margaret sank rather more into the background on her aunt's joining the conversation, she saw Henry Lennox directing his look towards a vacant seat near her; and she knew perfectly well that as soon as Edith released him from her questioning, he would take possession of that chair. She had not been quite sure, from her aunt's rather confused account of his engagements, whether he would come that night; it was almost a surprise to see him; and now she was sure of a pleasant evening. He liked and disliked pretty nearly the same things that she did. Margaret's face was lightened up into an honest, open brightness. By-and-by he came. She received him with a smile that had not a tinge of shyness or self-consciousness in it.

"Well, I suppose you are all in the depths of business—ladies' business, I mean. Very different to my business, which is the real true law business. Playing with shawls is very different work to drawing up settlements."

"Ah, I knew how you would be amused to find us all so occupied in admiring finery. But really Indian shawls are very perfect things of their kind."

"I have no doubt they are. Their prices are very perfect, too. Nothing wanting." The gentlemen came dropping in one by one, and the buzz and noise deepened in tone.

"This is your last dinner-party, is it not? There are no more before Thursday?"

"No. I think after this evening we shall feel at rest, which I am sure I have not done for many weeks; at least, that kind of rest when the hands have nothing more to do, and all the arrangements are complete for an event which must occupy one's head and heart. I shall be glad to have time to think, and I am sure Edith will."

"I am not so sure about her; but I can fancy that you will. Whenever I have seen you lately, you have been carried away by a whirlwind of some other person's making."

"Yes," said Margaret, rather sadly, remembering the never-ending commotion about trifles that had been going on for more than a month past: "I wonder if a marriage must always be preceded by what you call a whirlwind, or whether in some cases there might not rather be a calm and peaceful time just before it."

"Cinderella's godmother ordering the trousseau, the wedding-breakfast, writing the notes of invitation, for instance," said Mr. Lennox, laughing.

"But are all these quite necessary troubles?" asked Margaret, looking up straight at him for an answer. A sense of indescribable weariness of all the arrangements for a pretty effect, in which Edith had been busied as supreme authority for the last six weeks, oppressed her just now; and she really wanted some one to help her to a few pleasant, quiet ideas connected with a marriage.

"Oh, of course," he replied with a change to gravity in his tone. "There are forms and ceremonies to be gone through, not so much to satisfy oneself, as to stop the world's mouth, without which stoppage there would be very little satisfaction in life. But how would you have a wedding arranged?"

"Oh, I have never thought much about it; only I should like it to be a very fine summer morning; and I should like to walk to church through the shade of trees; and not to have so many bridesmaids, and to have no wedding-breakfast. I dare say I am resolving against the very things that have given me the most trouble just now."

"No, I don't think you are. The idea of stately simplicity accords well with your character."

Margaret did not quite like this speech; she winced away from it more, from remembering former occasions on which he had tried to lead her into a discussion (in which he took the complimentary part) about her own character and ways of going on. She cut his speech rather short by saying:

"It is natural for me to think of Helstone church, and the walk to it, rather than of driving up to a London church in the middle of a paved street."

"Tell me about Helstone. You have never described it to me. I should like to have some idea of the place you will be living in, when ninety-six Harley Street will be looking dingy and dirty, and dull, and shut up. Is Helstone a village, or a town, in the first place?"

"Oh, only a hamlet; I don't think I could call it a village at all. There is the church and a few houses near it on the green—cottages, rather—with roses growing all over them."

"And flowering all the year round, especially at Christmas—make your picture complete," said he.

"No," replied Margaret, somewhat annoyed, "I am not making a picture. I am trying to describe Helstone as it really is. You should not have said that."

"I am penitent," he answered. "Only it really sounded like a village in a tale rather than in real life."

"And so it is," replied Margaret, eagerly. "All the other places in England that I have seen seem so hard and prosaic-looking, after the New Forest. Helstone is like a village in a poem—in one of Tennyson's poems. But I won't try and describe it any more. You would only laugh at me if I told you what I think of it—what it really is."

"Indeed, I would not. But I see you are going to be very resolved. Well, then, tell me that which I should like still better to know what the parsonage is like."

"Oh, I can't describe my home. It is home, and I can't put its charm into words."

"I submit. You are rather severe to-night, Margaret."

"How?" said she, turning her large soft eyes round full upon him. "I did not know I was."

"Why, because I made an unlucky remark, you will neither tell me what Helstone is like, nor will you say anything about your home, though I have told you how much I want to hear about both, the latter especially."

"But indeed I cannot tell you about my own home. I don't quite think it is a thing to be talked about, unless you knew it."

"Well, then"—pausing for a moment—"tell me what you do there. Here you read, or have lessons, or otherwise improve your mind, till the middle of the day; take a walk before lunch, go a drive with your aunt after, and have some kind of engagement in the evening. There, now fill up your day at Helstone. Shall you ride, drive, or walk?"

"Walk, decidedly. We have no horse, not even for papa. He walks to the very extremity of his parish. The walks are so beautiful, it would be a shame to drive—almost a shame to ride."

"Shall you garden much? That, I believe, is a proper employment for young ladies in the country."

"I don't know. I am afraid I shan't like such hard work."

"Archery parties—pic-nics—race-balls—hunt-balls?"

"Oh no!" said she, laughing. "Papa's living is very small; and even if we were near such things, I doubt if I should go to them."

"I see, you won't tell me anything. You will only tell me that you are not going to do this and that. Before the vacation ends, I think I shall pay you a call, and see what you really do employ yourself in."

"I hope you will. Then you will see for yourself how beautiful Helstone is. Now I must go. Edith is sitting down to play, and I just know enough of music to turn over the leaves for her; and besides, Aunt Shaw won't like us to talk." Edith played brilliantly. In the middle of the piece the door half-opened, and Edith saw Captain Lennox hesitating whether to come in. She threw down her music, and rushed out of the room, leaving Margaret standing confused and blushing to explain to the astonished guests what vision had shown itself to cause Edith's sudden flight. Captain Lennox had come earlier than was expected; or was it really so late? They looked at their watches, were duly shocked, and took their leave.

Edith drew Captain Lennox away from the foyer and into a nearby corridor. Once away from the view of everyone she threw her arms around his neck.

"You're here!" She studied his face by the light from a nearby sconce as if she had forgotten his warm brown eyes, straight nose, and perfect teeth. He was the handsomest, most gallant man she had ever seen, not to mention an attentive lover. And he was hers, she thought, with no small amount of pride.

"I couldn't stay away. I know I'm early. I hope that's all right?" he said, his voice and eyes teasing.

His arms went round her waist, and he pulled her close. Edith sighed at the feel of his hard muscles against her own soft frame. She trembled, and her nipples pearled as desire began to simmer in her veins. "I've been longing to see you." She peeked around, but no one was nearby. "Quick, let's go in here."

Edith reached behind her for the handle of the door that led into a rarely used room where there was no chance of being disturbed. She pulled Captain Lennox in behind her and shut the door. Moonlight spilled in from the window on the far wall, revealing coverings draped over sofas and chairs. Edith paid it all little heed, turning her attention instead to her fiancé. She had surprised him, she could tell, by her bold action, but he seemed to have recovered sufficiently, for once again he pulled her into his arms.

"Did you miss me, then?" Captain Lennox asked, leaning down toward her.

Head tilted back, she said, "You know I did."

His mouth covered hers, a warm sweep of lips that sent a burst of pleasure through her. He had recently shaved, but his moustache tickled slightly, heightening the sensation. Edith moaned and pressed closer still. Her hands moved once more to caress the back of his neck and tug on his close-cropped hair. Captain Lennox drew back slightly and nipped at her lower lip before sucking it into his mouth. She felt that light caress between her thighs and knew a simple kiss would not be enough. When he released her, she opened her eyes in protest.

His gaze seared her, thrilling her as she beheld the tempered lust in its depths. A kiss would not be enough for him, either.

"I missed you as well," he murmured.

And he bent his head, capturing her mouth again, this time his tongue sweeping inside to mate with hers. Edith's breasts tingled and her nipples hardened further. She ached to have his rough palms cupping them, his thumbs brushing over the tight buds before he took them into his mouth. Just the thought of it sent another answering flare of heat to her nether regions.

"Yes," she sighed as his lips left hers once again.

His mouth travelling down to the base of her throat before moving to nibble at the sensitive flesh beneath her ear, Captain Lennox caught Edith by her buttocks and lifted her up against him. His arousal pressed against the juncture of her thighs while Edith trembled with desire as she imagined him sliding into her, filling her. Heat pooled in her belly and moisture dampened her core.

"I want to feel you inside me again."

His lips stilled near her ear, hot breath ghosting over her skin. "We can't. There's not enough time."

But Edith felt the slide of muslin over her silk stockings, then his hand brushing over them as he pushed her skirts up. She caught the material, bunching her skirts up in her fist. Captain Lennox's fingers eased into her drawers, brushing her thigh, and a tremor swept through her as she realized his target.

His fingers teased her flesh, parting her lips, circling her slick opening. At her whispered plea he pushed a digit up inside her. Her walls tightened and her thighs clenched together to hold him there as Captain Lennox began to slide it out again. But no! She wanted him to move, to feel that glorious friction that brought her such ecstasy. Edith relaxed and stepped further apart, and he pushed another finger inside her. He set a languid rhythm at first, gradually moving faster.

His mouth hovered near her ear again, his voice husky. "I love the way your cunny feels. So hot and tight. I can't wait to be inside you again."

Edith's pulse jolted at the naughty words. Her body moved with him as his touch commanded, thrumming with pleasure. His thumb found the bud of flesh at the apex of her cleft, softly stroking it and driving her mad. She caught at Captain Lennox's arm for support.

"Oh yes!" Edith gasped, just before Captain Lennox's mouth closed over hers again, swallowing the scream that followed with a scorching kiss.

Weak-kneed and breathless, she collapsed against Captain Lennox, but not before she saw him lick his fingers clean. She moaned and closed her eyes as another thrill rushed through her. When she had recovered somewhat she glanced at him. His expression was strained, and his smile tight. "You still need relief."

"I'll be fine," Captain Lennox murmured, bending down to kiss her yet again.

But he did not object when Edith undid his trousers and took his cock into her hand. With faltering strokes, then more sure ones, she moved her barely closed fist up and down his shaft. With a groan, he shoved himself into her hand until they were both panting. It was not long before Captain Lennox gasped her name, jerked, and Edith moaned again as his hot seed spilled over her hand.

She smiled, quite pleased and proud of herself that he had found release at her touch. He grinned back before fumbling for his handkerchief to clean her hand before wiping and tucking himself back into his trousers. Her skirts down and smooth, Edith quickly helped him right his clothing, and a moment later Captain Lennox drew her into a gentle embrace.

"I love you, Edith."

"I love you, too," she whispered. And though they wanted to linger, and make love without rushing, they hurried from the room hand in hand to return to the others.

Margaret, meanwhile, remembering the long absence of Edith and the Captain at another function, as well as Edith's confession, sought to keep her aunt and the remaining guests occupied with wedding talk. Henry added to the conversation, quite enthusiastically for a single man, but Margaret put it down to his happiness for his brother's coming marriage and thought no more of it. She kept up a steady stream of questions and responses, and wished that Edith and Captain Lennox would join them soon. She was just about to give up and go in search of them when she caught movement out of the corner of her eye.

Then Edith came back, glowing with pleasure, half-shyly, half-proudly leading in her tall handsome Captain. His brother shook hands with him, and Mrs. Shaw welcomed him in her gentle kindly way, which had always something plaintive in it, arising from the long habit of considering herself a victim to an uncongenial marriage. Now that, the General being gone, she had every good of life, with as few drawbacks as possible, she had been rather perplexed to find an anxiety, if not a sorrow. She had, however, of late settled upon her own health as a source of apprehension; she had a nervous little cough whenever she thought about it; and some complaisant doctor ordered her just what she desired,—a winter in Italy. Mrs. Shaw had as strong wishes as most people, but she never liked to do anything from the open and acknowledged motive of her own good will and pleasure; she preferred being compelled to gratify herself by some other person's command or desire. She really did persuade herself that she was submitting to some hard external necessity; and thus she was able to moan and complain in her soft manner, all the time she was in reality doing just what she liked.

It was in this way she began to speak of her own journey to Captain Lennox, who assented, as in duty bound, to all his future mother-in-law said, while his eyes sought Edith, who was busying herself in rearranging the tea-table, and ordering up all sorts of good things, in spite of his assurances that he had dined within the last two hours.

Mr. Henry Lennox stood leaning against the chimney-piece, amused with the family scene. He was close by his handsome brother; he was the plain one in a singularly good-looking family; but his face was intelligent, keen, and mobile; and now and then Margaret wondered what it was that he could be thinking about, while he kept silence, but was evidently observing, with an interest that was slightly sarcastic, all that Edith and she were doing. The sarcastic feeling was called out by Mrs. Shaw's conversation with his brother; it was separate from the interest which was excited by what he saw. He thought it a pretty sight to see the two cousins so busy in their little arrangements about the table. Edith chose to do most herself. She was in a humour to enjoy showing her lover how well she could behave as a soldier's wife. She found out that the water in the urn was cold, and ordered up the great kitchen tea-kettle; the only consequence of which was that when she met it at the door, and tried to carry it in, it was too heavy for her, and she came in pouting, with a black mark on her muslin gown, and a little round white hand indented by the handle, which she took to show to Captain Lennox, just like a hurt child, and, of course, the remedy was the same in both cases. Margaret's quickly-adjusted spirit-lamp was the most efficacious contrivance, though not so like the gypsy-encampment which Edith, in some of her moods, chose to consider the nearest resemblance to a barrack-life. After this evening all was bustle till the wedding was over.

# CHAPTER II—ROSES AND THORNS

"By the soft green light in the woody glade,
On the banks of moss where thy childhood played;
By the household tree, thro' which thine eye
First looked in love to the summer sky."
MRS. HEMANS.

Margaret was once more in her morning dress, travelling quietly home with her father, who had come up to assist at the wedding. Her mother had been detained at home by a multitude of half-reasons, none of which anybody fully understood, except Mr. Hale, who was perfectly aware that all his arguments in favour of a grey satin gown, which was midway between oldness and newness, had proved unavailing; and that, as he had not the money to equip his wife afresh, from top to toe, she would not show herself at her only sister's only child's wedding. If Mrs. Shaw had guessed at the real reason why Mrs. Hale did not accompany her husband, she would have showered down gowns upon her; but it was nearly twenty years since Mrs. Shaw had been the poor, pretty Miss Beresford, and she had really forgotten all grievances except that of the unhappiness arising from disparity of age in married life, on which she could descant by the half-hour. Dearest Maria had married the man of her heart, only eight years older than herself, with the sweetest temper, and that blue-black hair one so seldom sees. Mr. Hale was one of the most delightful preachers she had ever heard, and a perfect model of a parish priest. Perhaps it was not quite a logical deduction from all these premises, but it was still Mrs. Shaw's characteristic conclusion, as she thought over her sister's lot: "Married for love, what can dearest Maria have to wish for in this world?" Mrs. Hale, if she spoke truth, might have answered with a ready-made list, "a silver-grey glacé silk, a white chip bonnet, oh! Dozens of things for the wedding, and hundreds of things for the house." Margaret only knew that her mother had not found it convenient to come, and she was not sorry to think that their meeting and greeting would take place at Helstone parsonage, rather than, during the confusion of the last two or three days, in the house in Harley Street, where she herself had had to play the part of Figaro, and was wanted everywhere at one and the same time. Her mind and body ached now with the recollection of all she had done and said within the last forty-eight hours. The farewells so hurriedly taken, amongst all the other good-byes, of those she had lived with so long, oppressed her now with a sad regret for the times that were no more; it did not signify what those times had been, they were gone never to return. Margaret's heart felt more heavy than she could ever have thought it possible in going to her own dear home, the place and the life she had longed for years—at that time of all times for yearning and longing, just before the sharp senses lose their outlines in sleep. She took her mind away with a wrench from the recollection of the past to the bright serene contemplation of the hopeful future. Her eyes began to see, not visions of what had been, but the sight actually before her; her dear father leaning back asleep in the railway carriage. His blue-black hair was grey now, and lay thinly over his brows. The bones of his face were plainly to be seen—too plainly for beauty, if his features had been less finely cut; as it was, they had a grace if not a comeliness of their own. The face was in repose; but it was rather rest after weariness, than the serene calm of the countenance of one who led a placid, contented life. Margaret was painfully struck by the worn, anxious expression; and she went back over the open and avowed circumstances of her father's life, to find the cause for the lines that spoke so plainly of habitual distress and depression.

"Poor Frederick!" thought she, sighing. "Oh! If Frederick had but been a clergyman, instead of going into the navy, and being lost to us all! I wish I knew all about it. I never understood it from Aunt Shaw; I only knew he could not come back to England because of that terrible affair. Poor dear papa! How sad he looks! I am so glad I am going home, to be at hand to comfort him and mamma."

She was ready with a bright smile, in which there was not a trace of fatigue, to greet her father when he awakened. He smiled back again, but faintly, as if it were an unusual exertion. His face returned into its lines of habitual anxiety. He had a trick of half-opening his mouth as if to speak, which constantly unsettled the form of the lips, and gave the face an undecided expression. But he had the same large, soft eyes as his daughter,—eyes which moved slowly and almost grandly round in their orbits, and were well veiled by their transparent white eyelids. Margaret was more like him than like her mother. Sometimes people wondered that parents so handsome should have a daughter who was so far from regularly beautiful; not beautiful at all, was occasionally said. Her mouth was wide; no rosebud that could only open just enough to let out a "yes" and "no," and "an't please you, sir." But the wide mouth was one soft curve of rich red lips; and the skin, if not white and fair, was of an ivory smoothness and delicacy. If the look on her face was, in general, too dignified and reserved for one so young, now, talking to her father, it was bright as the morning,—full of dimples, and glances that spoke of childish gladness, and boundless hope in the future.

It was the latter part of July when Margaret returned home. The forest trees were all one dark, full, dusky green; the fern below them caught all the slanting sunbeams; the weather was sultry and broodingly still. Margaret used to tramp along by her father's side, crushing down the fern with a cruel glee, as she felt it yield under her light foot, and send up the fragrance peculiar to it,—out on the broad commons into the warm scented light, seeing multitudes of wild, free, living creatures, revelling in the sunshine, and the herbs and flowers it called forth. This life— at least these walks—realised all Margaret's anticipations. She took a pride in her forest. Its people were her people. She made hearty friends with them; learned and delighted in using their peculiar words; took up her freedom amongst them; nursed their babies; talked or read with slow distinctness to their old people; carried dainty messes to their sick; resolved before long to teach at the school, where her father went every day as to an appointed task, but she was continually tempted off to go and see some individual friend—man, woman, or child—in some cottage in the green shade of the forest. Her out-of-doors life was perfect. Her in-doors life had its drawbacks. With the healthy shame of a child, she blamed herself for her keenness of sight, in perceiving that all was not as it should be there. Her mother—her mother always so kind and tender towards her—seemed now and then so much discontented with their situation; thought that the bishop strangely neglected his episcopal duties, in not giving Mr. Hale a better living; and almost reproached her husband because he could not bring himself to say that he wished to leave the parish, and undertake the charge of a larger. He would sigh aloud as he answered, that if he could do what he ought in little Helstone, he should be thankful; but every day he was more overpowered; the world became more bewildering. At each repeated urgency of his wife, that he would put himself in the way of seeking some preferment, Margaret saw that her father shrank more and more; and she strove at such times to reconcile her mother to Helstone. Mrs. Hale said that the near neighbourhood of so many trees affected her health; and Margaret would try to tempt her forth on to the beautiful, broad, upland, sun-streaked, cloud-shadowed common; for she was sure that her mother had accustomed herself too much to an in-doors life, seldom extending her walks beyond the church, the school, and the neighbouring cottages. This did good for a time; but when the autumn drew on, and the weather became more changeable, her mother's idea of the unhealthiness of the place increased; and she repined even more frequently that her husband, who was more learned than Mr. Hume, a better parish priest than Mr. Houldsworth, should not have met with the preferment that these two former neighbours of theirs had done.

This marring of the peace of home, by long hours of discontent, was what Margaret was unprepared for. She knew, and had rather revelled in the idea, that she should have to give up many luxuries, which had only been troubles and trammels to her freedom in Harley Street. Her keen enjoyment of every sensuous pleasure, was balanced finely, if not overbalanced, by her conscious pride in being able to do without them all, if need were. But the cloud never comes in that quarter of the horizon from which we watch for it. There had been slight complaints and passing regrets on her mother's part, over some trifle connected with Helstone, and her father's position there, when Margaret had been spending her holidays at home before; but in the general happiness of the recollection of those times, she had forgotten the small details which were not so pleasant. In the latter half of September, the autumnal rains and storms came on, and Margaret was obliged to remain more in the house than she had hitherto done. Helstone was at some distance from any neighbours of their own standard of cultivation.

"It is undoubtedly one of the most out-of-the-way places in England," said Mrs. Hale, in one of her plaintive moods. "I can't help regretting constantly that papa has really no one to associate with here; he is so thrown away; seeing no one but farmers and labourers from week's end to week's end. If we only lived at the other side of the parish, it would be something; there we should be almost within walking distance of the Stansfields; certainly the Gormans would be within a walk."

"Gormans," said Margaret. "Are those the Gormans who made their fortunes in trade at Southampton? Oh! I'm glad we don't visit them. I don't like shoppy people. I think we are far better off, knowing only cottagers and labourers, and people without pretence."

"You must not be so fastidious, Margaret, dear!" said her mother, secretly thinking of a young and handsome Mr. Gorman whom she had once met at Mr. Hume's.

"No! I call mine a very comprehensive taste; I like all people whose occupations have to do with land; I like soldiers and sailors, and the three learned professions, as they call them. I'm sure you don't want me to admire butchers and bakers, and candlestick-makers, do you, mamma?"

"But the Gormans were neither butchers nor bakers, but very respectable coach-builders."

"Very well. Coach-building is a trade all the same, and I think a much more useless one than that of butchers or bakers. Oh! how tired I used to be of the drives every day in Aunt Shaw's carriage, and how I longed to walk!"

And walk Margaret did, in spite of the weather. She was so happy out of doors, at her father's side, that she almost danced; and with the soft violence of the west wind behind her, as she crossed some heath, she seemed to be borne onwards, as lightly and easily as the fallen leaf that was wafted along by the autumnal breeze.

But the evenings were rather difficult to fill up agreeably. Immediately after tea her father withdrew into his small library, and she and her mother were left alone. Mrs. Hale had never cared much for books, and had discouraged her husband, very early in their married life, in his desire of reading aloud to her, while she worked. At one time they had tried backgammon as a resource;

but as Mr. Hale grew to take an increasing interest in his school and his parishioners, he found that the interruptions which arose out of these duties were regarded as hardships by his wife, not to be accepted as the natural conditions of his profession, but to be regretted and struggled against by her as they severally arose. So he withdrew, while the children were yet young, into his library, to spend his evenings (if he were at home), in reading the speculative and metaphysical books which were his delight.

It had not always been so. There was one area in which Richard and Maria Hale were equally enthusiastic in those early years, and that was in sharing the pleasures of the flesh. There had been no separating after tea to pursue their different interests; like all young newlyweds their interest was each other. Mr. Hale did not say so, but he missed those days when a look, a touch, would have them dashing for the bedroom and tearing each other's clothes off. The days they did not make it so far he remembered with even more warmth.

Mrs. Hale was no less saddened by the loss of that closeness, for she too fondly recalled those days when they had been unable to keep their hands off each other. But like her husband, she did not speak of it, learning to be content with her children with each passing month. But, oh, the memories! Mrs. Hale brought them out every now and then to relive them, recalling every detail as if it had just occurred. There was one in particular which brought a blush to her face, and no small amount of pleasant tingles to her body, every time she thought of it.

They had been wed only three months. Dixon had been visiting family, and so they had the house to themselves. It was nearly noon, and Maria was busy in the kitchen preparing luncheon while Richard caught up on correspondence. One of the parishioners had brought a meat pie the day before, and Maria placed thick slices of it on two plates, and blueberries and pears in a bowl. She turned to find Richard watching her from the doorway, his gaze dark with a look that said he was hungry for more than food. Maria's pulse began to race and warmth curled in her belly.

"Why don't we have a pic-nic, Maria?"

"It's raining," she reminded him. "We'd be drenched and the food would be ruined."

"I've spread a blanket on the floor before the hearth." He moved forward and kissed her. "And I've opened a bottle of wine."

Maria smiled. "You planned this."

"Everything but the weather, dear." He searched in the cupboard and retrieved two glasses, setting them on the tray with the rest of the meal. Though they finished their meal quickly, they lingered over dessert, feeding each other pieces of fruit.

"Did you finish your letters?" she asked.

"Yes, quite."

She placed another berry in his mouth. Richard caught her hand as he chewed, and once he had swallowed, said, "Let's see if you taste sweeter than these berries." He brought her hand to his lips and pressed a hot, open-mouthed kiss on the back of it, turned it over and did the same to her palm. Maria's eyes closed and her breath left her in a shudder as he next flicked his tongue lightly across the smooth skin. His fingers now twined with hers, he kissed the inside of her wrist, suckling gently. The hot sensation travelled straight to her breasts, making her nipples pebble, and in her core she felt a tremor of anticipation.

Richard shoved the dishes haphazardly aside and drew her closer with a slight tug. She offered her lips, and he accepted, took control. He leaned back, drawing her with him until she lay sprawled atop his lean body. Maria moaned as her husband removed her cap and worked her hair from its pins. She loved the gentle pull on her scalp as he sifted the strands through his fingers before bunching it in his fists. Between them, the hard ridge of his erection pressed against the delta between her thighs, and Maria wriggled eagerly against him until he groaned and held her still, his hands cupping her bottom.

She raised her head smiled at him. "I can't help it, Richard. You feel so good."

In reply, he went to work on the buttons of her gown. "And I want to feel more of you, darling."

Her husband had become very skilled at undressing her, and she was no less proficient in removing his clothing; it was not long before she was bare and perched above him. She gasped in delight as he suckled at one breast while alternately palming and squeezing the other. His hands gliding downward to her hips, he urged her forward to straddle his face, and the hot slide of his tongue over her nether lips made her grasp the nearest piece of furniture to hold herself upright. For a few delicious moments Maria rode his mouth, but with a soft, "Stop," she shifted, turning round to face his feet.

Her knees once more on either side of Richard's head, she bent down and licked the bead of moisture glistening on his abdomen above his hard length. She loved the taste of him, the feel of him in her mouth. She caught his shaft in one hand and licked the head, swirling her tongue round it before she carefully took him in as much as she could. Richard groaned and his hands tightened on her buttocks, and Maria smiled.

She had quickly learned to please him this way, and now Maria raised her head, letting him slide almost from her mouth before taking him in again. But this time it was not so easy to concentrate on drawing on Richard's thick length, for he lapped at her wet folds, darted his tongue into her, then a finger. He repeated the motions again, and again. Tongue, fingers, in and out, lips suckling the sensitive bud of flesh, driving her closer and closer to the edge of release.

Richard's hips rose gently to meet her now, his hands once again on her hips as he re-doubled his efforts on her overly-sensitized flesh. Light flashed behind her eyelids, and she trembled violently as ecstasy swept over her.

Panting softly for breath now, she sucked harder on his turgid flesh, determined to give him the same pleasure, to feel him shake beneath her. It happened more quickly than she thought it might, for soon after her own release, he shuddered and grunted her name, his fingers digging into her skin. His hot seed filled her mouth a second later, dribbled over her chin as she gasped and swallowed. Maria licked her lips and wiped her face, smiling, as she moved into his waiting arms.

Richard caressed her limbs, her back, kissing her deeply, until her breath grew as ragged as his. She felt his flesh harden once more and nudge her thigh and her own swollen and damp flesh quivered in need. He rolled her over onto her back, entered her at last, and slowly made love to her again until she clutched at him as the world spun away.

Mrs. Hale came back to herself with a start and, her breath coming quickly, glanced guiltily at her daughter. To her relief, Margaret sat at the table, poring intently over a book and paid her no notice. Mrs. Hale pressed her thighs together to relieve the sharp ache, and with a sigh bent her head back to her own work.

When Margaret had been here before, she had brought down with her a great box of books, recommended by masters or governess, and had found the summer's day all too short to get through the reading she had to do before her return to town. Now there were only the well-bound little-read English Classics, which were weeded out of her father's library to fill up the small book-shelves in the drawing-room. Thomson's Seasons, Hayley's Cowper, Middleton's Cicero, were by far the lightest, newest, and most amusing. The book-shelves did not afford much resource. Margaret told her mother every particular of her London life, to all of which Mrs. Hale listened with interest, sometimes amused and questioning, at others a little inclined to compare her sister's circumstances of ease and comfort with the narrower means at Helstone vicarage. On such evenings Margaret was apt to stop talking rather abruptly, and listen to the drip-drip of the rain upon the leads of the little bow-window. Once or twice Margaret found herself mechanically counting the repetition of the monotonous sound, while she wondered if she might venture to put a question on a subject very near to her heart, and ask where Frederick was now; what he was doing; how long it was since they had heard from him. But a consciousness that her mother's delicate health, and positive dislike to Helstone, all dated from the time of the mutiny in which Frederick had been engaged,—the full account of which Margaret had never heard, and which now seemed doomed to be buried in sad oblivion,—made her pause and turn away from the subject each time she approached it. When she was with her mother, her father seemed the best person to apply to for information; and when with him, she thought that she could speak more easily to her mother. Probably there was nothing much to be heard that was new. In one of the letters she had received before leaving Harley Street, her father had told her that they had heard from Frederick; he was still at Rio, and very well in health, and sent his best love to her; which was dry bones, but not the living intelligence she longed for. Frederick was always spoken of, in the rare times when his name was mentioned, as "Poor Frederick." His room was kept exactly as he had left it; and was regularly dusted, and put into order by Dixon, Mrs. Hale's maid, who touched no other part of the household work, but always remembered the day when she had been engaged by Lady Beresford as ladies' maid to Sir John's wards, the pretty Miss Beresfords, the belles of Rutlandshire. Dixon had always considered Mr. Hale as the blight, which had fallen upon her young lady's prospects in life. If Miss Beresford had not been in such a hurry to marry a poor country clergyman, there was no knowing what she might not have become. But Dixon was too loyal to desert her in her affliction and downfall (alias her married life). She remained with her, and was devoted to her interests; always considering herself as the good and protecting fairy, whose duty it was to baffle the malignant giant, Mr. Hale. Master Frederick had been her favourite and pride; and it was with a little softening of her dignified look and manner, that she went in weekly to arrange the chamber as carefully as if he might be coming home that very evening. Margaret could not help believing that there had been some late intelligence of Frederick, unknown to her mother, which was making her father anxious and uneasy. Mrs. Hale did not seem to perceive any alteration in her husband's looks or ways. His spirits were always tender and gentle, readily affected by any small piece of intelligence concerning the welfare of others. He would be depressed for many days after witnessing a death-bed, or hearing of any crime. But now Margaret noticed an absence of mind, as if his thoughts were pre-occupied by some subject, the oppression of which could not be relieved by any daily action, such as comforting the survivors, or teaching at the school in hope of lessening the evils in the generation to come. Mr. Hale did not go out among his parishioners as much as usual; he was more shut up in his study; was anxious for the village postman, whose summons to the house-hold was a rap on the back-kitchen window-shutter—a signal which at one time had often to be repeated before any one was sufficiently alive to the hour of the day to understand what it was, and attend to him. Now Mr. Hale loitered about the garden if the morning was fine, and if not, stood dreamily by the study window until the postman had called, or gone down the lane, giving a half-respectful, half-confidential shake of the head to the parson, who watched him away beyond the sweet-briar hedge, and past the great arbutus, before he turned into the room to begin his day's work, with all the signs of a heavy heart and an occupied mind.

Margaret, meanwhile, continued her walks whenever the weather was fine enough, so that she could sort out what all this meant. It was on one of these that Margaret received an unexpected and quite shocking furtherance of the education Aunt Shaw had given her and Edith. She had decided to go alone, as her father could not be drawn from his study, and she could not bear to be shut up a moment longer in the house on such a pleasant day. It was early yet, not quite time for the noon meal, with a light breeze to counter the warmth of the sun. She walked farther than usual this morning, through one field after another, until she could not see the parsonage at all. Birds flew up from the grasses every now and then as she disturbed their nests. She stopped, turning to watch one as it rose in the air and flew toward the forest, and she decided to walk that way instead, as she had not been near the forest in some time. Margaret came to the tall hedge that bordered the next field and followed it along, searching for a way through, or for the end if she could not. She had just reached a gap in it and was about to pass through when she stopped short and stepped back behind the hawthorn.

She peered around the bush, certain that she had mistaken the scene before her, but she had not. There kneeling on the ground was a man and a woman, both about her age, and they were kissing and clutching at each other. The bodice of the woman's dress hung down around her waist. She wore no corset, only a chemise, and the man's sun-tanned hands were on her breasts, squeezing and cupping them through the material. Her face hot, Margaret took another careful step back to give them privacy, trying not to disturb any branches, but the fringe and part of her shawl had caught on one, and now held her where she was. She stood still, uncertain what to do. If she tried to free herself she might disturb wildlife that would undoubtedly alert them to her presence. But perhaps if she were cautious she could get away without them discovering her presence.

She had just managed to untangle the fringe a bit when a moan drew her attention to the pair once again, and her eyes widened.

Someone had tugged the woman's dress and chemise off. The woman's breasts were larger than her own, pale and pendulous. That much Margaret could see before the man lowered his head and caught one of the woman's nipples in his mouth. His jaws worked, drawing upon it, before moving to its twin.

Margaret's own breasts tightened, and she clapped her hand to her mouth to stop the unbidden gasp that rose to her lips. Her aunt had not spoken of such things, only of penetration, and Margaret watched in curiosity. Did such things often occur, she wondered, and quickly following, how would it feel, to be touched so by a man?

Margaret's nipples hardened and pushed against her chemise and corset, making her tremble. She knew that babes suckled at their mothers' breasts, but that a man would do the same had never occurred to her. But the man did not stop there, for as he drew on her nipples, one of his hands disappeared between the woman's thighs; Margaret could not tell what the man did, but the woman seemed to enjoy it. Her hips undulating, the woman clutched at the man's head, his shoulders. She spoke, but Margaret could not make out the words, everything was so hurried and jumbled together. A moment later the woman cried out loud enough to frighten a squirrel on a nearby tree, and Margaret ducked back behind the bushes a moment, heart beating fast, before she chanced another peek at them.

The man had begun undressing himself, pulling his shirt over his head in one quick movement. He was pale except for his face, neck and forearms, and Margaret could not help but admire his physique, the muscles honed by long hours of farm work, probably. And when he removed his shoes and trousers, Margaret's attention was caught and held by the length of flesh jutting upwards from a thatch of dark hair. She had never seen a naked man before, and more heat rose up her neck as she looked at him. Was that what her aunt had meant by a man being ready for lovemaking? And it fit inside a woman?

Margaret was still trying to work out how such a large instrument might penetrate the woman when she saw something that startled her even further. The woman took the man's penis (Margaret recalled now the word Aunt Shaw had used) into her hand and licked it up and down before taking it in her mouth to the root. Margaret glanced up at the man's face to see his eyes closed as if in some sort of pleasure-pain.

Aunt Shaw had never mentioned this, and Margaret watched in curiosity as the woman looked up at the man as she pulled away from him, until only the head of his shaft was in her mouth. The man reached down, caught the woman's head between his hands, and urged her back with a plea. For her part, the woman clasped his buttocks, drawing him even closer to her.

Margaret tore her gaze away. Her body was reacting strangely: she was warm all over, particularly between her thighs, and she became aware of dampness there. Her fingers trembling, her breath coming in short gasps, she managed to free herself and retreat. When she was far enough from them she turned and half-ran, half-walked, back to the parsonage. She never told anyone that it was more than the crisp autumn air that had brought a rosy hue to her face when it was remarked upon, and she never found out who the couple was, but she stayed away from that area the next time she walked and was grateful when even more rains came and kept her inside, where once again she began to fret over her parents', especially her father's, behaviour.

But Margaret was at an age when any apprehension, not absolutely based on a knowledge of facts, is easily banished for a time by a bright sunny day, or some happy outward circumstance. And when the brilliant fourteen fine days of October came on, her cares were all blown away as lightly as thistledown, and she thought of nothing but the glories of the forest. The fern-harvest was over, and now that the rain was gone, many a deep glade was accessible, into which Margaret had only peeped in July and

August weather. She had learnt drawing with Edith; and she had sufficiently regretted, during the gloom of the bad weather, her idle revelling in the beauty of the woodlands while it had yet been fine, to make her determined to sketch what she could before winter fairly set in. Accordingly, she was busy preparing her board one morning, when Sarah, the housemaid, threw wide open the drawing-room door and announced, "Mr. Henry Lennox."

# CHAPTER III—"THE MORE HASTE THE WORSE SPEED"

"Learn to win a lady's faith
Nobly, as the thing is high;
Bravely, as for life and death—
With a loyal gravity.
Lead her from the festive boards,
Point her to the starry skies,
Guard her, by your truthful words,
Pure from courtship's flatteries."
MRS. BROWNING.

"Mr. Henry Lennox." Margaret had been thinking of him only a moment before, and remembering his inquiry into her probable occupations at home. It was "parler du soleil et l'on en voit les rayons;" and the brightness of the sun came over Margaret's face as she put down her board, and went forward to shake hands with him. "Tell mamma, Sarah," said she. "Mamma and I want to ask you so many questions about Edith; I am so much obliged to you for coming."

"Did not I say that I should?" asked he, in a lower tone than that in which she had spoken.

"But I heard of you so far away in the Highlands that I never thought Hampshire could come in."

"Oh!" said he, more lightly, "our young couple were playing such foolish pranks, running all sorts of risks, climbing this mountain, sailing on that lake, that I really thought they needed a Mentor to take care of them. And indeed they did; they were quite beyond my uncle's management, and kept the old gentleman in a panic for sixteen hours out of the twenty-four. Indeed, when

I once saw how unfit they were to be trusted alone, I thought it my duty not to leave them till I had seen them safely embarked at Plymouth."

"Have you been at Plymouth? Oh! Edith never named that. To be sure, she has written in such a hurry lately. Did they really sail on Tuesday?"

"Really sailed, and relieved me from many responsibilities. Edith gave me all sorts of messages for you. I believe I have a little diminutive note somewhere; yes, here it is."

"Oh! Thank you," exclaimed Margaret; and then, half wishing to read it alone and unwatched, she made the excuse of going to tell her mother again (Sarah surely had made some mistake) that Mr. Lennox was there.

When she had left the room, he began in his scrutinising way to look about him. The little drawing-room was looking its best in the streaming light of the morning sun. The middle window in the bow was opened, and clustering roses and the scarlet honeysuckle came peeping round the corner; the small lawn was gorgeous with verbenas and geraniums of all bright colours. But the very brightness outside made the colours within seem poor and faded. The carpet was far from new; the chintz had been often washed; the whole apartment was smaller and shabbier than he had expected, as back-ground and frame-work for Margaret, herself so queenly. He took up one of the books lying on the table; it was the Paradiso of Dante, in the proper old Italian binding of white vellum and gold; by it lay a dictionary, and some words copied out in Margaret's hand-writing. They were a dull list of words, but somehow he liked looking at them. He put them down with a sigh.

"The living is evidently as small as she said. It seems strange, for the Beresfords belong to a good family."

Margaret meanwhile had found her mother. It was one of Mrs. Hale's fitful days, when everything was a difficulty and a hardship;

and Mr. Lennox's appearance took this shape, although secretly she felt complimented by his thinking it worth while to call.

"It is most unfortunate! We are dining early to-day, and having nothing but cold meat, in order that the servants may get on with their ironing; and yet, of course, we must ask him to dinner—Edith's brother-in-law and all. And your papa is in such low spirits this morning about something—I don't know what. I went into the study just now, and he had his face on the table, covering it with his hands. I told him I was sure Helstone air did not agree with him any more than with me, and he suddenly lifted up his head, and begged me not to speak a word more against Helstone, he could not bear it; if there was one place he loved on earth it was Helstone. But I am sure, for all that, it is the damp and relaxing air."

Margaret felt as if a thin cold cloud had come between her and the sun. She had listened patiently, in hopes that it might be some relief to her mother to unburden herself; but now it was time to draw her back to Mr. Lennox.

"Papa likes Mr. Lennox; they got on together famously at the wedding breakfast. I dare say his coming will do papa good. And never mind the dinner, dear mamma. Cold meat will do capitally for a lunch, which is the light in which Mr. Lennox will most likely look upon a two o'clock dinner."

"But what are we to do with him till then? It is only half-past ten now."

"I'll ask him to go out sketching with me. I know he draws, and that will take him out of your way, mamma. Only do come in now; he will think it so strange if you don't."

Mrs. Hale took off her black silk apron, and smoothed her face. She looked a very pretty lady-like woman, as she greeted Mr. Lennox with the cordiality due to one who was almost a relation. He evidently expected to be asked to spend the day, and accepted the invitation with a glad readiness that made Mrs. Hale wish she could add something to the cold beef. He was pleased with everything; delighted with Margaret's idea of going out sketching together; would not have Mr. Hale disturbed for the world, with the prospect of so soon meeting him at dinner. Margaret brought out her drawing materials for him to choose from; and after the paper and brushes had been duly selected, the two set out in the merriest spirits in the world.

"Now, please, just stop here for a minute or two, said Margaret. "These are the cottages that haunted me so during the rainy fortnight, reproaching me for not having sketched them."

"Before they tumbled down and were no more seen. Truly, if they are to be sketched—and they are very picturesque—we had better not put it off till next year. But where shall we sit?"

"Oh! You might have come straight from chambers in the Temple, instead of having been two months in the Highlands! Look at this beautiful trunk of a tree, which the wood-cutters have left just in the right place for the light. I will put my plaid over it, and it will be a regular forest throne."

"With your feet in that puddle for a regal footstool! Stay, I will move, and then you can come nearer this way. Who lives in these cottages?"

"They were built by squatters fifty or sixty years ago. One is uninhabited; the foresters are going to take it down, as soon as the old man who lives in the other is dead, poor old fellow! Look— there he is—I must go and speak to him. He is so deaf you will hear all our secrets."

The old man stood bareheaded in the sun, leaning on his stick at the front of his cottage. His stiff features relaxed into a slow smile as Margaret went up and spoke to him. Mr. Lennox hastily introduced the two figures into his sketch, and finished up the landscape with a subordinate reference to them—as Margaret perceived, when the time came for getting up, putting away water, and scraps of paper, and exhibiting to each other their sketches. She laughed and blushed: Mr. Lennox watched her countenance.

"Now, I call that treacherous," said she. "I little thought you were making old Isaac and me into subjects, when you told me to ask him the history of these cottages."

"It was irresistible. You can't know how strong a temptation it was. I hardly dare tell you how much I shall like this sketch."

He was not quite sure whether she heard this latter sentence before she went to the brook to wash her palette. She came back rather flushed, but looking perfectly innocent and unconscious. He was glad of it, for the speech had slipped from him unawares—a rare thing in the case of a man who premeditated his actions so much as Henry Lennox.

The aspect of home was all right and bright when they reached it. The clouds on her mother's brow had cleared off under the propitious influence of a brace of carp, most opportunely presented by a neighbour. Mr. Hale had returned from his morning's round, and was awaiting his visitor just outside the wicket gate that led into the garden. He looked a complete gentleman in his rather threadbare coat and well-worn hat.

Margaret was proud of her father; she had always a fresh and tender pride in seeing how favourably he impressed every stranger; still her quick eye sought over his face and found there traces of some unusual disturbance, which was only put aside, not cleared away.

Mr. Hale asked to look at their sketches.

"I think you have made the tints on the thatch too dark, have you not?" as he returned Margaret's to her, and held out his hand for Mr. Lennox's, which was withheld from him one moment, no more.

"No, papa! I don't think I have. The house-leek and stone-crop have grown so much darker in the rain. Is it not like, papa?" said she, peeping over his shoulder, as he looked at the figures in Mr. Lennox's drawing.

"Yes, very like. Your figure and way of holding yourself is capital. And it is just poor old Isaac's stiff way of stooping his long rheumatic back. What is this hanging from the branch of the tree? Not a bird's nest, surely."

"Oh no! That is my bonnet. I never can draw with my bonnet on; it makes my head so hot. I wonder if I could manage figures. There are so many people about here whom I should like to sketch."

"I should say that a likeness you very much wish to take you would always succeed in," said Mr. Lennox. "I have great faith in the power of will. I think myself I have succeeded pretty well in yours." Mr. Hale had preceded them into the house, while Margaret was lingering to pluck some roses, with which to adorn her morning gown for dinner.

"A regular London girl would understand the implied meaning of that speech," thought Mr. Lennox. "She would be up to looking through every speech that a young man made her for the *arriere-pensée* of a compliment. But I don't believe Margaret,— Stay!" exclaimed he, "Let me help you;" and he gathered for her some velvety cramoisy roses that were above her reach, and then dividing the spoil he placed two in his button-hole, and sent her in, pleased and happy, to arrange her flowers.

The conversation at dinner flowed on quietly and agreeably. There were plenty of questions to be asked on both sides—the latest intelligence which each could give of Mrs. Shaw's movements in Italy to be exchanged; and in the interest of what was said, the unpretending simplicity of the parsonage-ways—above all, in the neighbourhood of Margaret, Mr. Lennox forgot the little feeling of disappointment with which he had at first perceived that she had spoken but the simple truth when she had described her father's living as very small.

"Margaret, my child, you might have gathered us some pears for our dessert," said Mr. Hale, as the hospitable luxury of a freshly-decanted bottle of wine was placed on the table.

Mrs. Hale was hurried. It seemed as if desserts were impromptu and unusual things at the parsonage; whereas, if Mr. Hale would only have looked behind him, he would have seen biscuits and marmalade, and what not, all arranged in formal order on the sideboard. But the idea of pears had taken possession of Mr. Hale's mind, and was not to be got rid of.

"There are a few brown beurres against the south wall which are worth all foreign fruits and preserves. Run, Margaret, and gather us some."

"I propose that we adjourn into the garden, and eat them there" said Mr. Lennox.

"Nothing is so delicious as to set one's teeth into the crisp, juicy fruit, warm and scented by the sun. The worst is, the wasps are impudent enough to dispute it with one, even at the very crisis and summit of enjoyment."

He rose, as if to follow Margaret, who had disappeared through the window he only awaited Mrs. Hale's permission. She would rather have wound up the dinner in the proper way, and with all the ceremonies which had gone on so smoothly hitherto, especially as she and Dixon had got out the finger-glasses from the store-room on purpose to be as correct as became General Shaw's widow's sister, but as Mr. Hale got up directly, and prepared to accompany his guest, she could only submit.

"I shall arm myself with a knife," said Mr. Hale: "the days of eating fruit so primitively as you describe are over with me. I must pare it and quarter it before I can enjoy it."

Margaret made a plate for the pears out of a beetroot leaf, which threw up their brown gold colour admirably. Mr. Lennox looked more at her than at the pears; but her father, inclined to cull fastidiously the very zest and perfection of the hour he had stolen from his anxiety, chose daintily the ripest fruit, and sat down on the garden bench to enjoy it at his leisure. Margaret and Mr. Lennox strolled along the little terrace-walk under the south wall, where the bees still hummed and worked busily in their hives.

"What a perfect life you seem to live here! I have always felt rather contemptuously towards the poets before, with their wishes, 'Mine be a cot beside a hill,' and that sort of thing: but now I am afraid that the truth is, I have been nothing better than a cockney. Just now I feel as if twenty years' hard study of law would be amply rewarded by one year of such an exquisite serene life as this—such skies!" looking up—"such crimson and amber foliage, so perfectly motionless as that!" pointing to some of the great forest trees which shut in the garden as if it were a nest.

"You must please to remember that our skies are not always as deep a blue as they are now. We have rain, and our leaves do fall, and get sodden: though I think Helstone is about as perfect a place as any in the world. Recollect how you rather scorned my description of it one evening in Harley Street: 'a village in a tale.'"

"Scorned, Margaret! That is rather a hard word."

"Perhaps it is. Only I know I should have liked to have talked to you of what I was very full at the time, and you—what must I call it, then?—spoke disrespectfully of Helstone as a mere village in a tale."

"I will never do so again," said he, warmly. They turned the corner of the walk.

"I could almost wish, Margaret—" he stopped and hesitated. It was so unusual for the fluent lawyer to hesitate that Margaret looked up at him, in a little state of questioning wonder; but in an instant—from what about him she could not tell—she wished herself back with her mother—her father—anywhere away from him, for she was sure he was going to say something to which she should not know what to reply. In another moment the strong pride that was in her came to conquer her sudden agitation, which she hoped he had not perceived. Of course she could answer, and answer the right thing; and it was poor and despicable of her to shrink from hearing any speech, as if she had not power to put an end to it with her high maidenly dignity.

"Margaret," said he, taking her by surprise, and getting sudden possession of her hand, so that she was forced to stand still and listen, despising herself for the fluttering at her heart all the time; "Margaret, I wish you did not like Helstone so much—did not seem so perfectly calm and happy here. I have been hoping for these three months past to find you regretting London—and London friends, a little—enough to make you listen more kindly" (for she was quietly, but firmly, striving to extricate her hand from his grasp) "to one who has not much to offer, it is true—nothing but prospects in the future—but who does love you, Margaret, almost in spite of himself. Margaret, have I startled you too much? Speak!" For he saw her lips quivering almost as if she were going to cry. Then to Margaret's further dismayed surprise, he caught her by her upper arms and kissed her full on the lips. She recoiled at his touch. It was not the pleasant thing Edith had whispered of to her when they were alone. Henry's lips were damp and a little cool to the touch, and his kiss was soft and uncertain; it reminded her of the fish sometimes brought to her father and she turned her head away. She made a strong effort to be calm; she would not speak till she had succeeded in mastering her voice, and then she said:

"I was startled. I did not know that you cared for me in that way. I have always thought of you as a friend; and, please, I would rather go on thinking of you so. I don't like to be spoken to as you have been doing. I cannot answer you as you want me to do, and yet I should feel so sorry if I vexed you."

"Margaret," said he, looking into her eyes, which met his with their open, straight look, expressive of the utmost good faith and reluctance to give pain.

"Do you"—he was going to say—"love any one else?" But it seemed as if this question would be an insult to the pure serenity of those eyes. "Forgive me! I have been too abrupt. I am punished. Only let me hope. Give me the poor comfort of telling me you have never seen any one whom you could—" Again a pause. He could not end his sentence. Margaret reproached herself acutely as the cause of his distress.

"Ah! if you had but never got this fancy into your head! It was such a pleasure to think of you as a friend."

"But I may hope, may I not, Margaret, that some time you will think of me as a lover? Not yet, I see—there is no hurry—but some time———." She was silent for a minute or two, trying to discover the truth as it was in her own heart, before replying; then she said:

"I have never thought of—you, but as a friend. I like to think of you so; but I am sure I could never think of you as anything else. Pray, let us both forget that all this" ("disagreeable," she was going to say, but stopped short) "conversation has taken place."

He paused before he replied. Then, in his habitual coldness of tone, he answered:

"Of course, as your feelings are so decided, and as this conversation has been so evidently unpleasant to you, it had better not be remembered. That is all very fine in theory, that plan of forgetting whatever is painful, but it will be somewhat difficult for me, at least, to carry it into execution."

"You are vexed," said she, sadly; "yet how can I help it?"

She looked so truly grieved as she said this, that he struggled for a moment with his real disappointment, and then answered more cheerfully, but still with a little hardness in his tone:

"You should make allowances for the mortification, not only of a lover, Margaret, but of a man not given to romance in general— prudent, worldly, as some people call me—who has been carried out of his usual habits by the force of a passion—well, we will say no more of that; but in the one outlet which he has formed for the deeper and better feelings of his nature, he meets with rejection and repulse. I shall have to console myself with scorning my own folly. A struggling barrister to think of matrimony!"

Margaret could not answer this. The whole tone of it annoyed her. It seemed to touch on and call out all the points of difference which had often repelled her in him; while yet he was the pleasantest man, the most sympathising friend, the person of all others who understood her best in Harley Street. She felt a tinge of contempt mingle itself with her pain at having refused him. Her beautiful lip curled in a slight disdain. It was well that, having made the round of the garden, they came suddenly upon Mr. Hale, whose whereabouts had been quite forgotten by them. He had not yet finished the pear, which he had delicately peeled in one long strip of silver-paper thinness, and which he was enjoying in a deliberate manner. It was like the story of the eastern king, who dipped his head into a basin of water, at the magician's command, and ere he instantly took it out went through the experience of a lifetime. Margaret felt stunned, and unable to recover her self-possession enough to join in the trivial conversation that ensued between her father and Mr. Lennox. She was grave, and little disposed to speak; full of wonder when Mr. Lennox would go, and allow her to relax into thought on the events of the last quarter of an hour. He was almost as anxious to take his departure as she was for him to leave; but a few minutes light and careless talking, carried on at whatever effort, was a sacrifice which he owed to his mortified vanity, or his self-respect. He glanced from time to time at her sad and pensive face.

"I am not so indifferent to her as she believes," thought he to himself. "I do not give up hope."

Before a quarter of an hour was over, he had fallen into a way of conversing with quiet sarcasm; speaking of life in London and life in the country, as if he were conscious of his second mocking self, and afraid of his own satire. Mr. Hale was puzzled. His visitor was a different man to what he had seen him before at the wedding-breakfast, and at dinner to-day; a lighter, cleverer, more worldly man, and, as such, dissonant to Mr. Hale. It was a relief to all three when Mr. Lennox said that he must go directly if he meant to catch the five o'clock train. They proceeded to the house to find Mrs. Hale, and wish her good-bye. At the last moment, Henry Lennox's real self broke through the crust.

"Margaret, don't despise me; I have a heart, notwithstanding all this good-for-nothing way of talking. As a proof of it, I believe I love you more than ever—if I do not hate you—for the disdain with which you have listened to me during this last half-hour. Good-bye, Margaret—Margaret!"

# CHAPTER IV—DOUBTS AND DIFFICULTIES

"Cast me upon some naked shore,
Where I may tracke
Only the print of some sad wracke,
If thou be there, though the seas roare,
I shall no gentler calm implore."
HABINGTON.

He was gone. The house was shut up for the evening. No more deep blue skies or crimson and amber tints. Margaret went up to dress for the early tea, finding Dixon in a pretty temper from the interruption, which a visitor had naturally occasioned on a busy day. She showed it by brushing away viciously at Margaret's hair, under pretence of being in a great hurry to go to Mrs. Hale. Yet, after all, Margaret had to wait a long time in the drawing-room before her mother came down. She sat by herself at the fire, with unlighted candles on the table behind her, thinking over the day, the happy walk, happy sketching, cheerful pleasant dinner, and the uncomfortable, miserable walk in the garden.

How different men were to women! Here was she disturbed and unhappy, because her instinct had made anything but a refusal impossible; while he, not many minutes after he had met with a rejection of what ought to have been the deepest, holiest proposal of his life, could speak as if briefs, success, and all its superficial consequences of a good house, clever and agreeable society, were the sole avowed objects of his desires. Oh dear! How she could have loved him if he had but been different, with a difference which she felt, on reflection, to be one that went low—deep down. Then she took it into her head that, after all, his lightness might be but assumed, to cover a bitterness of disappointment which would have been stamped on her own heart if she had loved and been rejected. But there was no other answer she could have given. Henry Lennox was respectable and kind, and would have been a good match for anyone. But she was unwilling to settle for a marriage with no greater feeling than friendship. Margaret did want her husband to be a friend, but she wanted something more. She wanted love. She wanted passion like that of the couple she had seen in the meadow. The thought made her blush. Was it possible to find all three in a marriage?

Her mother came into the room before this whirl of thoughts was adjusted into anything like order. Margaret had to shake off the recollections of what had been done and said through the day, and turn a sympathising listener to the account of how Dixon had complained that the ironing-blanket had been burnt again; and how Susan Lightfoot had been seen with artificial flowers in her bonnet, thereby giving evidence of a vain and giddy character. Mr. Hale sipped his tea in abstracted silence; Margaret had the responses all to herself. She wondered how her father and mother could be so forgetful, so regardless of their companion through the day, as never to mention his name. She forgot that he had not made them an offer.

After tea Mr. Hale got up, and stood with his elbow on the chimney-piece, leaning his head on his hand, musing over something, and from time to time sighing deeply. Mrs. Hale went out to consult with Dixon about some winter clothing for the poor. Margaret was preparing her mother's worsted work, and rather shrinking from the thought of the long evening, and wishing bed-time were come that she might go over the events of the day again.

"Margaret!" said Mr. Hale, at last, in a sort of sudden desperate way that made her start. "Is that tapestry thing of immediate consequence? I mean, can you leave it and come into my study? I want to speak to you about something very serious to us all."

"Very serious to us all." Mr. Lennox had never had the opportunity of having any private conversation with her father after her refusal, or else that would indeed be a very serious affair. In the first place, Margaret felt guilty and ashamed of having grown so much into a woman as to be thought of in marriage; and secondly, she did not know if her father might not be displeased that she had taken upon herself to decline Mr. Lennox's proposal. But she soon felt it was not about anything, which having only lately and suddenly occurred, could have given rise to any complicated thoughts, that her father wished to speak to her. He made her take a chair by him; he stirred the fire, snuffed the candles, and sighed once or twice before he could make up his mind to say—and it came out with a jerk after all—"Margaret! I am going to leave Helstone."

That took her attention from lovers and would-be-husbands in a way her mother's conversation had not. He could not be serious! "Leave Helstone, papa! But why?"

Mr. Hale did not answer for a minute or two. He played with some papers on the table in a nervous and confused manner, opening his lips to speak several times, but closing them again without having the courage to utter a word. Margaret could not bear the sight of the suspense, which was even more distressing to her father than to herself.

"But why, dear papa? Do tell me!"

He looked up at her suddenly, and then said with a slow and enforced calmness:

"Because I must no longer be a minister in the Church of England."

Margaret had imagined nothing less than that some of the preferments which her mother so much desired had befallen her father at last—something that would force him to leave beautiful, beloved Helstone, and perhaps compel him to go and live in some of the stately and silent Closes which Margaret had seen from time to time in cathedral towns. They were grand and imposing places, but if, to go there, it was necessary to leave Helstone as a home for ever, that would have been a sad, long, lingering pain. But nothing to the shock she received from Mr. Hale's last speech. What could he mean? It was all the worse for being so mysterious. The aspect of piteous distress on his face, almost as imploring a merciful and kind judgment from his child, gave her a sudden sickening. Could he have become implicated in anything Frederick had done? Frederick was an outlaw. Had her father, out of a natural love for his son, connived at any—

"Oh! What is it? Do speak, papa! Tell me all! Why can you no longer be a clergyman? Surely, if the bishop were told all we know about Frederick, and the hard, unjust—"

"It is nothing about Frederick; the bishop would have nothing to do with that. It is all myself. Margaret, I will tell you about it. I will answer any questions this once, but after tonight let us never speak of it again. I can meet the consequences of my painful, miserable doubts; but it is an effort beyond me to speak of what has caused me so much suffering."

"Doubts, papa! Doubts as to religion?" asked Margaret, more shocked than ever.

"No! Not doubts as to religion; not the slightest injury to that." He paused. Margaret sighed, as if standing on the verge of some new horror. He began again, speaking rapidly, as if to get over a set task:

"You could not understand it all, if I told you—my anxiety, for years past, to know whether I had any right to hold my living—my efforts to quench my smouldering doubts by the authority of the Church. Oh! Margaret, how I love the holy Church from which I am to be shut out!" He could not go on for a moment or two.

Margaret could not tell what to say; it seemed to her as terribly mysterious as if her father were about to turn Mahometan.

"I have been reading to-day of the two thousand who were ejected from their churches,"—continued Mr. Hale, smiling faintly,—"trying to steal some of their bravery; but it is of no use—no use—I cannot help feeling it acutely."

"But, papa, have you well considered? Oh! it seems so terrible, so shocking," said Margaret, suddenly bursting into tears. The one staid foundation of her home, of her idea of her beloved father, seemed reeling and rocking. What could she say? What was to be done? The sight of her distress made Mr. Hale nerve himself, in order to try and comfort her. He swallowed down the dry choking sobs which had been heaving up from his heart hitherto, and going to his bookcase he took down a volume, which he had often been reading lately, and from which he thought he had derived strength to enter upon the course in which he was now embarked.

"Listen, dear Margaret," said he, putting one arm round her waist. She took his hand in hers and grasped it tight, but she could not lift up her head; nor indeed could she attend to what he read, so great was her internal agitation.

"This is the soliloquy of one who was once a clergyman in a country parish, like me; it was written by a Mr. Oldfield, minister of Carsington, in Derbyshire, a hundred and sixty years ago, or more. His trials are over. He fought the good fight." These last two sentences he spoke low, as if to himself. Then he read aloud,—

"When thou canst no longer continue in thy work without dishonour to God, discredit to religion, foregoing thy integrity, wounding conscience, spoiling thy peace, and hazarding the loss of thy salvation; in a word, when the conditions upon which thou must continue (if thou wilt continue) in thy employments are sinful, and unwarranted by the word of God, thou mayest, yea, thou must believe that God will turn thy very silence, suspension, deprivation, and laying aside, to His glory, and the advancement of the Gospel's interest. When God will not use thee in one kind, yet He will in another. A soul that desires to serve and honour Him shall never want opportunity to do it; nor must thou so limit the Holy One of Israel as to think He hath but one way in which He can glorify Himself by thee. He can do it by thy silence as well as by thy preaching; thy laying aside as well as thy continuance in thy work. It is not pretence of doing God the greatest service, or performing the weightiest duty, that will excuse the least sin, though that sin capacitated or gave us the opportunity for doing that duty. Thou wilt have little thanks, O my soul! if, when thou art charged with corrupting God's worship, falsifying thy vows, thou pretendest a necessity for it in order to a continuance in the ministry." As he read this, and glanced at much more which he did not read, he gained resolution for himself, and felt as if he too could be brave and firm in doing what he believed to be right; but as he ceased he heard Margaret's low convulsive sob; and his courage sank down under the keen sense of suffering.

"Margaret, dear!" said he, drawing her closer, "think of the early martyrs; think of the thousands who have suffered."

"But, father," said she, suddenly lifting up her flushed, tear-wet face, "the early martyrs suffered for the truth, while you—oh! dear, dear papa!"

"I suffer for conscience' sake, my child," said he, with a dignity that was only tremulous from the acute sensitiveness of his character; "I must do what my conscience bids. I have borne long with self-reproach that would have roused any mind less torpid and cowardly than mine." He shook his head as he went on. "Your poor mother's fond wish, gratified at last in the mocking way in which over-fond wishes are too often fulfilled—Sodom apples as they are—has brought on this crisis, for which I ought to be, and I hope I am thankful. It is not a month since the bishop offered me another living; if I had accepted it, I should have had to make a fresh declaration of conformity to the Liturgy at my institution.

Margaret, I tried to do it; I tried to content myself with simply refusing the additional preferment, and stopping quietly here,—strangling my conscience now, as I had strained it before. God forgive me!"

He rose and walked up and down the room, speaking low words of self-reproach and humiliation, of which Margaret was thankful to hear but few. At last he said,

"Margaret, I return to the old sad burden we must leave Helstone."

"Yes! I see. But when?"

"I have written to the bishop—I dare say I have told you so, but I forget things just now," said Mr. Hale, collapsing into his depressed manner as soon as he came to talk of hard matter-of-fact details, "informing him of my intention to resign this vicarage. He has been most kind; he has used arguments and expostulations, all in vain—in vain. They are but what I have tried upon myself, without avail. I shall have to take my deed of resignation, and wait upon the bishop myself, to bid him farewell. That will be a trial, but worse, far worse, will be the parting from my dear people. There is a curate appointed to read prayers—a Mr. Brown. He will come to stay with us to-morrow. Next Sunday I preach my farewell sermon."

Was it to be so sudden then? Thought Margaret; and yet perhaps it was as well. Lingering would only add stings to the pain; it was better to be stunned into numbness by hearing of all these arrangements, which seemed to be nearly completed before she had been told. "What does mamma say?" asked she, with a deep sigh.

To her surprise, her father began to walk about again before he answered. At length he stopped and replied:

"Margaret, I am a poor coward after all. I cannot bear to give pain. I know so well your mother's married life has not been all she hoped—all she had a right to expect—and this will be such a blow to her, that I have never had the heart, the power to tell her. She must be told though, now," said he, looking wistfully at his daughter. Margaret was almost overpowered with the idea that her mother knew nothing of it all, and yet the affair was so far advanced!

"Yes, indeed she must," said Margaret. "Perhaps, after all, she may not—Oh yes! she will, she must be shocked"—as the force of the blow returned upon herself in trying to realise how another would take it. "Where are we to go to?" said she at last, struck with a fresh wonder as to their future plans, if plans indeed her father had.

"To Milton-Northern," he answered, with a dull indifference, for he had perceived that, although his daughter's love had made her cling to him, and for a moment strive to soothe him with her love, yet the keenness of the pain was as fresh as ever in her mind.

"Milton-Northern! The manufacturing town in Darkshire?"

"Yes," said he, in the same despondent, indifferent way.

"Why there, papa?" asked she.

"Because there I can earn bread for my family. Because I know no one there, and no one knows Helstone, or can ever talk to me about it."

"Bread for your family! I thought you and mamma had"—and then she stopped, checking her natural interest regarding their future life, as she saw the gathering gloom on her father's brow. But he, with his quick intuitive sympathy, read in her face, as in a mirror, the reflections of his own moody depression, and turned it off with an effort.

"You shall be told all, Margaret. Only help me to tell your mother. I think I could do anything but that: the idea of her distress turns me sick with dread. If I tell you all, perhaps you could break it to her to-morrow. I am going out for the day, to bid Farmer Dobson and the poor people on Bracy Common good-bye. Would you dislike breaking it to her very much, Margaret?"

Margaret did dislike it, did shrink from it more than from anything she had ever had to do in her life before. She could not speak, all at once. Her father said, "You dislike it very much, don't you, Margaret?" Then she conquered herself, and said, with a bright strong look on her face:

"It is a painful thing, but it must be done, and I will do it as well as ever I can. You must have many painful things to do."

Mr. Hale shook his head despondingly: he pressed her hand in token of gratitude. Margaret was nearly upset again into a burst of crying. To turn her thoughts, she said: "Now tell me, papa, what our plans are. You and mamma have some money, independent of the income from the living, have not you? Aunt Shaw has, I know."

"Yes. I suppose we have about a hundred and seventy pounds a year of our own. Seventy of that has always gone to Frederick, since he has been abroad. I don't know if he wants it all," he continued in a hesitating manner. "He must have some pay for serving with the Spanish army."

"Frederick must not suffer," said Margaret, decidedly; "in a foreign country; so unjustly treated by his own. A hundred is left. Could not you, and I, and mamma live on a hundred a year in some very cheap—very quiet part of England? Oh! I think we could."

"No!" said Mr. Hale. "That would not answer. I must do something. I must make myself busy, to keep off morbid thoughts. Besides, in a country parish I should be so painfully reminded of Helstone, and my duties here. I could not bear it, Margaret. And a hundred a year would go a very little way, after the necessary wants of housekeeping are met, towards providing your mother with all the comforts she has been accustomed to, and ought to have. No: we must go to Milton. That is settled. I can always decide better by myself, and not influenced by those whom I love," said he, as a half apology for having arranged so much before he had told any one of his family of his intentions. "I cannot stand objections. They make me so undecided."

Margaret resolved to keep silence. After all, what did it signify where they went, compared to the one terrible change?

Mr. Hale continued: "A few months ago, when my misery of doubt became more than I could bear without speaking, I wrote to Mr. Bell—you remember Mr. Bell, Margaret?"

"No; I never saw him, I think. But I know who he is. Frederick's godfather—your old tutor at Oxford, don't you mean?"

"Yes. He is a Fellow of Plymouth College there. He is a native of Milton-Northern, I believe. At any rate, he has property there, which has very much increased in value since Milton has become such a large manufacturing town. Well, I had reason to suspect— to imagine—I had better say nothing about it, however. But I felt sure of sympathy from Mr. Bell. I don't know that he gave me much strength. He has lived an easy life in his college all his days. But he has been as kind as can be. And it is owing to him we are going to Milton."

"How?" said Margaret.

"Why he has tenants, and houses, and mills there; so, though he dislikes the place—too bustling for one of his habits—he is obliged to keep up some sort of connection; and he tells me that he hears there is a good opening for a private tutor there."

"A private tutor!" said Margaret, looking scornful: "What in the world do manufacturers want with the classics, or literature, or the accomplishments of a gentleman?"

"Oh," said her father, "some of them really seem to be fine fellows, conscious of their own deficiencies, which is more than many a man at Oxford is. Some want resolutely to learn, though they have come to man's estate. Some want their children to be better instructed than they themselves have been. At any rate, there is an opening, as I have said, for a private tutor. Mr. Bell has recommended me to a Mr. Thornton, a tenant of his, and a very intelligent man, as far as

I can judge from his letters. And in Milton, Margaret, I shall find a busy life, if not a happy one, and people and scenes so different that I shall never be reminded of Helstone."

There was the secret motive, as Margaret knew from her own feelings. It would be different. Discordant as it was—with almost a detestation for all she had ever heard of the North of England, the manufacturers, the people, the wild and bleak country—there was this one recommendation—it would be different from Helstone, and could never remind them of that beloved place.

"When do we go?" asked Margaret, after a short silence.

"I do not know exactly. I wanted to talk it over with you. You see, your mother knows nothing about it yet: but I think, in a fortnight;—after my deed of resignation is sent in, I shall have no right to remain."

Margaret was almost stunned.

"In a fortnight!"

"No—no, not exactly to a day. Nothing is fixed," said her father, with anxious hesitation, as he noticed the filmy sorrow that came over her eyes, and the sudden change in her complexion. But she recovered herself immediately.

"Yes, papa, it had better be fixed soon and decidedly, as you say. Only mamma to know nothing about it! It is that that is the great perplexity."

"Poor Maria!" replied Mr. Hale, tenderly. "Poor, poor Maria! Oh, if I were not married—if I were but myself in the world, how easy it would be! As it is—Margaret, I dare not tell her!"

"No," said Margaret, sadly, "I will do it. Give me till to-morrow evening to choose my time Oh, papa," cried she, with sudden passionate entreaty, "say—tell me it is a night-mare—a horrid dream—not the real waking truth! You cannot mean that you are really going to leave the Church—to give up Helstone—to be for ever separate from me, from mamma—led away by some delusion—some temptation! You do not really mean it!"

Mr. Hale sat in rigid stillness while she spoke.

Then he looked her in the face, and said in a slow, hoarse, measured way—"I do mean it, Margaret. You must not deceive yourself into doubting the reality of my words—my fixed intention and resolve." He looked at her in the same steady, stony manner, for some moments after he had done speaking. She, too, gazed back with pleading eyes before she would believe that it was irrevocable. Then she arose and went, without another word or look, towards the door. As her fingers were on the handle he called her back. He was standing by the fireplace, shrunk and stooping; but as she came near he drew himself up to his full height, and, placing his hands on her head, he said, solemnly:

"The blessing of God be upon thee, my child!"

"And may He restore you to His Church," responded she, out of the fulness of her heart. The next moment she feared lest this answer to his blessing might be irreverent, wrong—might hurt him as coming from his daughter, and she threw her arms round his neck. He held her to him for a minute or two. She heard him murmur to himself, "The martyrs and confessors had even more pain to bear—I will not shrink."

They were startled by hearing Mrs. Hale inquiring for her daughter. They started asunder in the full consciousness of all that was before them. Mr. Hale hurriedly said—"Go, Margaret, go. I shall be out all to-morrow. Before night you will have told your mother."

"Yes," she replied, and she returned to the drawing-room in a stunned and dizzy state.

# CHAPTER V—DECISION

"I ask Thee for a thoughtful love,
Through constant watching wise,
To meet the glad with joyful smiles,
And to wipe the weeping eyes;
And a heart at leisure from itself
To soothe and sympathise."
ANON.

Margaret made a good listener to all her mother's little plans for adding some small comforts to the lot of the poorer parishioners. She could not help listening, though each new project was a stab to her heart. By the time the frost had set in, they should be far away from Helstone. Old Simon's rheumatism might be bad and his eyesight worse; there would be no one to go and read to him, and comfort him with little porringers of broth and good red flannel: or if there was, it would be a stranger, and the old man would watch in vain for her. Mary Domville's little crippled boy would crawl in vain to the door and look for her coming through the forest. These poor friends would never understand why she had forsaken them; and there were many others besides. "Papa has always spent the income he derived from his living in the parish. I am, perhaps, encroaching upon the next dues, but the winter is likely to be severe, and our poor old people must be helped."

"Oh, mamma, let us do all we can," said Margaret eagerly, not seeing the prudential side of the question, only grasping at the idea that they were rendering such help for the last time; "we may not be here long."

"Do you feel ill, my darling?" asked Mrs. Hale, anxiously, misunderstanding Margaret's hint of the uncertainty of their stay at Helstone. "You look pale and tired. It is this soft, damp, unhealthy air."

"No—no, mamma, it is not that: it is delicious air. It smells of the freshest, purest fragrance, after the smokiness of Harley Street. But I am tired: it surely must be near bedtime."

"Not far off—it is half-past nine. You had better go to bed at once, dear. Ask Dixon for some gruel. I will come and see you as soon as you are in bed. I am afraid you have taken cold; or the bad air from some of the stagnant ponds—"

"Oh, mamma," said Margaret, faintly smiling as she kissed her mother, "I am quite well—don't alarm yourself about me; I am only tired."

Margaret went upstairs. To soothe her mother's anxiety she submitted to a basin of gruel. She was lying languidly in bed when Mrs. Hale came up to make some last inquiries and kiss her before going to her own room for the night. But the instant she heard her mother's door locked, she sprang out of bed, and throwing her dressing-gown on, she began to pace up and down the room, until the creaking of one of the boards reminded her that she must make no noise. She went and curled herself up on the window-seat in the small, deeply recessed window. That morning when she had looked out, her heart had danced at seeing the bright clear lights on the church tower, which foretold a fine and sunny day. This evening—sixteen hours at most had past by—she sat down, too full of sorrow to cry, but with a dull cold pain, which seemed to have pressed the youth and buoyancy out of her heart, never to return. Mr. Henry Lennox's visit—his offer—was like a dream, a thing beside her actual life. The hard reality was, that her father had so admitted tempting doubts into his mind as to become a schismatic—an outcast; all the changes consequent upon this grouped themselves around that one great blighting fact.

She looked out upon the dark-gray lines of the church tower, square and straight in the centre of the view, cutting against the deep blue transparent depths beyond, into which she gazed, and felt that she might gaze for ever, seeing at every moment some farther distance, and yet no sign of God! It seemed to her at the moment, as if the earth was more utterly desolate than if girt in by an iron dome, behind which there might be the ineffaceable peace and glory of the Almighty: those never-ending depths of space, in their still serenity, were more mocking to her than any material bounds could be—shutting in the cries of earth's sufferers, which now might ascend into that infinite splendour of vastness and be lost—lost for ever, before they reached His throne. In this mood her father came in unheard. The moonlight was strong enough to let him see his daughter in her unusual place and attitude. He came to her and touched her shoulder before she was aware that he was there.

"Margaret, I heard you were up. I could not help coming in to ask you to pray with me—to say the Lord's Prayer; that will do good to both of us."

Mr. Hale and Margaret knelt by the window-seat—he looking up, she bowed down in humble shame. God was there, close around them, hearing her father's whispered words. Her father might be a heretic; but had not she, in her despairing doubts not five minutes before, shown herself a far more utter sceptic? She spoke not a word, but stole to bed after her father had left her, like a child ashamed of its fault. If the world was full of perplexing problems she would trust, and only ask to see the one step needful for the hour. Mr. Lennox—his visit, his proposal—the remembrance of which had been so rudely pushed aside by the subsequent events of the day—haunted her dreams that night. He was climbing up some tree of fabulous height to reach the branch whereon was slung her bonnet: he was falling, and she was struggling to save him, but held back by some invisible powerful hand. He was dead. And yet, with a shifting of the scene, she was once more in the Harley Street drawing-room, talking to him as of old, and still with a consciousness all the time that she had seen him killed by that terrible fall.

Miserable, unresting night! Ill preparation for the coming day! She awoke with a start, unrefreshed, and conscious of some reality worse even than her feverish dreams. It all came back upon her; not merely the sorrow, but the terrible discord in the sorrow. Where, to what distance apart, had her father wandered, led by doubts, which were to her temptations of the Evil One? She longed to ask, and yet would not have heard for all the world.

The fine crisp morning made her mother feel particularly well and happy at breakfast-time. She talked on, planning village kindnesses, unheeding the silence of her husband and the monosyllabic answers of Margaret. Before the things were cleared away, Mr. Hale got up; he leaned one hand on the table, as if to support himself:

"I shall not be at home till evening. I am going to Bracy Common, and will ask Farmer Dobson to give me something for dinner. I shall be back to tea at seven." He did not look at either of them, but Margaret knew what he meant. By seven, the announcement must be made to her mother. Mr. Hale would have delayed making it till half-past six, but Margaret was of different stuff. She could not bear the impending weight on her mind all the day long: better get the worst over; the day would be too short to comfort her mother. But while she stood by the window, thinking how to begin, and waiting for the servant to have left the room, her mother had gone up-stairs to put on her things to go to the school. She came down ready equipped, in a brisker mood than usual.

"Mother, come round the garden with me this morning; just one turn," said Margaret, putting her arm round Mrs. Hale's waist.

They passed through the open window. Mrs. Hale spoke—said something—Margaret could not tell what. Her eye caught on a bee entering a deep-belled flower: when that bee flew forth with his spoil she would begin—that should be the sign. Out he came.

"Mamma! Papa is going to leave Helstone!" she blurted forth. "He's going to leave the Church, and live in Milton-Northern." There were the three hard facts hardly spoken.

"What makes you say so?" asked Mrs. Hale, in a surprised incredulous voice. "Who has been telling you such nonsense?"

"Papa himself," said Margaret, longing to say something gentle and consoling, but literally not knowing how. They were close to a garden-bench. Mrs. Hale sat down, and began to cry.

"I don't understand you," she said. "Either you have made some great mistake, or I don't quite understand you."

"No, mother, I have made no mistake. Papa has written to the bishop, saying that he has such doubts that he cannot conscientiously remain a priest of the Church of England, and that he must give up Helstone. He has also consulted Mr. Bell—Frederick's godfather, you know, mamma; and it is arranged that we go to live in Milton-Northern." Mrs. Hale looked up in Margaret's face all the time she was speaking these words: the shadow on her countenance told that she, at least, believed in the truth of what she said.

"I don't think it can be true," said Mrs. Hale, at length. "He would surely have told me before it came to this."

It came strongly upon Margaret's mind that her mother ought to have been told: that whatever her faults of discontent and repining might have been, it was an error in her father to have left her to learn his change of opinion, and his approaching change of life, from her better-informed child. Margaret sat down by her mother, and took her unresisting head on her breast, bending her own soft cheeks down caressingly to touch her face.

"Dear, darling mamma! We were so afraid of giving you pain. Papa felt so acutely—you know you are not strong, and there must have been such terrible suspense to go through."

"When did he tell you, Margaret?"

"Yesterday, only yesterday," replied Margaret, detecting the jealousy, which prompted the inquiry. "Poor papa!"—trying to divert her mother's thoughts into compassionate sympathy for all her father had gone through. Mrs. Hale raised her head.

"What does he mean by having doubts?" she asked. "Surely, he does not mean that he thinks differently—that he knows better than the Church." Margaret shook her head, and the tears came into her eyes, as her mother touched the bare nerve of her own regret.

"Can't the bishop set him right?" asked Mrs. Hale, half impatiently.

"I'm afraid not," said Margaret. "But I did not ask. I could not bear to hear what he might answer. It is all settled at any rate. He is going to leave Helstone in a fortnight. I am not sure if he did not say he had sent in his deed of resignation."

"In a fortnight!" exclaimed Mrs. Hale, "I do think this is very strange—not at all right. I call it very unfeeling," said she, beginning to take relief in tears. "He has doubts, you say, and gives up his living, and all without consulting me. I dare say, if he had told me his doubts at the first I could have nipped them in the bud."

Mistaken as Margaret felt her father's conduct to have been, she could not bear to hear it blamed by her mother. She knew that his very reserve had originated in a tenderness for her, which might be cowardly, but was not unfeeling.

"I almost hoped you might have been glad to leave Helstone, mamma," said she, after a pause. "You have never been well in this air, you know."

"You can't think the smoky air of a manufacturing town, all chimneys and dirt like Milton-Northern, would be better than this air, which is pure and sweet, if it is too soft and relaxing. Fancy living in the middle of factories, and factory people! Though, of course, if your father leaves the Church, we shall not be admitted into society anywhere. It will be such a disgrace to us! Poor dear Sir John! It is well he is not alive to see what your father has come to! Every day after dinner, when I was a girl, living with your Aunt Shaw, at Beresford Court, Sir John used to give for the first toast—'Church and King, and down with the Rump.'"

Margaret was glad that her mother's thoughts were turned away from the fact of her husband's silence to her on the point, which must have been so near his heart. Next to the serious vital anxiety as to the nature of her father's doubts, this was the one circumstance of the case that gave Margaret the most pain.

"You know, we have very little society here, mamma. The Gormans, who are our nearest neighbours (to call society—and we hardly ever see them), have been in trade just as much as these Milton-Northern people."

"Yes," said Mrs. Hale, almost indignantly, "but, at any rate, the Gormans made carriages for half the gentry of the county, and were brought into some kind of intercourse with them; but these factory people, who on earth wears cotton that can afford linen?"

"Well, mamma, I give up the cotton-spinners; I am not standing up for them, any more than for any other trades-people. Only we shall have little enough to do with them."

"Why on earth has your father fixed on Milton-Northern to live in?"

"Partly," said Margaret, sighing, "because it is so very different from Helstone—partly because Mr. Bell says there is an opening there for a private tutor."

"Private tutor in Milton! Why can't he go to Oxford, and be a tutor to gentlemen?"

"You forget, mamma! He is leaving the Church on account of his opinions—his doubts would do him no good at Oxford."

Mrs. Hale was silent for some time, quietly crying. At last she said:—

"And the furniture—How in the world are we to manage the removal? I never removed in my life, and only a fortnight to think about it!"

Margaret was inexpressibly relieved to find that her mother's anxiety and distress was lowered to this point, so insignificant to herself, and on which she could do so much to help. She planned and promised, and led her mother on to arrange fully as much as could be fixed before they knew somewhat more definitively what Mr. Hale intended to do. Throughout the day Margaret never left her mother; bending her whole soul to sympathise in all the various turns her feelings took; towards evening especially, as she became more and more anxious that her father should find a soothing welcome home awaiting him, after his return from his day of fatigue and distress. She dwelt upon what he must have borne in secret for long; her mother only replied coldly that he ought to have told her, and that then at any rate he would have had an adviser to give him counsel; and Margaret turned faint at heart when she heard her father's step in the hall. She dared not go to meet him, and tell him what she had done all day, for fear of her mother's jealous annoyance. She heard him linger, as if awaiting her, or some sign of her; and she dared not stir; she saw by her mother's twitching lips, and changing colour, that she too was aware that her husband had returned. Presently he opened the room-door, and stood there uncertain whether to come in. His face was gray and pale; he had a timid, fearful look in his eyes; something almost pitiful to see in a man's face; but that look of despondent uncertainty, of mental and bodily languor, touched his wife's heart. She went to him, and threw herself on his breast, crying out—

"Oh! Richard, Richard, you should have told me sooner!"

And then, in tears, Margaret left her, as she rushed up-stairs to throw herself on her bed, and hide her face in the pillows to stifle the hysteric sobs that would force their way at last, after the rigid self-control of the whole day. How long she lay thus she could not tell. She heard no noise, though the housemaid came in to arrange the room. The affrighted girl stole out again on tip-toe, and went and told Mrs. Dixon that Miss Hale was crying as if her heart would break: she was sure she would make herself deadly ill if she went on at that rate. In consequence of this, Margaret felt herself touched, and started up into a sitting posture; she saw the accustomed room, the figure of Dixon in shadow, as the latter stood holding the candle a little behind her, for fear of the effect on Miss Hale's startled eyes, swollen and blinded as they were.

"Oh, Dixon! I did not hear you come into the room!" said Margaret, resuming her trembling self-restraint. "Is it very late?" continued she, lifting herself languidly off the bed, yet letting her feet touch the ground without fairly standing down, as she shaded her wet ruffled hair off her face, and tried to look as though nothing were the matter; as if she had only been asleep.

"I hardly can tell what time it is," replied Dixon, in an aggrieved tone of voice. "Since your mamma told me this terrible news, when I dressed her for tea, I've lost all count of time. I'm sure I don't know what is to become of us all. When Charlotte told me just now you were sobbing, Miss Hale, I thought, no wonder, poor thing! And master thinking of turning Dissenter at his time of life, when, if it is not to be said he's done well in the Church, he's not done badly after all. I had a cousin, miss, who turned Methodist preacher after he was fifty years of age, and a tailor all his life; but then he had never been able to make a pair of trousers to fit, for as long as he had been in the trade, so it was no wonder; but for master! as I said to missus, 'What would poor Sir John have said? He never liked your marrying Mr. Hale, but if he could have known it would have come to this, he would have sworn worse oaths than ever, if that was possible!'"

Dixon had been so much accustomed to comment upon Mr. Hale's proceedings to her mistress (who listened to her, or not, as she was in the humour), that she never noticed Margaret's flashing eye and dilating nostril. To hear her father talked of in this way by a servant to her face!

"Dixon," she said, in the low tone she always used when much excited, which had a sound in it as of some distant turmoil, or threatening storm breaking far away. "Dixon! you forget to whom you are speaking." She stood upright and firm on her feet now, confronting the waiting-maid, and fixing her with her steady discerning eye. "I am Mr. Hale's daughter. Go! You have made a strange mistake, and one that I am sure your own good feeling will make you sorry for when you think about it."

Dixon hung irresolutely about the room for a minute or two. Margaret repeated, "You may leave me, Dixon. I wish you to go." Dixon did not know whether to resent these decided words or to cry; either course would have done with her mistress: but, as she said to herself, "Miss Margaret has a touch of the old gentleman about her, as well as poor Master Frederick; I wonder where they get it from?" and she, who would have resented such words from any one less haughty and determined in manner, was subdued enough to say, in a half humble, half injured tone:

"Mayn't I unfasten your gown, miss, and do your hair?"

"No! Not to-night, thank you." And Margaret gravely lighted her out of the room, and bolted the door. From henceforth Dixon obeyed and admired Margaret. She said it was because she was so like poor Master Frederick; but the truth was, that Dixon, as do many others, liked to feel herself ruled by a powerful and decided nature.

Margaret needed all Dixon's help in action, and silence in words; for, for some time, the latter thought it her duty to show her sense of affront by saying as little as possible to her young lady; so the energy came out in doing rather than in speaking. A fortnight was a very short time to make arrangements for so serious a removal; as Dixon said, "Any one but a gentleman—indeed almost any other gentleman—" but catching a look at Margaret's straight, stern brow just here, she coughed the remainder of the sentence away, and meekly took the horehound drop that Margaret offered her, to stop the "little tickling at my chest, miss." But almost any one but Mr. Hale would have had practical knowledge enough to see, that in so short a time it would be difficult to fix on any house in Milton-Northern, or indeed elsewhere, to which they could remove the furniture that had of necessity to be taken out of Helstone vicarage. Mrs. Hale, overpowered by all the troubles and necessities for immediate household decisions that seemed to come upon her at once, became really ill, and Margaret almost felt it as a relief when her mother fairly took to her bed, and left the management of affairs to her. Dixon, true to her post of body-guard, attended most faithfully to her mistress, and only emerged from Mrs. Hale's bed-room to shake her head, and murmur to herself in a manner which Margaret did not choose to hear. For, the one thing clear and straight before her, was the necessity for leaving Helstone. Mr. Hale's successor in the living was appointed; and, at any rate, after her father's decision; there must be no lingering now, for his sake, as well as from every other consideration. For he came home every evening more and more depressed, after the necessary leave-taking which he had resolved to have with every individual parishioner. Margaret, inexperienced as she was in all the necessary matter-of-fact business to be got through, did not know to whom to apply for advice. The cook and Charlotte worked away with willing arms and stout hearts at all the moving and packing; and as far as that went, Margaret's admirable sense enabled her to see what was best, and to direct how it should be done. But where were they to go to? In a week they must be gone. Straight to Milton, or where? So many arrangements depended on this decision that Margaret resolved to ask her father one evening, in spite of his evident fatigue and low spirits. He answered:

"My dear! I have really had too much to think about to settle this. What does your mother say? What does she wish? Poor Maria!"

He met with an echo even louder than his sigh. Dixon had just come into the room for another cup of tea for Mrs. Hale, and catching Mr. Hale's last words, and protected by his presence from Margaret's upbraiding eyes, made bold to say, "My poor mistress!"

"You don't think her worse to-day," said Mr. Hale, turning hastily.

"I'm sure I can't say, sir. It's not for me to judge. The illness seems so much more on the mind than on the body."

Mr. Hale looked infinitely distressed.

"You had better take mamma her tea while it is hot, Dixon," said Margaret, in a tone of quiet authority.

"Oh! I beg your pardon, miss! My thoughts were otherwise occupied in thinking of my poor——of Mrs. Hale."

"Papa!" said Margaret, "it is this suspense that is bad for you both. Of course, mamma must feel your change of opinions: we can't help that," she continued, softly; "but now the course is clear, at least to a certain point. And I think, papa, that I could get mamma to help me in planning, if you could tell me what to plan for. She has never expressed any wish in any way, and only thinks of what can't be helped. Are we to go straight to Milton? Have you taken a house there?"

"No," he replied. "I suppose we must go into lodgings, and look about for a house."

"And pack up the furniture so that it can be left at the railway station, till we have met with one?"

"I suppose so. Do what you think best. Only remember, we shall have much less money to spend."

They had never had much superfluity, as Margaret knew. She felt that it was a great weight suddenly thrown upon her shoulders. Four months ago, all the decisions she needed to make were what dress she would wear for dinner, and to help Edith to draw out the lists of who should take down whom in the dinner parties at home. Nor was the household in which she lived one that called for much decision. Except in the one grand case of Captain Lennox's offer, everything went on with the regularity of clockwork. Once a year, there was a long discussion between her aunt and Edith as to whether they should go to the Isle of Wight, abroad, or to Scotland; but at such times Margaret herself was secure of drifting, without any exertion of her own, into the quiet harbour of home. Now, since that day when Mr. Lennox came, and startled her into a decision, every day brought some question, momentous to her, and to those whom she loved, to be settled.

Her father went up after tea to sit with his wife. Margaret remained alone in the drawing-room. Suddenly she took a candle and went into her father's study for a great atlas, and lugging it back into the drawing-room, she began to pore over the map of England. She was ready to look up brightly when her father came down stairs.

"I have hit upon such a beautiful plan. Look here—in Darkshire, hardly the breadth of my finger from Milton, is Heston, which I have often heard of from people living in the north as such a pleasant little bathing-place. Now, don't you think we could get mamma there with Dixon, while you and I go and look at houses, and get one all ready for her in Milton? She would get a breath of sea air to set her up for the winter, and be spared all the fatigue, and Dixon would enjoy taking care of her."

"Is Dixon to go with us?" asked Mr. Hale, in a kind of helpless dismay.

"Oh, yes!" said Margaret. "Dixon quite intends it, and I don't know what mamma would do without her."

"But we shall have to put up with a very different way of living, I am afraid. Everything is so much dearer in a town. I doubt if Dixon can make herself comfortable. To tell you the truth Margaret, I sometimes feel as if that woman gave herself airs."

"To be sure she does, papa," replied Margaret; "and if she has to put up with a different style of living, we shall have to put up with her airs, which will be worse. But she really loves us all, and would be miserable to leave us, I am sure—especially in this change; so, for mamma's sake, and for the sake of her faithfulness, I do think she must go."

"Very well, my dear. Go on. I am resigned. How far is Heston from Milton? The breadth of one of your fingers does not give me a very clear idea of distance."

"Well, then, I suppose it is thirty miles; that is not much!"

"Not in distance, but in——. Never mind! If you really think it will do your mother good, let it be fixed so."

This was a great step. Now Margaret could work, and act, and plan in good earnest. And now Mrs. Hale could rouse herself from her languor, and forget her real suffering in thinking of the pleasure and the delight of going to the sea-side. Her only regret was that Mr. Hale could not be with her all the fortnight she was to be there, as he had been for a whole fortnight once, when they were engaged, and she was staying with Sir John and Lady Beresford at Torquay.

# CHAPTER VI—FAREWELL

"Unwatch'd the garden bough shall sway,
The tender blossom flutter down,
Unloved that beech will gather brown,
The maple burn itself away;
Unloved, the sun-flower, shining fair,
Ray round with flames her disk of seed,
And many a rose-carnation feed
With summer spice the humming air;

• • •

Till from the garden and the wild
A fresh association blow,
And year by year the landscape grow
Familiar to the stranger's child;
As year by year the labourer tills
His wonted glebe, or lops the glades;
And year by year our memory fades
From all the circle of the hills."
TENNYSON.

The last day came; the house was full of packing-cases, which were being carted off at the front door, to the nearest railway station. Even the pretty lawn at the side of the house was made unsightly and untidy by the straw that had been wafted upon it through the open door and windows. The rooms had a strange echoing sound in them,—and the light came harshly and strongly in through the uncurtained windows,—seeming already unfamiliar and strange. Mrs. Hale's dressing-room was left untouched to the last; and

78

there she and Dixon were packing up clothes, and interrupting each other every now and then to exclaim at, and turn over with fond regard, some forgotten treasure, in the shape of some relic of the children while they were yet little. They did not make much progress with their work. Down-stairs, Margaret stood calm and collected, ready to counsel or advise the men who had been called in to help the cook and Charlotte. These two last, crying between whiles, wondered how the young lady could keep up so this last day, and settled it between them that she was not likely to care much for Helstone, having been so long in London. There she stood, very pale and quiet, with her large grave eyes observing everything,—up to every present circumstance, however small. They could not understand how her heart was aching all the time, with a heavy pressure that no sighs could lift off or relieve, and how constant exertion for her perceptive faculties was the only way to keep herself from crying out with pain. Moreover, if she gave way, who was to act? Her father was examining papers, books, registers, what not, in the vestry with the clerk; and when he came in, there were his own books to pack up, which no one but himself could do to his satisfaction. Besides, was Margaret one to give way before strange men, or even household friends like the cook and Charlotte! Not she. But at last the four packers went into the kitchen to their tea; and Margaret moved stiffly and slowly away from the place in the hall where she had been standing so long, out through the bare echoing drawing-room, into the twilight of an early November evening. There was a filmy veil of soft dull mist obscuring, but not hiding, all objects, giving them a lilac hue, for the sun had not yet fully set; a robin was singing,—perhaps, Margaret thought, the very robin that her father had so often talked of as his winter pet, and for which he had made, with his own hands, a kind of robin-house by his study-window. The leaves were more gorgeous than ever; the first touch of frost would lay them all low on the ground. Already one or two kept constantly floating down, amber and golden in the low slanting sun-rays.

Margaret went along the walk under the pear-tree wall. She had never been along it since she paced it at Henry Lennox's side. Here, at this bed of thyme, he began to speak of what she must not think of now. Her eyes were on that late-blowing rose as she was trying to answer; and she had caught the idea of the vivid beauty of the feathery leaves of the carrots in the very middle of his last sentence. Only a fortnight ago! And all so changed! Where was he now? In London,—going through the old round; dining with the old Harley Street set, or with gayer young friends of his own. Even now, while she walked sadly through that damp and drear garden in the dusk, with everything falling and fading, and turning to decay around her, he might be gladly putting away his law-books after a day of satisfactory toil, and freshening himself up, as he had told her he often did, by a run in the Temple Gardens, taking in the while the grand inarticulate mighty roar of tens of thousands of busy men, nigh at hand, but not seen, and catching ever, at his quick turns, glimpses of the lights of the city coming up out of the depths of the river. He had often spoken to Margaret of these hasty walks, snatched in the intervals between study and dinner. At his best times and in his best moods had he spoken of them; and the thought of them had struck upon her fancy. Here there was no sound. The robin had gone away into the vast stillness of night. Now and then, a cottage door in the distance was opened and shut, as if to admit the tired labourer to his home; but that sounded very far away.

Margaret sighed and sat upon a low bench, leaning back against the wall and willing her body and mind to relax after such a tumultuous fortnight. At last the familiar evening sounds and her fatigue overwhelmed her, and her eyelids drooped shut. She opened them with a start; it was not yet time for tea and she did not want to miss the last one in the parsonage. But a moment later, they fell shut again and before she could rouse herself she fell asleep.

She was in a room she did not know, but she felt no alarm, for somehow she understood that she belonged there. The night was warm, but not overly so. A soft breeze came through the open windows every now and then, making the candlelight near the bed flicker. Margaret turned her head and caught sight of a man half-reclining atop a dark brown coverlet, long legs stretching out before him. She could not see his face, for it was in shadow, but she knew he watched her move about the room, putting things away. As she looked at him he rose from the bed and walked with purposeful steps toward her, his bare feet silent on the floor.

"Margaret."

He had a nice voice, a strong and deep one, different from Henry's, more like that of a man used to giving orders and having them obeyed without question. Rough hands closed over her shoulders, drawing her close to him, and she went without hesitation to meet him. Firm, warm lips closed over hers, gentle and demanding all at once. She moaned, and his tongue teased at her parted lips, sweeping in and touching hers, sending little jolts of pleasure to her breasts. Her nipples peaked, wanting his attention, while a further caress of his tongue into her mouth sent heat rushing through her limbs. Margaret clung to his broad shoulders afraid she might collapse at his feet otherwise, for her knees had buckled at the passionate kiss. His mouth moved from hers, forcing a murmur of protest from her and then another moan as first his breath, then his tongue, brushed the sensitive skin below her ear.

"Come to bed."

"Yes." There was no thought of protest, of being coy. She wanted him too. No, she burned for him in a way she had never imagined possible and that she would have thought shameful with anyone else.

His hands were at her back now, drawing her close to him as he ravaged her mouth again, but it was not enough. There was too much clothing between them, and Margaret wanted to feel his skin against hers. To ease this ache that filled her, to cool the heat that flushed her body. Her mysterious lover must have had the same thought, for she felt him undoing the fastenings of her dress with the expertise of a lady's maid. She did not care how he had learned to undress a woman, she was only glad that he knew how, for her fingers could not have managed the buttons. He drew her dress up and over her head, and tossed it onto the nearby chair. Margaret closed her eyes as his hands brushed over her shoulders, burning her there with the heat of them, even through the soft barrier of her chemise. Would they feel the same on her bare skin?

"Look at me," he said.

Margaret did, or tried to, but his face was still obscured. She reached for him and cupped his face between her palms, the stubble pleasantly abrading her skin as she touched him. He kissed her again, devouring her as if he were starved, his tongue plundering every part of her mouth. Margaret could not think; she could only feel, every part of her quivering and longing for more. She released a little mewl of protest as he drew away. He stood behind her now, his quick breaths fanning her neck, sending goose bumps down her spine, and then his lips touched her skin, sucking softly. Margaret's heart pounded and more blood surged through her, settling in her core, and between her thighs she felt moisture gather inside her swollen nether lips. Her lover quickly worked the rest of her garments from her body, and his moan joined hers as his hands cupped her breasts, his thumbs brushing her nipples until they ached.

"You fill my hands so well," he whispered, "as if you were made for me."

Margaret trembled at the desire in his voice and arched toward his hands, needing more of his touch. But he held her trapped, his muscular body pressing against hers. Her head fell back against his shoulder, lost in sensation as he cupped her breasts and kneaded them as if that was enough for him. It was not enough for her.

"Please."

"Ay, my Margaret."

Her lover began to undress. Margaret stared at his broad chest and lean waist but before she could see more he lifted her in his arms and carried her to the bed as if she were a tiny thing and did not reach nearly up to his chin in height. She laid back, legs parted indecently, and he joined her, settling between them. Her lover bent his head to hers again, claiming her lips, his tongue delving inside again to taste her. Breathless, Margaret drew him close and threaded her fingers through the short strands of his hair. He moved his lips away from hers again, until they trailed over her right breast and his tongue circled the nipple. She gasped and raised her torso off the blanket when he closed his lips over her flesh and tugged tenderly. The action sent another hot bolt of desire to her core and another rush of moisture to the place between her thighs. If he did not take her soon she thought she might go mad.

She whispered something even she could barely hear, but her lover did, and understood, for he moved a hand down, brushed the damp curls before teasing her lips apart. A finger slipped inside, and then another, and her need grew with each teasing stroke.

"More," she begged. "Please."

He moved back, and Margaret was about to protest, but it was only to shed the rest of his clothing. Then he was back above her, easing her thighs farther apart. He entered her swiftly, capturing her soft cry, though no one was nearby to hear. For a moment he held still, watching her, but then he began to move, long slow thrusts that drove her further toward the promise his eyes had offered earlier. Without warning it was there, pleasure spiralling through her, washing over her. She clung to him, riding the waves of ecstasy as she splintered apart, her fingernails digging into his back, while above her he shuddered and groaned, and he whispered her name over and over. "Margaret. Margaret!"

She awoke with a start. Something nearby moved again, and she listened, holding her still-unsteady breath, wondering at the tingles still coursing through her body.

A stealthy, creeping, cranching sound among the crisp fallen leaves of the forest, beyond the garden, seemed almost close at hand. Margaret knew it was some poacher. Sitting up in her bedroom this past autumn, with the light of her candle extinguished, and purely revelling in the solemn beauty of the heavens and the earth, she had many a time seen the light noiseless leap of the poachers over the garden-fence, their quick tramp across the dewy moonlit lawn, their disappearance in the black still shadow beyond. The wild adventurous freedom of their life had taken her fancy; she felt inclined to wish them success; she had no fear of them. But to-night she was afraid, she knew not why. She heard Charlotte shutting the windows, and fastening up for the night, unconscious that any one had gone out into the garden. A small branch—it might be of rotten wood, or it might be broken by force—came heavily down in the nearest part of the forest, Margaret ran, swift as Camilla, down to the window, and rapped at it with a hurried tremulousness which startled Charlotte within.

"Let me in! Let me in! It is only me, Charlotte!" Her heart did not still its fluttering till she was safe in the drawing-room, with the windows fastened and bolted, and the familiar walls hemming her round, and shutting her in. She had sate down upon a packing case; cheerless, Chill was the dreary and dismantled room—no fire nor other light, but Charlotte's long unsnuffed candle. Charlotte looked at Margaret with surprise; and Margaret, feeling it rather than seeing it, rose up.

"I was afraid you were shutting me out altogether, Charlotte," said she, half-smiling. "And then you would never have heard me in the kitchen, and the doors into the lane and churchyard are locked long ago."

"Oh, miss, I should have been sure to have missed you soon. The men would have wanted you to tell them how to go on. And I have put tea in master's study, as being the most comfortable room, so to speak."

"Thank you, Charlotte. You are a kind girl. I shall be sorry to leave you. You must try and write to me, if I can ever give you any little help or good advice. I shall always be glad to get a letter from Helstone, you know. I shall be sure and send you my address when I know it."

The study was all ready for tea. There was a good blazing fire, and unlighted candles on the table. Margaret sat down on the rug, partly to warm herself, for the dampness of the evening hung about her dress, and over-fatigue had made her chilly. She kept herself balanced by clasping her hands together round her knees; her head dropped a little towards her chest; the attitude was one of despondency, whatever her frame of mind might be. But when she heard her father's step on the gravel outside, she started up, and hastily shaking her heavy black hair back, and wiping a few tears away that had come on her cheeks she knew not how, she went out to open the door for him. He showed far more depression than she did. She could hardly get him to talk, although she tried to speak on subjects that would interest him, at the cost of an effort every time which she thought would be her last.

"Have you been a very long walk to-day?" asked she, on seeing his refusal to touch food of any kind.

"As far as Fordham Beeches. I went to see Widow Maltby; she is sadly grieved at not having wished you good-bye. She says little Susan has kept watch down the lane for days past.—Nay, Margaret, what is the matter, dear?" The thought of the little child watching for her, and continually disappointed—from no forgetfulness on her part, but from sheer inability to leave home—was the last drop in poor Margaret's cup, and she was sobbing away as if her heart would break. Mr. Hale was distressingly perplexed. He rose, and walked nervously up and down the room. Margaret tried to check herself, but would not speak until she could do so with firmness. She heard him talking, as if to himself.

"I cannot bear it. I cannot bear to see the sufferings of others. I think I could go through my own with patience. Oh, is there no going back?"

"No, father," said Margaret, looking straight at him, and speaking low and steadily. "It is bad to believe you in error. It would be infinitely worse to have known you a hypocrite." She dropped her voice at the last few words, as if entertaining the idea of hypocrisy for a moment in connection with her father savoured of irreverence.

"Besides," she went on, "it is only that I am tired to-night; don't think that I am suffering from what you have done, dear papa. We can't either of us talk about it to-night, I believe," said she, finding that tears and sobs would come in spite of herself. "I had better go and take mamma up this cup of tea. She had hers very early, when I was too busy to go to her, and I am sure she will be glad of another now."

Railroad time inexorably wrenched them away from lovely, beloved Helstone, the next morning. They were gone; they had seen the last of the long low parsonage home, half-covered with China-roses and pyracanthus—more homelike than ever in the morning sun that glittered on its windows, each belonging to some well-loved room. Almost before they had settled themselves into the car, sent from Southampton to fetch them to the station, they were gone away to return no more. A sting at Margaret's heart made her strive to look out to catch the last glimpse of the old church tower at the turn where she knew it might be seen above a wave of the forest trees; but her father remembered this too, and she silently acknowledged his greater right to the one window from which it could be seen. She leant back and shut her eyes, and the tears welled forth, and hung glittering for an instant on the shadowing eye-lashes before rolling slowly down her cheeks, and dropping, unheeded, on her dress.

They were to stop in London all night at some quiet hotel. Poor Mrs. Hale had cried in her way nearly all day long; and Dixon showed her sorrow by extreme crossness, and a continual irritable attempt to keep her petticoats from even touching the unconscious Mr. Hale, whom she regarded as the origin of all this suffering.

They went through the well-known streets, past houses which they had often visited, past shops in which she had lounged, impatient, by her aunt's side, while that lady was making some important and interminable decision-nay, absolutely past acquaintances in the streets; for though the morning had been of an incalculable length to them, and they felt as if it ought long ago to have closed in for the repose of darkness, it was the very busiest time of a London afternoon in November when they arrived there. It was long since Mrs. Hale had been in London; and she roused up, almost like a child, to look about her at the different streets, and to gaze after and exclaim at the shops and carriages.

"Oh, there's Harrison's, where I bought so many of my wedding-things. Dear! How altered! They've got immense plate-glass windows, larger than Crawford's in Southampton. Oh, and there, I declare—no, it is not—yes, it is—Margaret, we have just passed Mr. Henry Lennox. Where can he be going, among all these shops?"

Margaret started forwards, and as quickly fell back, half-smiling at herself for the sudden motion. They were a hundred yards away by this time; but he seemed like a relic of Helstone—he was associated with a bright morning, an eventful day, and she should have liked to have seen him, without his seeing her—without the chance of their speaking.

The evening, without employment, passed in a room high up in an hotel, was long and heavy. Mr. Hale went out to his bookseller's, and to call on a friend or two. Every one they saw, either in the house or out in the streets, appeared hurrying to some appointment, expected by, or expecting somebody. They alone seemed strange and friendless, and desolate. Yet within a mile, Margaret knew of house after house, where she for her own sake, and her mother for her Aunt Shaw's, would be welcomed, if they came in gladness, or even in peace of mind. If they came sorrowing, and wanting sympathy in a complicated trouble like the present, then they would be felt as a shadow in all these houses of intimate acquaintances, not friends. London life is too whirling and full to admit of even an hour of that deep silence of feeling which the friends of Job showed, when "they sat with him on the ground seven days and seven nights, and none spake a word unto him; for they saw that his grief was very great."

# CHAPTER VII—
# NEW SCENES AND FACES

"Mist clogs the sunshine,
Smoky dwarf houses
Have we round on every side."
MATTHEW ARNOLD.

The next afternoon, about twenty miles from Milton-Northern, they entered on the little branch railway that led to Heston. Heston itself was one long straggling street, running parallel to the seashore. It had a character of its own, as different from the little bathing-places in the south of England as they again from those of the continent. To use a Scotch word, every thing looked more "purposelike." The country carts had more iron, and less wood and leather about the horse-gear; the people in the streets, although on pleasure bent, had yet a busy mind. The colours looked grayer—more enduring, not so gay and pretty. There were no smock-frocks, even among the country folk; they retarded motion, and were apt to catch on machinery, and so the habit of wearing them had died out. In such towns in the south of England, Margaret had seen the shopmen, when not employed in their business, lounging a little at their doors, enjoying the fresh air, and the look up and down the street. Here, if they had any leisure from customers, they made themselves business in the shop—even, Margaret fancied, to the unnecessary unrolling and rerolling of ribbons. All these differences struck upon her mind, as she and her mother went out next morning to look for lodgings.

Their two nights at hotels had cost more than Mr. Hale had anticipated, and they were glad to take the first clean, cheerful rooms they met with that were at liberty to receive them. There, for the first time for many days, did Margaret feel at rest. There was a dreaminess in the rest, too, which made it still more perfect and luxurious to repose in. The distant sea, lapping the sandy shore with measured sound; the nearer cries of the donkey-boys; the unusual scenes moving before her like pictures, which she cared not in her laziness to have fully explained before they passed away; the stroll down to the beach to breathe the sea-air, soft and warm on that sandy shore even to the end of November; the great long misty sea-line touching the tender-coloured sky; the white sail of a distant boat turning silver in some pale sunbeam:—it seemed as if she could dream her life away in such luxury of pensiveness, in which she made her present all in all, from not daring to think of the past, or wishing to contemplate the future.

But the future must be met, however stern and iron it be. One evening it was arranged that Margaret and her father should go the next day to Milton-Northern, and look out for a house. Mr. Hale had received several letters from Mr. Bell, and one or two from Mr. Thornton, and he was anxious to ascertain at once a good many particulars respecting his position and chances of success there, which he could only do by an interview with the latter gentleman. Margaret knew that they ought to be removing; but she had a repugnance to the idea of a manufacturing town, and believed that her mother was receiving benefit from Heston air, so she would willingly have deferred the expedition to Milton.

For several miles before they reached Milton, they saw a deep lead-coloured cloud hanging over the horizon in the direction in which it lay. It was all the darker from contrast with the pale gray-blue of the wintry sky; for in Heston there had been the earliest signs of frost. Nearer to the town, the air had a faint taste and smell of smoke; perhaps, after all, more a loss of the fragrance of grass and herbage than any positive taste or smell. Quick they were whirled over long, straight, hopeless streets of regularly-built houses, all small and of brick. Here and there a great oblong many-windowed factory stood up, like a hen among her chickens, puffing out black "unparliamentary" smoke, and sufficiently accounting for the cloud, which Margaret had taken to foretell rain. As they drove through the larger and wider streets, from the station to the hotel, they had to stop constantly; great loaded lurries blocked up the not over-wide thoroughfares. Margaret had now and then been into the city in her drives with her aunt. But there the heavy lumbering vehicles seemed various in their purposes and intent; here every van, every waggon and truck, bore cotton, either in the raw shape in bags, or the woven shape in bales of calico. People thronged the footpaths, most of them well-dressed as regarded the material, but with a slovenly looseness which struck Margaret as different from the shabby, threadbare smartness of a similar class in London.

"New Street," said Mr. Hale. "This, I believe, is the principal street in Milton. Bell has often spoken to me about it. It was the opening of this street from a lane into a great thoroughfare, thirty years ago, which has caused his property to rise so much in value. Mr. Thornton's mill must be somewhere not very far off, for he is Mr. Bell's tenant. But I fancy he dates from his warehouse."

"Where is our hotel, papa?"

"Close to the end of this street, I believe. Shall we have lunch before or after we have looked at the houses we marked in the Milton Times?"

"Oh, let us get our work done first."

"Very well. Then I will only see if there is any note or letter for me from Mr. Thornton, who said he would let me know anything he might hear about these houses, and then we will set off. We will keep the cab; it will be safer than losing ourselves, and being too late for the train this afternoon."

There were no letters awaiting him. They set out on their house-hunting. Thirty pounds a-year was all they could afford to give, but in Hampshire they could have met with a roomy house and pleasant garden for the money. Here, even the necessary accommodation of two sitting-rooms and four bed-rooms seemed unattainable. They went through their list, rejecting each as they visited it. Then they looked at each other in dismay.

"We must go back to the second, I think. That one,—in Crampton, don't they call the suburb? There were three sitting-rooms; don't you remember how we laughed at the number compared with the three bed-rooms? But I have planned it all. The front room down-stairs is to be your study and our dining-room (poor papa!), for, you know, we settled mamma is to have as cheerful a sitting-room as we can get; and that front room up-stairs, with the atrocious blue and pink paper and heavy cornice, had really a pretty view over the plain, with a great bend of river, or canal, or whatever it is, down below. Then I could have the little bed-room behind, in that projection at the head of the first flight of stairs—over the kitchen, you know—and you and mamma the room behind the drawing-room, and that closet in the roof will make you a splendid dressing-room."

"But Dixon, and the girl we are to have to help?"

"Oh, wait a minute. I am overpowered by the discovery of my own genius for management. Dixon is to have—let me see, I had it once—the back sitting-room. I think she will like that. She grumbles so much about the stairs at Heston; and the girl is to have that sloping attic over your room and mamma's. Won't that do?"

"I dare say it will. But the papers. What taste! And the overloading such a house with colour and such heavy cornices!"

"Never mind, papa! Surely, you can charm the landlord into re-papering one or two of the rooms—the drawing-room and your bed-room—for mamma will come most in contact with them; and your book-shelves will hide a great deal of that gaudy pattern in the dining-room."

"Then you think it the best? If so, I had better go at once and call on this Mr. Donkin, to whom the advertisement refers me. I will take you back to the hotel, where you can order lunch, and rest, and by the time it is ready, I shall be with you. I hope I shall be able to get new papers."

Margaret hoped so too, though she said nothing. She had never come fairly in contact with the taste that loves ornament, however bad, more than the plainness and simplicity which are of themselves the framework of elegance. Her father took her through the entrance of the hotel, and leaving her at the foot of the staircase, went to the address of the landlord of the house they had fixed upon. Just as Margaret had her hand on the door of their sitting-room, she was followed by a quick-stepping waiter:

"I beg your pardon, ma'am. The gentleman was gone so quickly, I had no time to tell him. Mr. Thornton called almost directly after you left; and, as I understood from what the gentleman said, you would be back in an hour, I told him so, and he came again about five minutes ago, and said he would wait for Mr. Hale. He is in your room now, ma'am."

"Thank you. My father will return soon, and then you can tell him." Margaret opened the door and went in with the straight, fearless, dignified presence habitual to her. She felt no awkwardness; she had too much the habits of society for that. Here was a person come on business to her father; and, as he was one who had shown himself obliging, she was disposed to treat him with a full measure of civility. Mr. Thornton was a good deal more surprised and discomfited than she. Instead of a quiet, middle-aged clergyman, a young lady came forward with frank dignity,—a young lady of a different type to most of those he was in the habit of seeing. Her dress was very plain: a close straw bonnet of the best material and shape, trimmed with white ribbon; a dark silk gown, without any trimming or flounce; a large Indian shawl, which hung about her in long heavy folds, and which she wore as an empress wears her drapery. He did not understand who she was, as he caught the simple, straight, unabashed look, which showed that his being there was of no concern to the beautiful countenance, and called up no flush of surprise to the pale ivory of the complexion. He had heard that Mr. Hale had a daughter, but he had imagined that she was a little girl.

Instead, here before him was a full-grown woman. Her wide red lips were curved into a slight smile, and his gaze lingered there a moment as he recovered from the not unpleasant jolt to his senses her appearance had caused. He looked back up into her eyes. She still regarded him in an even, open way, as though she were weighing *him* rather than the contents of his pocketbook, which was a novel thing of late. He did not know what to make of her, but he thought he should like to get to know her, if she were anything like he had heard of her father.

As for Margaret, her composure faltered and she stood still. Society had not prepared her for meeting such a man as the one who stood before her now, for she had never encountered one who seemed so vigorous. He seemed to suck the air out of the room, only to release it again charged as if before a storm. She had imagined Mr. Thornton to be her father's age at least, if not older, perhaps even a little stooped from sitting at a desk tallying figures. This man was anything but what she had pictured. He was older than she, but only by a few years, she supposed, with not a bit of gray hair to be seen. But what drew her attention most were his eyes; they were as clear and intent as the man she had dreamt of only a few nights before, and her skin tingled where his gaze wandered. Heat rose up her neck as she tried to force the images from the dream away, and she drew in as deep a breath as she could in a corset that seemed suddenly too tight, in an effort to regain her self-control and her manners. "Mr. Thornton, I believe!" said Margaret, after a half-instant's pause, during which his unready words would not come. "Will you sit down. My father brought me to the door, not a minute ago, but unfortunately he was not told that you were here, and he has gone away on some business.

But he will come back almost directly. I am sorry you have had the trouble of calling twice."

Mr. Thornton was in habits of authority himself, but she seemed to assume some kind of rule over him at once. He had been getting impatient at the loss of his time on a market-day, the moment before she appeared, yet now he calmly took a seat at her bidding.

"Do you know where it is that Mr. Hale has gone to? Perhaps I might be able to find him."

"He has gone to a Mr. Donkin's in Canute Street. He is the land-lord of the house my father wishes to take in Crampton."

Mr. Thornton knew the house. He had seen the advertisement, and been to look at it, in compliance with a request of Mr. Bell's that he would assist Mr. Hale to the best of his power: and also instigated by his own interest in the case of a clergyman who had given up his living under circumstances such as those of Mr. Hale. Mr. Thornton had thought that the house in Crampton was really just the thing; but now that he saw Margaret, with her superb ways of moving and looking, he began to feel ashamed of having imagined that it would do very well for the Hales, in spite of a certain vulgarity in it which had struck him at the time of his looking it over.

Margaret could not help her looks; but the short curled upper lip, the round, massive up-turned chin, the manner of carrying her head, her movements, full of a soft feminine defiance, always gave strangers the impression of haughtiness. She was tired now, and would rather have remained silent, and taken the rest her father had planned for her; but, of course, she owed it to herself to be a gentlewoman, and to speak courteously from time to time to this stranger; not over-brushed, nor over-polished, it must be confessed, after his rough encounter with Milton streets and crowds. She wished that he would go, as he had once spoken of doing, instead of sitting there, answering with curt sentences all the remarks she made. She had taken off her shawl, and hung it over the back of her chair. She sat facing him and facing the light; her full beauty met his eye; her round white flexile throat rising out of the full, yet lithe figure; her lips, moving so slightly as she spoke, not breaking the cold serene look of her face with any variation from the one lovely haughty curve; her eyes, with their soft gloom, meeting his with quiet maiden freedom. He almost said to himself that he did not like her, before their conversation ended; he tried so to compensate himself for the mortified feeling, that while he looked upon her with an admiration he could not repress, she looked at him with proud indifference, taking him, he thought, for what, in his irritation, he told himself he was—a great rough fellow, with not a grace or a refinement about him. Her quiet coldness of demeanour he interpreted into contemptuousness, and resented it in his heart to the pitch of almost inclining him to get up and go away, and have nothing more to do with these Hales, and their superciliousness.

Just as Margaret had exhausted her last subject of conversation— and yet conversation that could hardly be called which consisted of so few and such short speeches—her father came in, and with his pleasant gentlemanly courteousness of apology, reinstated his name and family in Mr. Thornton's good opinion.

Mr. Hale and his visitor had a good deal to say respecting their mutual friend, Mr. Bell; and Margaret, glad that her part of entertaining the visitor was over, went to the window to try and make herself more familiar with the strange aspect of the street. She got so much absorbed in watching what was going on outside that she hardly heard her father when he spoke to her, and he had to repeat what he said:

"Margaret! The landlord will persist in admiring that hideous paper, and I am afraid we must let it remain."

"Oh dear! I am sorry!" she replied, and began to turn over in her mind the possibility of hiding part of it, at least, by some of her sketches, but gave up the idea at last, as likely only to make bad worse. Her father, meanwhile, with his kindly country hospitality, was pressing Mr. Thornton to stay to luncheon with them. It would have been very inconvenient to him to do so, yet he felt that he should have yielded, if Margaret by word or look had seconded her father's invitation; he was glad she did not, and yet he was irritated at her for not doing it, and he was irritated at himself for hoping she would have offered when he found her whole manner toward him vexing. She gave him a low, grave bow when he left, and he felt more awkward and self-conscious in every limb than he had ever done in all his life before.

"Well, Margaret, now to luncheon, as fast we can. Have you ordered it?"

Margaret had been watching Mr. Thornton walk away from beneath her lashes, and for the first time since entering the room she felt as if she could breathe properly. But now she wrenched her attention away from him and turned to her father. "No, papa; that man was here when I came home, and I have never had an opportunity."

"Then we must take anything we can get. He must have been waiting a long time, I'm afraid."

"It seemed exceedingly long to me. I was just at the last gasp when you came in. He never went on with any subject, but gave little, short, abrupt answers."

"Very much to the point though, I should think. He is a clearheaded fellow. He said (did you hear?) that Crampton is on gravelly soil, and by far the most healthy suburb in the neighbour hood of Milton."

When they returned to Heston, there was the day's account to be given to Mrs. Hale, who was full of questions which they answered in the intervals of tea-drinking.

"And what is your correspondent, Mr. Thornton, like?"

"Ask Margaret," said her husband. "She and he had a long attempt at conversation, while I was away speaking to the landlord."

"Oh! I hardly know what he is like," said Margaret, lazily; too tired to tax her powers of description much. And then rousing herself, she said, "He is a tall, broad-shouldered man, about—how old, papa?"

"I should guess about thirty."

"About thirty—with a face that is neither exactly plain, nor yet handsome, nothing remarkable—not quite a gentleman; but that was hardly to be expected." She stopped her little speech and looked down, pretending to be interested in the room's carpet and not the man whose voice had made her senses hum with such strange awareness. What had come over her? No man had ever had that effect upon her.

"Not vulgar, or common though," put in her father, rather jealous of any disparagement of the sole friend he had in Milton.

"Oh no!" said Margaret. "With such an expression of resolution and power, no face, however plain in feature, could be either vulgar or common. I should not like to have to bargain with him; he looks very inflexible. Altogether a man who seems made for his niche, mamma; sagacious, and strong, as becomes a great tradesman."

"Don't call the Milton manufacturers tradesmen, Margaret," said her father.

"They are very different."

"Are they? I apply the word to all who have something tangible to sell; but if you think the term is not correct, papa, I won't use it. But, oh mamma! Speaking of vulgarity and commonness, you must prepare yourself for our drawing-room paper. Pink and blue roses, with yellow leaves! And such a heavy cornice round the room!"

But when they removed to their new house in Milton, the obnoxious papers were gone. The landlord received their thanks very composedly; and let them think, if they liked, that he had relented from his expressed determination not to repaper. There was no particular need to tell them, that what he did not care to do for a Reverend Mr. Hale, unknown in Milton, he was only too glad to do at the one short sharp remonstrance of Mr. Thornton, the wealthy manufacturer.

# CHAPTER VIII—HOME SICKNESS

"And it's hame, hame; hame,
Hame fain wad I be."

It needed the pretty light papering of the rooms to reconcile them to Milton. It needed more—more that could not be had. The thick yellow November fogs had come on; and the view of the plain in the valley, made by the sweeping bend of the river, was all shut out when Mrs. Hale arrived at her new home.

Margaret and Dixon had been at work for two days, unpacking and arranging, but everything inside the house still looked in disorder; and outside a thick fog crept up to the very windows, and was driven in to every open door in choking white wreaths of unwholesome mist.

"Oh, Margaret! Are we to live here?" asked Mrs. Hale in blank dismay. Margaret's heart echoed the dreariness of the tone in which this question was put. She could scarcely command herself enough to say, "Oh, the fogs in London are sometimes far worse!"

"But then you knew that London itself, and friends lay behind it. Here—well! We are desolate. Oh Dixon, what a place this is!"

"Indeed, ma'am, I'm sure it will be your death before long, and then I know who'll—stay! Miss Hale, that's far too heavy for you to lift."

"Not at all, thank you, Dixon," replied Margaret, coldly. "The best thing we can do for mamma is to get her room quite ready for her to go to bed, while I go and bring her a cup of coffee."

Mr. Hale was equally out of spirits, and equally came upon Margaret for sympathy.

"Margaret, I do believe this is an unhealthy place. Only suppose that your mother's health or yours should suffer. I wish I had gone into some country place in Wales; this is really terrible," said he, going up to the window. There was no comfort to be given. They were settled in Milton, and must endure smoke and fogs for a season; indeed, all other life seemed shut out from them by as thick a fog of circumstance. Only the day before, Mr. Hale had been reckoning up with dismay how much their removal and fortnight at Heston had cost, and he found it had absorbed nearly all his little stock of ready money. No! Here they were, and here they must remain.

At night when Margaret realised this, she felt inclined to sit down in a stupor of despair. The heavy smoky air hung about her bedroom, which occupied the long narrow projection at the back of the house. The window, placed at the side of the oblong, looked to the blank wall of a similar projection, not above ten feet distant. It loomed through the fog like a great barrier to hope. Inside the room everything was in confusion. All their efforts had been directed to make her mother's room comfortable. Margaret sat down on a box, the direction card upon which struck her as having been written at Helstone—beautiful, beloved Helstone! She lost herself in dismal thought: but at last she determined to take her mind away from the present; and suddenly remembered that she had a letter from Edith which she had only half read in the bustle of the morning. It was to tell of their arrival at Corfu; their voyage along the Mediterranean—their music, and dancing on board ship; the gay new life opening upon her; her house with its trellised balcony, and its views over white cliffs and deep blue sea. Edith wrote fluently and well, if not graphically. She could not only seize the salient and characteristic points of a scene, but she could enumerate enough of indiscriminate particulars for Margaret to make it out for herself Captain Lennox and another lately married officer shared a villa, high up on the beautiful precipitous rocks overhanging the sea. Their days, late as it was in the year, seemed spent in boating or land pic-nics;

all out-of-doors, pleasure-seeking and glad, Edith's life seemed like the deep vault of blue sky above her, free—utterly free from fleck or cloud. Her husband had to attend drill, and she, the most musical officer's wife there, had to copy the new and popular tunes out of the most recent English music, for the benefit of the bandmaster; those seemed their most severe and arduous duties. She expressed an affectionate hope that, if the regiment stopped another year at Corfu, Margaret might come out and pay her a long visit. She asked Margaret if she remembered the day twelve-month on which she, Edith, wrote—how it rained all day long in Harley Street; and how she would not put on her new gown to go to a stupid dinner, and get it all wet and splashed in going to the carriage; and how at that very dinner they had first met Captain Lennox.

Yes! Margaret remembered it well. Edith and Mrs. Shaw had gone to dinner. Margaret had joined the party in the evening. The recollection of the plentiful luxury of all the arrangements, the stately handsomeness of the furniture, the size of the house, the peaceful, untroubled ease of the visitors—all came vividly before her, in strange contrast to the present time. The smooth sea of that old life closed up, without a mark left to tell where they had all been. The habitual dinners, the calls, the shopping, the dancing evenings, were all going on, going on for ever, though her Aunt Shaw and Edith were no longer there; and she, of course, was even less missed. She doubted if any one of that old set ever thought of her, except Henry Lennox. He too, she knew, would strive to forget her, because of the pain she had caused him. She had heard him often boast of his power of putting any disagreeable thought far away from him. Then she penetrated farther into what might have been. If she had cared for him as a lover, and had accepted him, and this change in her father's opinions and consequent station had taken place, she could not doubt but that it would have been impatiently received by Mr. Lennox. It was a bitter mortification to her in one sense; but she could bear it patiently, because she knew her father's purity of purpose, and that strengthened her to endure his errors, grave and serious though in her estimation they were. But the fact of the world esteeming her father degraded, in its rough wholesale judgment, would have oppressed and irritated Mr. Lennox. As she realised what might have been, she grew to be thankful for what was. They were at the lowest now; they could not be worse. Edith's astonishment and her Aunt Shaw's dismay would have to be met bravely, when their letters came. So Margaret rose up and began slowly to undress herself, feeling the full luxury of acting leisurely, late as it was, after all the past hurry of the day. She fell asleep, hoping for some brightness, either internal or external. But if she had known how long it would be before the brightness came, her heart would have sunk low down. The time of the year was most unpropitious to health as well as to spirits. Her mother caught a severe cold, and Dixon herself was evidently not well, although Margaret could not insult her more than by trying to save her, or by taking any care of her. They could hear of no girl to assist her; all were at work in the factories; at least, those who applied were well scolded by Dixon, for thinking that such as they could ever be trusted to work in a gentleman's house. So they had to keep a charwoman in almost constant employ. Margaret longed to send for Charlotte; but besides the objection of her being a better servant than they could now afford to keep, the distance was too great.

Mr. Hale met with several pupils, recommended to him by Mr. Bell, or by the more immediate influence of Mr. Thornton. They were mostly of the age when many boys would be still at school, but, according to the prevalent, and apparently well-founded notions of Milton, to make a lad into a good tradesman he must be caught young, and acclimated to the life of the mill, or office, or warehouse. If he were sent to even the Scotch Universities, he came back unsettled for commercial pursuits; how much more so if he went to Oxford or Cambridge, where he could not be entered till he was eighteen? So most of the manufacturers placed their sons in sucking situations" at fourteen or fifteen years of age, unsparingly cutting away all off-shoots in the direction of literature or high mental cultivation, in hopes of throwing the whole strength and vigour of the plant into commerce. Still there were some wiser parents; and some young men, who had sense enough to perceive their own deficiencies, and strive to remedy them. Nay, there were a few no longer youths, but men in the prime of life, who had the stern wisdom to acknowledge their own ignorance, and to learn late what they should have learnt early. Mr. Thornton was perhaps the oldest of Mr. Hale's pupils. He was certainly the favourite. He came to the house frequently, and every now and then his voice drifted up to Margaret as he was admitted. She found herself listening for him and when she realised it, she firmly put an end to it by being in a part of the house where she could not hear him. Not that she could forget his existence. And one afternoon proved how deeply he had staked his claim on her thoughts. She had been helping Dixon whenever needed for the tasks she thought beneath her and which the charwoman they had employed refused to do. Margaret was used to keeping busy but manual labour was more tiring than her other pursuits, and she often rested in her room for a little while each day. This particular day, Margaret was more tired than usual, and it was not long before she was asleep.

Margaret was back in the house. She walked down a long hallway until she came to a door that was slightly ajar. Opening it all the way, she peeked inside and found a room filled with steam and the scent of lavender. She moved forward, and in the centre of it saw a large, claw-footed tub that looked as if two could easily fit inside it. A stack of cloths and various soaps were set upon a table near it, ready for use. Ah, this was just what she needed, a relaxing bath.

She quickly untied the belt of her dressing robe and stepped into it. Margaret sighed and laid back, her head resting on the edge of the tub, letting the heat of the water and the pleasant aroma of the herbs ease her tired muscles. She had no idea how long she had lain there when the door opened and a deep, masculine voice sounded in the room.

"There you are."

Margaret's heart tripped and began to pound loudly; her mystery lover had returned! She opened her eyes, anticipation sizzling through her when he turned and slid the bolt into place, locking out intruders. He moved closer and stopped just at the end of the tub. As before, his face was mostly in shadow, but the heat of his gaze made the water seem cool as it roamed over her face, her limbs, her breasts, to the delta between her thighs. Her skin pebbled in response, her nipples tightening. Never would she have imagined that one look could have such an effect upon her! Margaret drew her legs in to give him room in the bath, whispering, "Join me?"

He grinned back at her and began removing his clothes. Margaret let her own gaze wander his tall, broad-shouldered and thick-limbed frame as he undressed, and she sighed appreciatively. He was beautiful, this mysterious man that she somehow knew— and did not. She bit her lip to control the desire already flowing in her veins as he stepped into the tub. She wanted him, wanted to feel his hands on her, wanted to feel him deep inside her again. He did not reach for her as she hoped he would; instead, her lover took a bar of soap from the bowl in hand and picked up a washcloth. These he dipped into the water and made a rich lather, watching her with hooded eyes.

"Turn around."

She did as he urged, leaning over the edge of the tub and trembling as she waited for his touch. The cloth was slightly abrasive as he smoothed it over the skin of her nape, her shoulders.

His free hand caressed where he had already washed as he moved the cloth, and his attention, lower. Tingles worked their way up her spine and spread, within as well as without, as the cloth softly scraped and the pads of his fingers brushed her skin. Margaret closed her eyes and purred, arching her back toward him for more of his touch. She felt his hand tremble as he continued plying the soapy cloth, now smoothing the indentation above her buttocks. Margaret thought she would combust if he kept this up much longer. She wished he would kiss her and that he would touch her there, between her legs, where she ached.

His hands stilled, left her. A moment later, water trickled over her skin and her lover leaned forward, his rigid length nestling between her thighs. He pressed an open-mouthed kiss to the back of her neck. His warm breath and tongue sent another quiver of desire through her, and she tilted her neck toward him, offering more access. His hot mouth worked its way up toward her ear, a nip here, a lick there. Her breath grew more uneven, and she felt coiled tight as a spring. She turned her head and his lips captured hers. One rough palm caressed her cheek, the other, a breast. His fingers found her nipple and teased it into an unbearable point of sensation that seemed to echo in her moistened, swollen core. Margaret whimpered and pressed herself back against him.

She must have begged, for his hand moved down, finding her dampness and caressing within and without, deftly flicking the bud buried within her folds. Darts of pleasure burst from her centre, shutting down her mind so that her only thought was the hope that this should never end. That this man and the exquisite feelings he wrought in her should always be a part of her life. She cried out as ecstasy overwhelmed her, catching his other hand and twining her fingers with his as she flew apart, though he held her close and safe all the while against him.

"I want you," she whispered when she could breathe normally again.

"What do you want, love?"

She swallowed, closed her eyes. "You, inside me."

"God, yes, I want that too," he murmured. "Look at me, Margaret."

She turned round. He had moved slightly away from her. Margaret leaned forward, cupped his face, and pressed her lips to his. She slid them back and forth, teasing and caressing. His breath hitched, and she opened her eyes and smiled at him. Mr. Thornton gazed back at her, his expression determined, hungry. Her chest rose and fell on a deep breath, desire coiling through her, hot and heady, as he caught one of her hands and tugged her gently toward him. She straddled him, his erection teasing her cleft as she settled on his lap, and the rapid thud of his heart matched her own as her breasts crushed against his hard chest, sending more thrilling sensations rushing through her body. He drew her face down toward his again, and she licked her lips, parting them for the coming kiss. His mouth closed over hers. His tongue delved inside to claim and coax hers, while his hands moved to her hair, his fingers uncoiling and sifting through the thick strands.

His mouth gentled, his tongue dancing with hers, gliding around, stroking along it. Margaret trembled and ached more than she had before with each caress. When he began to leave her, heedless of her own need for breath, her hands moved to his shoulders, and her lips closed around the agile muscle, drew it into her mouth, and suckled. His low groan reverberated throughout her body, and Margaret, encouraged, repeated the caress.

Mr. Thornton broke away to stare at her, his face as flushed as hers no doubt was. "I have to have you now."

His voice shook, but his movements were sure as he lifted her and positioned her over his shaft. Margaret lowered herself, sighing as she took him inside her moist and aching core. His hands tangled in her hair again as she bent her head, seeking his lips. His tongue darted into her mouth again, mimicking his thrusts into her eager body as she moved downward to meet him. Water sloshed around them, a musical background to their rhythmic moans. Margaret gasped and held on to him for support as pleasure began to build. Mr. Thornton's hands caught her hips and he drove up into her, harder and faster. As if he could not get enough of her any more than she could get enough of him. Margaret's head fell back and she shivered all over, her body exploding with delight as another shattering release obliterated her control making her motions almost erratic as she rode him.

"Oh, Mr. Thornton!" she panted, clutching at his shoulders, once more letting him be her anchor.

In reply, he grunted her own name, driving so hard up into her that water splashed over the edge of the tub. At last he fell still and rested his head against her, his face buried in her throat, his breathing ragged. He lifted his head and gazed at her, this time with tenderness, as he lifted a hand to caress her cheek.

Margaret started awake with a gasp. Panting, heat rising to her face, she sat up and glanced around the room, disoriented. Where was the tub? Where was Mr. Thornton? Margaret, blinked, looked again, and sighed in relief. She was in her own bedroom, in her house in Crampton. Light slanted in through her window, much lower than when she had lain down. It must be late afternoon. Good heavens, she had not meant to sleep so long. Her limbs shook as she rose and made her way to it, pulling the curtains aside to raise the sash.

The winter air did nothing to cool her face, or her body. She closed her eyes again, almost able to feel his body against hers, his lips hot as fire as he kissed her. She pressed her palms to her face, trying to blot out the images that continued to play in her mind. It did no good. She drew another deep breath and expelled it slowly. "It was just a dream," she reminded herself.

But why dream of Mr. Thornton at all, a man she did not know, and did not want to know? It made no sense. If only she had someone to confide in, but she doubted Edith would understand much beyond the physical aspect of it.

Margaret comforted herself with the fact that she could avoid him when he came to the house, and she never went near the mills in town, so she was safe there, too. If only her father would stop talking of him in between his lessons.

Mr. Hale got into the habit of quoting his opinions so frequently, and with such regard, that it became a little domestic joke to wonder what time, during the hour appointed for instruction, could be given to absolute learning, so much of it appeared to have been spent in conversation.

Margaret rather encouraged this light, merry way of viewing her father's acquaintance with Mr. Thornton, because she felt that her mother was inclined to look upon this new friendship of her husband's with jealous eyes. As long as his time had been solely occupied with his books and his parishioners, as at Helstone, she had appeared to care little whether she saw much of him or not; but now that he looked eagerly forward to each renewal of his intercourse with Mr. Thornton, she seemed hurt and annoyed, as if he were slighting her companionship for the first time. Mr. Hale's over-praise had the usual effect of over-praise upon his auditors; they were a little inclined to rebel against Aristides being always called the Just.

After a quiet life in a country parsonage for more than twenty years, there was something dazzling to Mr. Hale in the energy which conquered immense difficulties with ease; the power of the machinery of Milton, the power of the men of Milton, impressed him with a sense of grandeur, which he yielded to without caring to inquire into the details of its exercise. But Margaret went less abroad, among machinery and men; saw less of power in its public effect, and, as it happened, she was thrown with one or two of those who, in all measures affecting masses of people, must be acute sufferers for the good of many. The question always is, has everything been done to make the sufferings of these exceptions as small as possible? Or, in the triumph of the crowded procession, have the helpless been trampled on, instead of being gently lifted aside out of the roadway of the conqueror, whom they have no power to accompany on his march?

It fell to Margaret's share to have to look out for a servant to assist Dixon, who had at first undertaken to find just the person she wanted to do all the rough work of the house. But Dixon's ideas of helpful girls were founded on the recollection of tidy elder scholars at Helstone school, who were only too proud to be allowed to come to the parsonage on a busy day, and treated Mrs. Dixon with all the respect, and a good deal more of fright, which they paid to Mr. and Mrs. Hale. Dixon was not unconscious of this awed reverence, which was given to her; nor did she dislike it; it flattered her much as Louis the Fourteenth was flattered by his courtiers shading their eyes from the dazzling light of his presence. But nothing short of her faithful love for Mrs. Hale could have made her endure the rough independent way in which all the Milton girls, who made application for the servant's place, replied to her inquiries respecting their qualifications. They even went the length of questioning her back again; having doubts and fears of their own, as to the solvency of a family who lived in a house of thirty pounds a-year, and yet gave themselves airs, and kept two servants, one of them so very high and mighty. Mr. Hale was no longer looked upon as Vicar of Helstone, but as a man who only spent at a certain rate. Margaret was weary and impatient of the accounts which Dixon perpetually brought to Mrs. Hale of the behaviour of these would-be servants. Not but what Margaret was repelled by the rough uncourteous manners of these people; not but what she shrunk with fastidious pride from their hail-fellow accost and severely resented their unconcealed curiosity as to the means and position of any family who lived in Milton, and yet were not engaged in trade of some kind. But the more Margaret felt impertinence, the more likely she was to be silent on the subject; and, at any rate, if she took upon herself to make inquiry for a servant, she could spare her mother the recital of all her disappointments and fancied or real insults.

Margaret accordingly went up and down to butchers and grocers, seeking for a nonpareil of a girl; and lowering her hopes and expectations every week, as she found the difficulty of meeting with any one in a manufacturing town who did not prefer the better wages and greater independence of working in a mill. It was something of a trial to Margaret to go out by herself in this busy bustling place. Mrs. Shaw's ideas of propriety and her own helpless dependence on others, had always made her insist that a footman should accompany Edith and Margaret, if they went beyond Harley Street or the immediate neighbourhood. The limits by which this rule of her aunt's had circumscribed Margaret's independence had been silently rebelled against at the time: and she had doubly enjoyed the free walks and rambles of her forest life, from the contrast, which they presented. She went along there with a bounding fearless step, that occasionally broke out into a run, if she were in a hurry, and occasionally was stilled into perfect repose, as she stood listening to, or watching any of the wild creatures who sang in the leafy courts, or glanced out with their keen bright eyes from the low brushwood or tangled furze. It was a trial to come down from such motion or such stillness, only guided by her own sweet will, to the even and decorous pace necessary in streets. But she could have laughed at herself for minding this change, if it had not been accompanied by what was a more serious annoyance. The side of the town on which Crampton lay was especially a thoroughfare for the factory people. In the back streets around them there were many mills, out of which poured streams of men and women two or three times a day. Until Margaret had learnt the times of their ingress and egress, she was very unfortunate in constantly falling in with them. They came rushing along, with bold, fearless faces, and loud laughs and jests, particularly aimed at all those who appeared to be above them in rank or station. The tones of their unrestrained voices, and their carelessness of all common rules of street politeness, frightened Margaret a little at first. The girls, with their rough, but not unfriendly freedom, would comment on her dress, even touch her shawl or gown to ascertain the exact material; nay, once or twice she was asked questions relative to some article which they particularly admired. There was such a simple reliance on her womanly sympathy with their love of dress, and on her kindliness, that she gladly replied to these inquiries, as soon as she understood them; and half smiled back at their remarks. She did not mind meeting any number of girls, loud spoken and boisterous though they might be. But she alternately dreaded and fired up against the workmen, who commented not on her dress, but on her looks, in the same open fearless manner. She, who had hitherto felt that even the most refined remark on her personal appearance was an impertinence, had to endure undisguised admiration from these outspoken men. But the very out-spokenness marked their innocence of any intention to hurt her delicacy, as she would have perceived if she had been less frightened by the disorderly tumult. Out of her fright came a flash of indignation which made her face scarlet, and her dark eyes gather flame, as she heard some of their speeches. Yet there were other sayings of theirs, which, when she reached the quiet safety of home, amused her even while they irritated her.

For instance, one day, after she had passed a number of men, several of whom had paid her the not unusual compliment of wishing she was their sweetheart, one of the lingerers added, "Your bonny face, my lass, makes the day look brighter." And another day, as she was unconsciously smiling at some passing thought, she was addressed by a poorly-dressed, middle-aged workman, with "You may well smile, my lass; many a one would smile to have such a bonny face." This man looked so careworn that Margaret could not help giving him an answering smile, glad to think that her looks, such as they were, should have had the power to call up a pleasant thought. He seemed to understand her acknowledging glance, and a silent recognition was established between them whenever the chances of the day brought them across each other's paths. They had never exchanged a word; nothing had been said but that first compliment; yet somehow Margaret looked upon this man with more interest than upon any one else in Milton. Once or twice, on Sundays, she saw him walking with a girl, evidently his daughter, and, if possible, still more unhealthy than he was himself.

One day Margaret and her father had been as far as the fields that lay around the town; it was early spring, and she had gathered some of the hedge and ditch flowers, dog-violets, lesser celandines, and the like, with an unspoken lament in her heart for the sweet profusion of the South. Her father had left her to go into Milton upon some business; and on the road home she met her humble friends. The girl looked wistfully at the flowers, and, acting on a sudden impulse, Margaret offered them to her. Her pale blue eyes lightened up as she took them, and her father spoke for her.

"Thank yo, Miss. Bessy'll think a deal o' them flowers; that hoo will; and I shall think a deal o' yor kindness. Yo're not of this country, I reckon?"

"No!" said Margaret, half sighing. "I come from the South—from Hampshire," she continued, a little afraid of wounding his consciousness of ignorance, if she used a name which he did not understand.

"That's beyond London, I reckon? And I come fro' Burnley-ways, and forty mile to th' North. And yet, yo see, North and

South has both met and made kind o' friends in this big smoky place."

Margaret had slackened her pace to walk alongside of the man and his daughter, whose steps were regulated by the feebleness of the latter. She now spoke to the girl, and there was a sound of tender pity in the tone of her voice as she did so that went right to the heart of the father.

"I'm afraid you are not very strong."

"No," said the girl, "nor never will be."

"Spring is coming," said Margaret, as if to suggest pleasant, hopeful thoughts.

"Spring nor summer will do me good," said the girl quietly.

Margaret looked up at the man, almost expecting some contradiction from him, or at least some remark that would modify his daughter's utter hopelessness. But, instead, he added—

"I'm afeared hoo speaks truth. I'm afeared hoo's too far gone in a waste."

"I shall have a spring where I'm boun to, and flowers, and amaranths, and shining robes besides."

"Poor lass, poor lass!" said her father in a low tone. "I'm none so sure o' that; but it's a comfort to thee, poor lass, poor lass. Poor father! It'll be soon."

Margaret was shocked by his words—shocked but not repelled; rather attracted and interested.

"Where do you live? I think we must be neighbours, we meet so often on this road."

"We put up at nine Frances Street, second turn to th' left at after yo've past th' Goulden Dragon."

"And your name? I must not forget that."

"I'm none ashamed o' my name. It's Nicholas Higgins. Hoo's called Bessy Higgins. Whatten yo' asking for?"

Margaret was surprised at this last question, for at Helstone it would have been an understood thing, after the inquiries she had made, that she intended to come and call upon any poor neighbour whose name and habitation she had asked for.

"I thought—I meant to come and see you." She suddenly felt rather shy of offering the visit, without having any reason to give for her wish to make it, beyond a kindly interest in a stranger. It seemed all at once to take the shape of an impertinence on her part; she read this meaning too in the man's eyes.

"I'm none so fond of having strange folk in my house." But then relenting, as he saw her heightened colour, he added, "Yo're a foreigner, as one may say, and maybe don't know many folk here, and yo've given my wench here flowers out of yo'r own hand;—yo may come if yo like."

Margaret was half-amused, half-nettled at this answer. She was not sure if she would go where permission was given so like a favour conferred. But when they came to the town into Frances Street, the girl stopped a minute, and said,

"Yo'll not forget yo're to come and see us."

"Aye, aye," said the father, impatiently, "hoo'll come. Hoo's a bit set up now, because hoo thinks I might ha' spoken more civilly; but hoo'll think better on it, and come. I can read her proud bonny face like a book. Come along, Bess; there's the mill bell ringing."

Margaret went home, wondering at her new friends, and smiling at the man's insight into what had been passing in her mind. From that day Milton became a brighter place to her. It was not the long, bleak sunny days of spring, nor yet was it that time was reconciling her to the town of her habitation. It was that in it she had found a human interest.

# CHAPTER IX—DRESSING FOR TEA

"Let China's earth, enrich'd with colour'd stains,
Pencil'd with gold, and streak'd with azure veins,
The grateful flavour of the Indian leaf,
Or Mocho's sunburnt berry glad receive."
MRS. BARBAULD.

The day after this meeting with Higgins and his daughter, Mr. Hale came upstairs into the little drawing-room at an unusual hour. He went up to different objects in the room, as if examining them, but Margaret saw that it was merely a nervous trick—a way of putting off something he wished, yet feared to say. Out it came at last—

"My dear! I've asked Mr. Thornton to come to tea to-night."

Mrs. Hale was leaning back in her easy chair, with her eyes shut, and an expression of pain on her face, which had become habitual to her of late. But she roused up into querulousness at this speech of her husband's.

"Mr. Thornton!—and to-night! What in the world does the man want to come here for? And Dixon is washing my muslins and laces, and there is no soft water with these horrid east winds, which I suppose we shall have all the year round in Milton."

"The wind is veering round, my dear," said Mr. Hale, looking out at the smoke, which drifted right from the east, only he did not yet understand the points of the compass, and rather arranged them ad libitum, according to circumstances.

"Don't tell me!" said Mrs. Hale, shuddering up, and wrapping her shawl about her still more closely. "But, east or west wind, I suppose this man comes."

"Oh, mamma, that shows you never saw Mr. Thornton. He looks like a person who would enjoy battling with every adverse thing he could meet with—enemies, winds, or circumstances. The more it rains and blows, the more certain we are to have him. But I'll go and help Dixon. I'm getting to be a famous clear-starcher. And he won't want any amusement beyond talking to papa. Papa, I am really longing to see the Pythias to your Damon. You know I never saw him but once, and then we were so puzzled to know what to say to each other that we did not get on particularly well."

"I don't know that you would ever like him, or think him agreeable, Margaret. He is not a lady's man."

Margaret wreathed her throat in a scornful curve.

"I don't particularly admire ladies' men, papa. But Mr. Thornton comes here as your friend—as one who has appreciated you"—

"The only person in Milton," said Mrs. Hale.

"So we will give him a welcome, and some cocoa-nut cakes. Dixon will be flattered if we ask her to make some; and I will undertake to iron your caps, mamma."

Many a time that morning did Margaret wish Mr. Thornton far enough away. She had planned other employments for herself: a letter to Edith, a good piece of Dante, a visit to the Higginses. But, instead, she ironed away, listening to Dixon's complaints, and only hoping that by an excess of sympathy she might prevent her from carrying the recital of her sorrows to Mrs. Hale. Every now and then, Margaret had to remind herself of her father's regard for Mr. Thornton, to subdue the irritation of weariness that was stealing over her, and bringing on one of the bad headaches to which she had lately become liable. She could hardly speak when she sat down at last, and told her mother that she was no longer Peggy the laundry-maid, but Margaret Hale the lady. She meant this speech for a little joke, and was vexed enough with her busy tongue when she found her mother taking it seriously.

"Yes! if any one had told me, when I was Miss Beresford, and one of the belles of the county, that a child of mine would have to stand half a day, in a little poky kitchen, working away like any servant, that we might prepare properly for the reception of a tradesman, and that this tradesman should be the only"—"Oh, mamma!" said Margaret, lifting herself up, "don't punish me so for a careless speech. I don't mind ironing, or any kind of work, for you and papa. I am myself a born and bred lady through it all, even though it comes to scouring a floor, or washing dishes. I am tired now, just for a little while; but in half an hour I shall be ready to do the same over again. And as to Mr. Thornton's being in trade, why he can't help that now, poor fellow. I don't suppose his education would fit him for much else." Margaret lifted herself slowly up, and went to her own room; for just now she could not bear much more.

In Mr. Thornton's house, at this very same time, a similar, yet different, scene was going on. A large-boned lady, long past middle age, sat at work in a grim handsomely-furnished dining-room. Her features, like her frame, were strong and massive, rather than heavy. Her face moved slowly from one decided expression to another equally decided. There was no great variety in her countenance; but those who looked at it once, generally looked at it again; even the passers-by in the street, half-turned their heads to gaze an instant longer at the firm, severe, dignified woman, who never gave way in street-courtesy, or paused in her straight-onward course to the clearly-defined end which she proposed to herself. She was handsomely dressed in stout black silk, of which not a thread was worn or discoloured. She was mending a large long table-cloth of the finest texture, holding it up against the light occasionally to discover thin places, which required her delicate care. There was not a book about in the room, with the exception of Matthew Henry's Bible Commentaries, six volumes of which lay in the centre of the massive side-board, flanked by a tea-urn on one side, and a lamp on the other. In some remote apartment, there was exercise upon the piano going on. Some one was practising up a morceau de salon, playing it very rapidly; every third note, on an average, being either indistinct, or wholly missed out, and the loud chords at the end being half of them false, but not the less satisfactory to the performer. Mrs. Thornton heard a step, like her own in its decisive character, pass the dining-room door.

"John! Is that you?"

Her son opened the door and showed himself.

"What has brought you home so early? I thought you were going to tea with that friend of Mr. Bell's; that Mr. Hale."

"So I am, mother; I am come home to dress!"

"Dress! humph! When I was a girl, young men were satisfied with dressing once in a day. Why should you dress to go and take a cup of tea with an old parson?"

"Mr. Hale is a gentleman, and his wife and daughter are ladies."

"Wife and daughter! Do they teach too? What do they do? You have never mentioned them."

"No! mother, because I have never seen Mrs. Hale; I have only seen Miss Hale for half an hour."

"Take care you don't get caught by a penniless girl, John."

"I am not easily caught, mother, as I think you know. But I must not have Miss Hale spoken of in that way, which, you know, is offensive to me. I never was aware of any young lady trying to catch me yet, nor do I believe that any one has ever given themselves that useless trouble."

Mrs. Thornton did not choose to yield the point to her son; or else she had, in general, pride enough for her sex.

"Well! I only say, take care. Perhaps our Milton girls have too much spirit and good feeling to go angling after husbands; but this Miss Hale comes out of the aristocratic counties, where, if all tales be true, rich husbands are reckoned prizes."

Mr. Thornton's brow contracted, and he came a step forward into the room.

"Mother" (with a short scornful laugh), "you will make me confess. The only time I saw Miss Hale, she treated me with a haughty civility, which had a strong flavour of contempt in it. She held herself aloof from me as if she had been a queen, and I her humble, unwashed vassal. Be easy, mother."

"No! I am not easy, nor content either. What business had she, a renegade clergyman's daughter, to turn up her nose at you! I would dress for none of them—a saucy set! If I were you." As he was leaving the room, he said:—

"Mr. Hale is good, and gentle, and learned. He is not saucy. As for Mrs. Hale, I will tell you what she is like to-night, if you care to hear." He shut the door and was gone.

"Despise my son! Treat him as her vassal, indeed! Humph! I should like to know where she could find such another! Boy and man, he's the noblest, stoutest heart I ever knew. I don't care if I am his mother; I can see what's what, and not be blind. I know what Fanny is; and I know what John is. Despise him! I hate her!"

# CHAPTER X—WROUGHT IRON AND GOLD

"We are the trees whom shaking fastens more."
GEORGE HERBERT.

Mr. Thornton left the house without coming into the dining-room again. He was rather late, and walked rapidly out to Crampton. He was anxious not to slight his new friend by any disrespectful unpunctuality. The church-clock struck half-past seven as he stood at the door awaiting Dixon's slow movements; always doubly tardy when she had to degrade herself by answering the door-bell. He was ushered into the little drawing-room, and kindly greeted by Mr. Hale, who led him up to his wife, whose pale face, and shawl-draped figure made a silent excuse for the cold languor of her greeting. Margaret was lighting the lamp when he entered, for the darkness was coming on. Mr. Thornton paused and his ready greeting caught in his throat when she completed her task and turned toward him, a soft smile upon her face. Her gaze met his and held an instant, and his heart leapt, starting up again at a rapid pace. But then she lowered her eyes and moved to where the tea things stood, and he felt strangely as if he had lost something. He glanced around to clear his head. The lamp threw a pretty light into the centre of the dusky room, from which, with country habits, they did not exclude the night-skies, and the outer darkness of air. Somehow, that room contrasted itself with the one he had lately left; handsome, ponderous, with no sign of feminine habitation, except in the one spot where his mother sate, and no convenience for any other employment than eating and drinking. To be sure, it was a dining-room; his mother preferred to sit in it; and her will was a household law. But the drawing-room was not like this. It was twice—twenty times as fine; not one quarter as comfortable. Here were no mirrors, not even a scrap of glass to reflect the light, and answer the same purpose as water in a landscape; no gilding; a warm, sober breadth of colouring, well relieved by the dear old Helstone chintz-curtains and chair covers. An open davenport stood in the window opposite the door; in the other there was a stand, with a tall white china vase, from which drooped wreaths of English ivy, pale-green birch, and copper-coloured beech-leaves. Pretty baskets of work stood about in different places: and books, not cared for on account of their binding solely, lay on one table, as if recently put down. Behind the door was another table, decked out for tea, with a white tablecloth, on which flourished the cocoa-nut cakes, and a basket piled with oranges and ruddy American apples, heaped on leaves.

It appeared to Mr. Thornton that all these graceful cares were habitual to the family; and especially of a piece with Margaret. She stood by the tea-table in a light-coloured muslin gown, which had a good deal of pink about it. She looked as if she was not attending to the conversation, but solely busy with the tea-cups, among which her round ivory hands moved with pretty, noiseless, daintiness. She had a bracelet on one taper arm, which would fall down over her round wrist. Mr. Thornton watched the replacing of this troublesome ornament with far more attention than he listened to her father. It seemed as if it fascinated him to see her push it up impatiently, until it tightened her soft flesh; and then to mark the loosening—the fall. He could almost have exclaimed— "There it goes, again!" There was so little left to be done after he arrived at the preparation for tea, that he was almost sorry the obligation of eating and drinking came so soon to prevent his watching Margaret. But he was equally relieved, for again he had let himself become entranced in her presence and near unable to speak. Worse, to his dismay, his trousers had become snug in front. This would not do, he rebuked himself, shifting slightly in his chair. Miss Hale was a lady, and he had best not let the unexpected desire that had rushed through him as he had watched her let him forget that. She handed him his cup of tea with the proud air of an unwilling slave; but her eye caught the moment when he was ready for another cup; and he almost longed to ask her to do for him what he saw her compelled to do for her father, who took her little finger and thumb in his masculine hand, and made them serve as sugar-tongs. Mr. Thornton saw her beautiful eyes lifted to her father, full of light, half-laughter and half-love, as this bit of pantomime went on between the two, unobserved, as they fancied, by any. Margaret's head still ached, as the paleness of her complexion, and her silence might have testified; but she was resolved to throw herself into the breach, if there was any long untoward pause, rather than that her father's friend, pupil, and guest should have cause to think himself in any way neglected. But the conversation went on; and Margaret drew into a corner, near her mother, with her work, after the tea-things were taken away; and felt that she might let her thoughts roam, without fear of being suddenly wanted to fill up a gap.

Mr. Thornton and Mr. Hale were both absorbed in the continuation of some subject, which had been started at their last meeting. Margaret was recalled to a sense of the present by some trivial, low-spoken remark of her mother's; and on suddenly looking up from her work, her eye was caught by the difference of outward appearance between her father and Mr. Thornton, as betokening such distinctly opposite natures. Her father was of slight figure, which made him appear taller than he really was, when not contrasted, as at this time, with the tall, massive frame of another. The lines in her father's face were soft and waving, with a frequent undulating kind of trembling movement passing over them, showing every fluctuating emotion; the eyelids were large and arched, giving to the eyes a peculiar languid beauty, which was almost feminine. The brows were finely arched, but were, by the very size of the dreamy lids, raised to a considerable distance from the eyes. Now, in Mr. Thornton's face the straight brows fell low over the clear, deep-set earnest eyes, which, without being unpleasantly sharp, seemed intent enough to penetrate into the very heart and core of what he was looking at. The lines in the face were few but firm, as if they were carved in marble, and lay principally about the lips, which were slightly compressed over a set of teeth so faultless and beautiful as to give the effect of sudden sunlight when the rare bright smile, coming in an instant and shining out of the eyes, changed the whole look from the severe and resolved expression of a man ready to do and dare everything, to the keen honest enjoyment of the moment, which is seldom shown so fearlessly and instantaneously except by children. Margaret liked this smile; it was the first thing she had admired in this new friend of her father's; and the opposition of character, shown in all these details of appearance she had just been noticing, seemed to explain the attraction they evidently felt towards each other. He turned toward her, as if sensing her scrutiny, and once again she felt unable to breathe as their gazes met, and held. Her heart fluttered as images from her dream rose in her mind. Before she could stop herself, she wondered if his kisses were as wonderful in reality. Margaret frowned and jerked her attention from him, determined to ignore him as much as civility allowed for the remainder of the evening. She rearranged her mother's worsted-work, and fell back into her own thoughts— as completely forgotten by Mr. Thornton as if she had not been in the room, so thoroughly was he occupied in explaining to Mr. Hale the magnificent power, yet delicate adjustment of the might of the steam-hammer, which was recalling to Mr. Hale some of the wonderful stories of subservient genii in the Arabian Nights— one moment stretching from earth to sky and filling all the width of the horizon, at the next obediently compressed into a vase small enough to be borne in the hand of a child.

"And this imagination of power, this practical realisation of a gigantic thought, came out of one man's brain in our good town. That very man has it within him to mount, step by step, on each wonder he achieves to higher marvels still. And I'll be bound to say, we have many among us who, if he were gone, could spring into the breach and carry on the war which compels, and shall compel, all material power to yield to science."

"Your boast reminds me of the old lines—
'I've a hundred
captains in England,' he said,
'As good as ever was he.'"

At her father's quotation Margaret looked suddenly up, with inquiring wonder in her eyes. How in the world had they got from cog-wheels to Chevy Chace?

"It is no boast of mine," replied Mr. Thornton; "it is plain matter-of-fact. I won't deny that I am proud of belonging to a town—or perhaps I should rather say a district—the necessities of which give birth to such grandeur of conception. I would rather be a man toiling, suffering—nay, failing and successless—here, than lead a dull prosperous life in the old worn grooves of what you call more aristocratic society down in the South, with their slow days of careless ease. One may be clogged with honey and unable to rise and fly."

"You are mistaken," said Margaret, roused by the aspersion on her beloved South to a fond vehemence of defence that brought the colour into her cheeks and the angry tears into her eyes. "You do not know anything about the South. If there is less adventure or less progress—I suppose I must not say less excitement—from the gambling spirit of trade, which seems requisite to force out these wonderful inventions, there is less suffering also. I see men here going about in the streets who look ground down by some pinching sorrow or care—who are not only sufferers but haters. Now, in the South we have our poor, but there is not that terrible expression in their countenances of a sullen sense of injustice, which I see here. You do not know the South, Mr. Thornton," she concluded, collapsing into a determined silence, and angry with herself for having said so much.

"And may I say you do not know the North?" asked he, with an inexpressible gentleness in his tone, as he saw that he had really hurt her. She continued resolutely silent; yearning after the lovely haunts she had left far away in Hampshire, with a passionate longing that made her feel her voice would be unsteady and trembling if she spoke.

"At any rate, Mr. Thornton," said Mrs. Hale, "you will allow that Milton is a much more smoky, dirty town than you will ever meet with in the South."

"I'm afraid I must give up its cleanliness," said Mr. Thornton, with the quick gleaming smile. "But we are bidden by parliament to burn our own smoke; so I suppose, like good little children, we shall do as we are bid—some time."

"But I think you told me you had altered your chimneys so as to consume the smoke, did you not?" asked Mr. Hale.

"Mine were altered by my own will, before parliament meddled with the affair. It was an immediate outlay, but it repays me in the saving of coal. I'm not sure whether I should have done it, if I had waited until the act was passed. At any rate, I should have waited to be informed against and fined, and given all the trouble in yielding that I legally could. But all laws which depend for their enforcement upon informers and fines, become inert from the odiousness of the machinery. I doubt if there has been a chimney in Milton informed against for five years past, although some are constantly sending out one-third of their coal in what is called here unparliamentary smoke."

"I only know it is impossible to keep the muslin blinds clean here above a week together; and at Helstone we have had them up for a month or more, and they have not looked dirty at the end of that time. And as for hands—Margaret, how many times did you say you had washed your hands this morning before twelve o'clock? Three times, was it not?"

"Yes, mamma."

"You seem to have a strong objection to acts of parliament and all legislation affecting your mode of management down here at Milton," said Mr. Hale.

"Yes, I have; and many others have as well. And with justice, I think. The whole machinery—I don't mean the wood and iron machinery now—of the cotton trade is so new that it is no wonder if it does not work well in every part all at once. Seventy years ago what was it? And now what is it not? Raw, crude materials came together; men of the same level, as regarded education and station, took suddenly the different positions of masters and men, owing to the motherwit, as regarded opportunities and probabilities, which distinguished some, and made them far-seeing as to what great future lay concealed in that rude model of Sir Richard Arkwright's. The rapid development of what might be called a new trade, gave those early masters enormous power of wealth and command. I don't mean merely over the workmen; I mean over purchasers—over the whole world's market. Why, I may give you, as an instance, an advertisement, inserted not fifty years ago in a Milton paper, that so-and-so (one of the half-dozen calico-printers of the time) would close his warehouse at noon each day; therefore, that all purchasers must come before that hour. Fancy a man dictating in this manner the time when he would sell and when he would not sell. Now, I believe, if a good customer chose to come at midnight, I should get up, and stand hat in hand to receive his orders."

Margaret's lip curled, but somehow she was compelled to listen; she could no longer abstract herself in her own thoughts.

"I only name such things to show what almost unlimited power the manufacturers had about the beginning of this century. The men were rendered dizzy by it. Because a man was successful in his ventures, there was no reason that in all other things his mind should be well-balanced. On the contrary, his sense of justice, and his simplicity, were often utterly smothered under the glut of wealth that came down upon him; and they tell strange tales of the wild extravagance of living indulged in on gala-days by those early cotton-lords. There can be no doubt, too, of the tyranny they exercised over their work-people. You know the proverb, Mr. Hale, 'set a beggar on horseback, and he'll ride to the devil,'— well, some of these early manufacturers did ride to the devil in a magnificent style—crushing human bone and flesh under their horses' hoofs without remorse. But by-and-by came a re-action, there were more factories, more masters; more men were wanted. The power of masters and men became more evenly balanced; and now the battle is pretty fairly waged between us. We will hardly submit to the decision of an umpire, much less to the interference of a meddler with only a smattering of the knowledge of the real facts of the case, even though that meddler be called the High Court of Parliament."

"Is there necessity for calling it a battle between the two classes?" asked Mr. Hale. "I know, from your using the term, it is one which gives a true idea of the real state of things to your mind."

"It is true; and I believe it to be as much a necessity as that prudent wisdom and good conduct are always opposed to, and doing battle with ignorance and improvidence. It is one of the great beauties of our system, that a working-man may raise himself into the power and position of a master by his own exertions and behaviour; that, in fact, every one who rules himself to decency and sobriety of conduct, and attention to his duties, comes over to our ranks; it may not be always as a master, but as an over-looker, a cashier, a book-keeper, a clerk, one on the side of authority and order."

"You consider all who are unsuccessful in raising themselves in the world, from whatever cause, as your enemies, then, if I understand you rightly," said Margaret in a clear, cold voice.

"As their own enemies, certainly," said he, quickly, not a little piqued by the haughty disapproval her form of expression and tone of speaking implied. But, in a moment, his straightforward honesty made him feel that his words were but a poor and quibbling answer to what she had said; and, be she as scornful as she liked, it was a duty he owed to himself to explain, as truly as he could, what he did mean. Yet it was very difficult to separate her interpretation, and keep it distinct from his meaning. He could best have illustrated what he wanted to say by telling them something of his own life; but was it not too personal a subject to speak about to strangers? Still, it was the simple straightforward way of explaining his meaning; so, putting aside the touch of shyness that brought a momentary flush of colour into his dark cheek, he said:

"I am not speaking without book. Sixteen years ago, my father died under very miserable circumstances. I was taken from school, and had to become a man (as well as I could) in a few days. I had such a mother as few are blest with; a woman of strong power, and firm resolve. We went into a small country town, where living was cheaper than in Milton, and where I got employment in a draper's shop (a capital place, by the way, for obtaining a knowledge of goods). Week by week our income came to fifteen shillings, out of which three people had to be kept. My mother managed so that I put by three out of these fifteen shillings regularly. This made the beginning; this taught me self-denial. Now that I am able to afford my mother such comforts as her age, rather than her own wish, requires, I thank her silently on each occasion for the early training she gave me. Now when I feel that in my own case it is no good luck, nor merit, nor talent,—but simply the habits of life which taught me to despise indulgences not thoroughly earned,—indeed, never to think twice about them,—I believe that this suffering, which Miss Hale says is impressed on the countenances of the people of Milton, is but the natural punishment of dishonestly-enjoyed pleasure, at some former period of their lives. I do not look on self-indulgent, sensual people as worthy of my hatred; I simply look upon them with contempt for their poorness of character."

"But you have had the rudiments of a good education," remarked Mr. Hale. "The quick zest with which you are now reading Homer, shows me that you do not come to it as an unknown book; you have read it before, and are only recalling your old knowledge."

"That is true,—I had blundered along it at school; I dare say, I was even considered a pretty fair classic in those days, though my Latin and Greek have slipt away from me since. But I ask you, what preparation they were for such a life as I had to lead? None at all. Utterly none at all. On the point of education, any man who can read and write starts fair with me in the amount of really useful knowledge that I had at that time."

"Well! I don't agree with you. But there I am perhaps somewhat of a pedant. Did not the recollection of the heroic simplicity of the Homeric life nerve you up?"

"Not one bit!" exclaimed Mr. Thornton, laughing. "I was too busy to think about any dead people, with the living pressing alongside of me, neck to neck, in the struggle for bread. Now that I have my mother safe in the quiet peace that becomes her age, and duly rewards her former exertions, I can turn to all that old narration and thoroughly enjoy it."

"I dare say, my remark came from the professional feeling of there being nothing like leather," replied Mr. Hale.

When Mr. Thornton rose up to go away, after shaking hands with Mr. and Mrs. Hale, he made an advance to Margaret to wish her good-bye in a similar manner. It was the frank familiar custom of the place; but Margaret was not prepared for it. She simply bowed her farewell; although the instant she saw the hand, half put out, quickly drawn back, she was sorry she had not been aware of the intention. Mr. Thornton, however, knew nothing of her sorrow, and, drawing himself up to his full height, walked off, muttering as he left the house—

"A more proud, disagreeable girl I never saw. Even her great beauty is blotted out of one's memory by her scornful ways."

He stepped out onto the street, his teeth set and his brows drawn together. He needed to cool his thoughts and was glad of the distance he had to walk to reach Marlborough Street.

Once again Miss Hale had managed to irritate him. He did not mind that she had challenged his opinions. In fact, he admired her spirit, for not many people disputed what he had to say, and certainly not women. Margaret Hale was different; there was no doubt of that. A man would not be bored with such a woman to argue with every day, and she was attractive; there was no doubt about that either. But she treated him as if he were a small boy who had not washed his ears, or his hands, properly. He shoved his fists into his pockets and slowed his gait. It was just as well. A woman like that was not for the likes of him. She was too fine, and he too rough.

His mother was not up when he let himself into the house a while later, nor was his sister, and he was glad, for he would have to face no questions tonight. Tomorrow, perhaps, after he had put his thoughts into order, but not tonight. He lit a candle from a sconce near the door and made his way upstairs to his room trying to push thoughts of Miss Hale from his mind. But his thoughts wandered back to her in spite of his efforts, and he recalled the spots of colour on her cheeks when she had defended her old home: how it had made her beauty seem less cold and somehow more approachable, than how she had appeared when he had first entered her home. Following rapidly as a train, the memory of Margaret pouring tea, and the way she had kept pushing that bracelet back into place upon her arm, rose before him, and he felt himself stir.

He shut the door to his room with more force than he should have and paused to make sure he had not awakened anyone. Satisfied, Mr. Thornton shoved himself away from the door and set the candle down on his night table. He tugged at the end of his cravat and tossed it aside when it came loose. He had better keep such things, as the way Margaret Hale poured tea, from entering his head. She was a lady, and he would not think of her as he had tonight. He had been too long without a woman. That was all. Not since he had made that business trip to Liverpool, and that was nearly a year ago.

Her name had been Tilly, or at least that was what she had told him. He had been tired from meetings with the dock manager and a group of ship captains and not looking forward to a solitary meal and a night alone in his hotel room. He had been wishing he had accepted the invitation to stay and sup with them instead when her bright red hair had caught his eye. His first instinct had been to walk past, but something had compelled him to follow her up to her room. She had known how to awaken a man's appetite and how to please his body. More blood rushed to his groin at the memory.

He was hard long before he let his braces fall and slipped his shirttails from his waistband. The shirt landed behind him and he undid his trousers, pushing them down along with his underwear. He pictured it now: the way she had grasped his penis, and stroked down, her mouth closing over him in one quick movement, and he knew he would not sleep without relief.

One hand against the nearest wall he spat in his other and closed it around his cock. Down he pumped as he closed his eyes, picturing her. She had a pretty, bow-shaped pair of lips that stretched around him. He closed his eyes, remembered the suction of her mouth as she drew back nearly to the tip. His hand slipped up, his thumb gliding across the head of his shaft and gathering the wetness seeping from the slit. His hips jerked and he pressed his own lips together to stifle the little grunt of pleasure he could not hold back.

Short fingernails stroked his balls as she cupped and caressed them, and Mr. Thornton opened his eyes, glancing down. Dark eyes gleamed back up at him as rich red lips drew him back into her mouth. *Margaret.* His hand stilled. He did not want thoughts of her, of all people, intruding, with her airs and contempt. But again he recalled the pretty bracelet falling down her pale arm, and the way she had kept pushing it back up. Down and up again. His strokes resumed, his mind now working with his body against him as he imagined Margaret's hand sliding over his cock along with her mouth, and that she enjoyed pleasuring him as much he enjoyed receiving such from her.

Mr. Thornton fisted his cock faster, his hand tight. He reached down to uncoil the black hair twisted neatly at the back of her head. The pins fell away and his fingers sifted through the thick, silken strands. With a growl he pulled her to her feet and crushed his mouth to hers. In a moment, she was on the bed beneath him, begging him to take her. And as he imagined himself pushing into her tight, wet heat, he came. His hot release spurted over his hand as he shook from the force of it.

"Margaret."

It was barely a whisper but it seemed as loud to his ears as the thudding of his heart. The hand that splayed against the wall curled into a fist and he stood still, his breathing heavy, until he recalled himself and where he was. He toed off his shoes and stepped out of his trousers, stumbling to the washstand on unsteady legs before cleaning himself in the water he had left behind earlier that evening. His reflection stared back at him, as if mocking him for his weakness. If it could speak he knew what it would say, so he uttered the words himself.

"Fool. She would never have you, John Thornton."

No, she would never have him. She was above him, in breeding and manners. Her father had said she had lived in London for a time. Mr. Thornton imagined the kind of man she would think good enough: He would be more handsome than himself, with a fortune inherited rather than gained, and no doubt he would be so polite as to ask permission for each kiss. That was the sort of man she would want. The scornful laugh that rose in his throat hung there, until he swallowed it back. No, he was not for Margaret Hale any more than she was for him, and if the thought made his gut twist, he put it down to anger and annoyance at her scornful behaviour.

At length he blew out the candle and climbed into bed, staring at the ceiling until exhaustion claimed him.

# CHAPTER XI—FIRST IMPRESSIONS

"There's iron, they say, in all our blood,
And a grain or two perhaps is good;
But his, he makes me harshly feel,
Has got a little too much of steel."
ANON.

"Margaret!" said Mr. Hale, as he returned from showing his guest downstairs; "I could not help watching your face with some anxiety, when Mr. Thornton made his confession of having been a shop-boy. I knew it all along from Mr. Bell; so I was aware of what was coming; but I half expected to see you get up and leave the room."

"Oh, papa! You don't mean that you thought me so silly? I really liked that account of himself better than anything else he said. Everything else revolted me, from its hardness; but he spoke about himself so simply—with so little of the pretence that makes the vulgarity of shop-people, and with such tender respect for his mother, that I was less likely to leave the room then than when he was boasting about Milton, as if there was not such another place in the world; or quietly professing to despise people for careless, wasteful improvidence, without ever seeming to think it his duty to try to make them different,—to give them anything of the training which his mother gave him, and to which he evidently owes his position, whatever that may be. No! His statement of having been a shop-boy was the thing I liked best of all."

"I am surprised at you, Margaret," said her mother. "You who were always accusing people of being shoppy at Helstone! I don't think, Mr. Hale, you have done quite right in introducing such a person to us without telling us what he had been. I really was very much afraid of showing him how much shocked I was at some parts of what he said. His father 'dying in miserable circumstances.' Why it might have been in the workhouse."

"I am not sure if it was not worse than being in the workhouse," replied her husband. "I heard a good deal of his previous life from Mr. Bell before we came here; and as he has told you a part, I will fill up what he left out. His father speculated wildly, failed, and then killed himself, because he could not bear the disgrace. All his former friends shrunk from the disclosures that had to be made of his dishonest gambling—wild, hopeless struggles, made with other people's money, to regain his own moderate portion of wealth. No one came forwards to help the mother and this boy. There was another child, I believe, a girl; too young to earn money, but of course she had to be kept. At least, no friend came forwards immediately, and Mrs. Thornton is not one, I fancy, to wait till tardy kindness comes to find her out. So they left Milton. I knew he had gone into a shop, and that his earnings, with some fragment of property secured to his mother, had been made to keep them for a long time. Mr. Bell said they absolutely lived upon water-porridge for years—how, he did not know; but long after the creditors had given up hope of any payment of old Mr. Thornton's debts (if, indeed, they ever had hoped at all about it, after his suicide,) this young man returned to Milton, and went quietly round to each creditor, paying him the first instalment of the money owing to him. No noise—no gathering together of creditors—it was done very silently and quietly, but all was paid at last; helped on materially by the circumstance of one of the creditors, a crabbed old fellow (Mr. Bell says), taking in Mr. Thornton as a kind of partner."

"That really is fine," said Margaret. "What a pity such a nature should be tainted by his position as a Milton manufacturer."

"How tainted?" asked her father.

"Oh, papa, by that testing everything by the standard of wealth. When he spoke of the mechanical powers, he evidently looked upon them only as new ways of extending trade and making money. And the poor men around him—they were poor because they were vicious—out of the pale of his sympathies because they had not his iron nature, and the capabilities that it gives him for being rich."

"Not vicious; he never said that. Improvident and self-indulgent were his words."

Margaret was collecting her mother's working materials, and preparing to go to bed. Just as she was leaving the room, she hesitated—she was inclined to make an acknowledgment which she thought would please her father, but which to be full and true must include a little annoyance. However, out it came.

"Papa, I do think Mr. Thornton a very remarkable man; but personally I don't like him at all."

"And I do!" said her father laughing. "Personally, as you call it, and all. I don't set him up for a hero, or anything of that kind. But good night, child. Your mother looks sadly tired to-night, Margaret."

Margaret had noticed her mother's jaded appearance with anxiety for some time past, and this remark of her father's sent her up to bed with a dim fear lying like a weight on her heart. The life in Milton was so different from what Mrs. Hale had been accustomed to live in Helstone, in and out perpetually into the fresh and open air; the air itself was so different, deprived of all revivifying principle as it seemed to be here; the domestic worries pressed so very closely, and in so new and sordid a form, upon all the women in the family, that there was good reason to fear that her mother's health might be becoming seriously affected. There were several other signs of something wrong about Mrs. Hale. She and Dixon held mysterious consultations in her bedroom, from which Dixon would come out crying and cross, as was her custom when any distress of her mistress called upon her sympathy. Once Margaret had gone into the chamber soon after Dixon left it, and found her mother on her knees, and as Margaret stole out she caught a few words, which were evidently a prayer for strength and patience to endure severe bodily suffering. Margaret yearned to re-unite the bond of intimate confidence which had been broken by her long residence at her Aunt Shaw's, and strove by gentle caresses and softened words to creep into the warmest place in her mother's heart. But though she received caresses and fond words back again, in such profusion as would have gladdened her formerly, yet she felt that there was a secret withheld from her, and she believed it bore serious reference to her mother's health. She lay awake very long this night, planning how to lessen the evil influence of their Milton life on her mother. A servant to give Dixon permanent assistance should be got, if she gave up her whole time to the search; and then, at any rate, her mother might have all the personal attention she required, and had been accustomed to her whole life.

Visiting register offices, seeing all manner of unlikely people, and very few in the least likely, absorbed Margaret's time and thoughts for several days. One afternoon she met Bessy Higgins in the street, and stopped to speak to her.

"Well, Bessy, how are you? Better, I hope, now the wind has changed."

"Better and not better, if yo' know what that means."

"Not exactly," replied Margaret, smiling.

"I'm better in not being torn to pieces by coughing o'nights, but I'm weary and tired o' Milton, and longing to get away to the land o' Beulah; and when I think I'm farther and farther off, my heart sinks, and I'm no better; I'm worse." Margaret turned round to walk alongside of the girl in her feeble progress homeward. But for a minute or two she did not speak. At last she said in a low voice,

"Bessy, do you wish to die?" For she shrank from death herself, with all the clinging to life so natural to the young and healthy.

Bessy was silent in her turn for a minute or two. Then she replied,

"If yo'd led the life I have, and getten as weary of it as I have, and thought at times, 'maybe it'll last for fifty or sixty years—it does wi' some,'—and got dizzy and dazed, and sick, as each of them sixty years seemed to spin about me, and mock me with its length of hours and minutes, and endless bits o' time—oh, wench! I tell thee thou'd been glad enough when th' doctor said he feared thou'd never see another winter."

"Why, Bessy, what kind of a life has yours been?"

"Nought worse than many others, I reckon. Only I fretted again it, and they didn't."

"But what was it? You know, I'm a stranger here, so perhaps I'm not so quick at understanding what you mean as if I'd lived all my life at Milton."

"If yo'd ha' come to our house when yo' said yo' would, I could maybe ha' told you. But father says yo're just like th' rest on 'em; it's out o' sight out o' mind wi' you."

"I don't know who the rest are; and I've been very busy; and, to tell the truth, I had forgotten my promise—"

"Yo' offered it! We asked none of it."

"I had forgotten what I said for the time," continued Margaret quietly. "I should have thought of it again when I was less busy. May I go with you now?" Bessy gave a quick glance at Margaret's face, to see if the wish expressed was really felt. The sharpness in her eye turned to a wistful longing as she met Margaret's soft and friendly gaze.

"I ha' none so many to care for me; if yo' care yo' may come."

So they walked on together in silence. As they turned up into a small court, opening out of a squalid street, Bessy said,

"Yo'll not be daunted if father's at home, and speaks a bit gruffish at first. He took a mind to ye, yo' see, and he thought a deal o' your coming to see us; and just because he liked yo' he were vexed and put about."

"Don't fear, Bessy."

But Nicholas was not at home when they entered. A great slatternly girl, not so old as Bessy, but taller and stronger, was busy at the wash-tub, knocking about the furniture in a rough capable way, but altogether making so much noise that Margaret shrunk, out of sympathy with poor Bessy, who had sat down on the first chair, as if completely tired out with her walk. Margaret asked the sister for a cup of water, and while she ran to fetch it (knocking down the fire-irons, and tumbling over a chair in her way), she unloosed Bessy's bonnet strings, to relieve her catching breath.

"Do you think such life as this is worth caring for?" gasped Bessy, at last. Margaret did not speak, but held the water to her lips. Bessy took a long and feverish draught, and then fell back and shut her eyes. Margaret heard her murmur to herself: "they shall hunger no more, neither thirst any more; neither shall the sun light on them, nor any heat."

Margaret bent over and said, "Bessy, don't be impatient with your life, whatever it is—or may have been. Remember who gave it you, and made it what it is!" She was startled by hearing Nicholas speak behind her; he had come in without her noticing him.

"Now, I'll not have my wench preached to. She's bad enough as it is, with her dreams and her methodee fancies, and her visions of cities with goulden gates and precious stones. But if it amuses her I let it a be, but I'm none going to have more stuff poured into her."

"But surely," said Margaret, facing round, "you believe in what I said, that God gave her life, and ordered what kind of life it was to be?"

"I believe what I see, and no more. That's what I believe, young woman. I don't believe all I hear—no! Not by a big deal. I did hear a young lass make an ado about knowing where we lived, and coming to see us. And my wench here thought a deal about it, and flushed up many a time, when hoo little knew as I was looking at her, at the sound of a strange step. But hoo's come at last,—and hoo's welcome, as long as hoo'll keep from preaching on what hoo knows nought about." Bessy had been watching Margaret's face; she half sate up to speak now, laying her hand on Margaret's arm with a gesture of entreaty. "Don't be vexed wi' him—there's many a one thinks like him; many and many a one here. If yo' could hear them speak, yo'd not be shocked at him; he's a rare good man, is father—but oh!" said she, falling back in despair, "what he says at times makes me long to die more than ever, for I want to know so many things, and am so tossed about wi' wonder."

"Poor wench—poor old wench,—I'm loth to vex thee, I am; but a man mun speak out for the truth, and when I see the world going all wrong at this time o' day, bothering itself wi' things it knows nought about, and leaving undone all the things that lie in disorder close at its hand—why, I say, leave a' this talk about religion alone, and set to work on what yo' see and know. That's my creed. It's simple, and not far to fetch, nor hard to work."

But the girl only pleaded the more with Margaret.

"Don't think hardly on him—he's a good man, he is. I sometimes think I shall be moped wi' sorrow even in the City of God, if father is not there." The feverish colour came into her cheek, and the feverish flame into her eye. "But you will be there, father! you shall! Oh! My heart!" She put her hand to it, and became ghastly pale.

Margaret held her in her arms, and put the weary head to rest upon her bosom. She lifted the thin soft hair from off the temples, and bathed them with water. Nicholas understood all her signs for different articles with the quickness of love, and even the round-eyed sister moved with laborious gentleness at Margaret's "hush!" Presently the spasm that foreshadowed death had passed away, and Bessy roused herself and said,—

"I'll go to bed,—it's best place; but," catching at Margaret's gown, "yo'll come again,—I know yo' will—but just say it!"

"I will come to-morrow, said Margaret.

Bessy leant back against her father, who prepared to carry her upstairs; but as Margaret rose to go, he struggled to say something: "I could wish there were a God, if it were only to ask Him to bless thee."

Margaret went away very sad and thoughtful.

She was late for tea at home. At Helstone unpunctuality at meal-times was a great fault in her mother's eyes; but now this, as well as many other little irregularities, seemed to have lost their power of irritation, and Margaret almost longed for the old complainings.

"Have you met with a servant, dear?"

"No, mamma; that Anne Buckley would never have done."

"Suppose I try," said Mr. Hale. "Everybody else has had their turn at this great difficulty. Now let me try. I may be the Cinderella to put on the slipper after all."

Margaret could hardly smile at this little joke, so oppressed was she by her visit to the Higginses.

"What would you do, papa? How would you set about it?"

"Why, I would apply to some good house-mother to recommend me one known to herself or her servants."

"Very good. But we must first catch our house-mother."

"You have caught her. Or rather she is coming into the snare, and you will catch her to-morrow, if you're skilful."

"What do you mean, Mr. Hale?" asked his wife, her curiosity aroused.

"Why, my paragon pupil (as Margaret calls him), has told me that his mother intends to call on Mrs. and Miss Hale to-morrow."

"Mrs. Thornton!" exclaimed Mrs. Hale.

"The mother of whom he spoke to us?" said Margaret.

"Mrs. Thornton; the only mother he has, I believe," said Mr. Hale quietly.

"I shall like to see her. She must be an uncommon person," her mother added.

"Perhaps she may have a relation who might suit us, and be glad of our place. She sounded to be such a careful economical person, that I should like any one out of the same family."

"My dear," said Mr. Hale alarmed. "Pray don't go off on that idea. I fancy Mrs. Thornton is as haughty and proud in her way, as our little Margaret here is in hers, and that she completely ignores that old time of trial, and poverty, and economy, of which he speaks so openly. I am sure, at any rate, she would not like strangers to know anything about It."

"Take notice that is not my kind of haughtiness, papa, if I have any at all; which I don't agree to, though you're always accusing me of it."

"I don't know positively that it is hers either; but from little things I have gathered from him, I fancy so."

They cared too little to ask in what manner her son had spoken about her. Margaret only wanted to know if she must stay in to receive this call, as it would prevent her going to see how Bessy was, until late in the day, since the early morning was always occupied in household affairs; and then she recollected that her mother must not be left to have the whole weight of entertaining her visitor.

# CHAPTER XII—MORNING CALLS

"Well—I suppose we must."
FRIENDS IN COUNCIL.

Mr. Thornton had had some difficulty in working up his mother to the desired point of civility. She did not often make calls; and when she did, it was in heavy state that she went through her duties. Her son had given her a carriage; but she refused to let him keep horses for it; they were hired for the solemn occasions, when she paid morning or evening visits. She had had horses for three days, not a fortnight before, and had comfortably "killed off" all her acquaintances, who might now put themselves to trouble and expense in their turn. Yet Crampton was too far off for her to walk; and she had repeatedly questioned her son as to whether his wish that she should call on the Hales was strong enough to bear the expense of cab-hire. She would have been thankful if it had not; for, as she said, "she saw no use in making up friendships and intimacies with all the teachers and masters in Milton; why, he would be wanting her to call on Fanny's dancing-master's wife, the next thing!"

"And so I would, mother, if Mr. Mason and his wife were friendless in a strange place, like the Hales."

"Oh! You need not speak so hastily. I am going to-morrow. I only wanted you exactly to understand about it."

"If you are going to-morrow, I shall order horses."

"Nonsense, John. One would think you were made of money."

"Not quite, yet. But about the horses I'm determined. The last time you were out in a cab, you came home with a headache from the jolting."

"I never complained of it, I'm sure."

"No. My mother is not given to complaints," said he, a little proudly. "But so much the more I have to watch over you. Now as for Fanny there, a little hardship would do her good."

"She is not made of the same stuff as you are, John. She could not bear it." Mrs. Thornton was silent after this; for her last words bore relation to a subject which mortified her. She had an unconscious contempt for a weak character; and Fanny was weak in the very points in which her mother and brother were strong. Mrs. Thornton was not a woman much given to reasoning; her quick judgment and firm resolution served her in good stead of any long arguments and discussions with herself; she felt instinctively that nothing could strengthen Fanny to endure hardships patiently, or face difficulties bravely; and though she winced as she made this acknowledgment to herself about her daughter, it only gave her a kind of pitying tenderness of manner towards her; much of the same description of demeanour with which mothers are wont to treat their weak and sickly children. A stranger, a careless observer might have considered that Mrs. Thornton's manner to her children betokened far more love to Fanny than to John. But such a one would have been deeply mistaken. The very daringness with which mother and son spoke out unpalatable truths, the one to the other, showed a reliance on the firm centre of each other's souls, which the uneasy tenderness of Mrs. Thornton's manner to her daughter, the shame with which she thought to hide the poverty of her child in all the grand qualities which she herself possessed unconsciously, and which she set so high a value upon in others—this shame, I say, betrayed the want of a secure resting-place for her affection. She never called her son by any name but John; "love," and "dear," and such like terms, were reserved for Fanny. But her heart gave thanks for him day and night; and she walked proudly among women for his sake.

"Fanny dear, I shall have horses to the carriage to-day, to go and call on these Hales. Should not you go and see nurse? It's in the same direction, and she's always so glad to see you. You could go on there while I am at Mrs. Hale's."

"Oh! Mamma, it's such a long way, and I am so tired."

"With what?" asked Mrs. Thornton, her brow slightly contracting.

"I don't know—the weather, I think. It is so relaxing. Couldn't you bring nurse here, mamma? The carriage could fetch her, and she could spend the rest of the day here, which I know she would like."

Mrs. Thornton did not speak; but she laid her work on the table, and seemed to think.

"It will be a long way for her to walk back at night!" she remarked, at last.

"Oh, but I will send her home in a cab. I never thought of her walking." At this point, Mr. Thornton came in, just before going to the mill.

"Mother! I need hardly say, that if there is any little thing that could serve Mrs. Hale as an invalid, you will offer it, I'm sure."

"If I can find it out, I will. But I have never been ill myself, so I am not much up to invalids' fancies."

"Well! Here is Fanny then, who is seldom without an ailment. She will be able to suggest something, perhaps—won't you, Fan?"

"I have not always an ailment," said Fanny, pettishly; "and I am not going with mamma. I have a headache to-day, and I shan't go out."

Mr. Thornton looked annoyed. His mother's eyes were bent on her work, at which she was now stitching away busily.

"Fanny! I wish you to go," said he, authoritatively. "It will do you good, instead of harm. You will oblige me by going, without my saying anything more about it."

He went abruptly out of the room after saying this.

If he had staid a minute longer, Fanny would have cried at his tone of command, even when he used the words, "You will oblige me." As it was, she grumbled.

"John always speaks as if I fancied I was ill, and I am sure I never do fancy any such thing. Who are these Hales that he makes such a fuss about?"

"Fanny, don't speak so of your brother. He has good reasons of some kind or other, or he would not wish us to go. Make haste and put your things on."

But the little altercation between her son and her daughter did not incline Mrs. Thornton more favourably towards "these Hales." Her jealous heart repeated her daughter's question, "Who are they, that he is so anxious we should pay them all this attention?" It came up like a burden to a song, long after Fanny had forgotten all about it in the pleasant excitement of seeing the effect of a new bonnet in the looking-glass.

Mrs. Thornton was shy. It was only of late years that she had had leisure enough in her life to go into society; and as society she did not enjoy it. As dinner-giving, and as criticising other people's dinners, she took satisfaction in it. But this going to make acquaintance with strangers was a very different thing. She was ill at ease, and looked more than usually stern and forbidding as she entered the Hales" little drawing-room.

Margaret was busy embroidering a small piece of cambric for some little article of dress for Edith's expected baby—"Flimsy, useless work," as Mrs. Thornton observed to herself. She liked Mrs. Hale's double knitting far better; that was sensible of its kind. The room altogether was full of knick-knacks, which must take a long time to dust; and time to people of limited income was money. She made all these reflections as she was talking in her stately way to Mrs. Hale, and uttering all the stereotyped commonplaces that most people can find to say with their senses blindfolded. Mrs. Hale was making rather more exertion in her answers, captivated by some real old lace which Mrs. Thornton wore; "lace," as she afterwards observed to Dixon, "of that old English point which has not been made for this seventy years, and which cannot be bought. It must have been an heir-loom, and shows that she had ancestors." So the owner of the ancestral lace became worthy of something more than the languid exertion to be agreeable to a visitor, by which Mrs. Hale's efforts at conversation would have been otherwise bounded. And presently, Margaret, racking her brain to talk to Fanny, heard her mother and Mrs. Thornton plunge into the interminable subject of servants.

"I suppose you are not musical," said Fanny, "as I see no piano."

"I am fond of hearing good music; I cannot play well myself; and papa and mamma don't care much about it; so we sold our old piano when we came here."

"I wonder how you can exist without one. It almost seems to me a necessary of life."

"Fifteen shillings a week, and three saved out of them!" thought Margaret to herself. "But she must have been very young. She probably has forgotten her own personal experience. But she must know of those days." Margaret's manner had an extra tinge of coldness in it when she next spoke.

"You have good concerts here, I believe."

"Oh, yes! Delicious! Too crowded, that is the worst. The directors admit so indiscriminately. But one is sure to hear the newest music there. I always have a large order to give to Johnson's, the day after a concert."

"Do you like new music simply for its newness, then?"

"Oh; one knows it is the fashion in London, or else the singers would not bring it down here. You have been in London, of course."

"Yes," said Margaret, "I have lived there for several years."

"Oh! London and the Alhambra are the two places I long to see!"

"London and the Alhambra!"

"Yes! Ever since I read the Tales of the Alhambra. Don't you know them?"

"I don't think I do. But surely, it is a very easy journey to London."

"Yes; but somehow," said Fanny, lowering her voice, "mamma has never been to London herself, and can't understand my longing. She is very proud of Milton; dirty, smoky place, as I feel it to be. I believe she admires it the more for those very qualities."

"If it has been Mrs. Thornton's home for some years, I can well understand her loving it," said Margaret, in her clear bell-like voice.

"What are you saying about me, Miss Hale? May I inquire?"

Margaret had not the words ready for an answer to this question, which took her a little by surprise, so Miss Thornton replied:

"Oh, mamma! we are only trying to account for your being so fond of Milton."

"Thank you," said Mrs. Thornton. "I do not feel that my very natural liking for the place where I was born and brought up,—and which has since been my residence for some years, requires any accounting for."

Margaret was vexed. As Fanny had put it, it did seem as if they had been impertinently discussing Mrs. Thornton's feelings; but she also rose up against that lady's manner of showing that she was offended.

Mrs. Thornton went on after a moment's pause:

"Do you know anything of Milton, Miss Hale? Have you seen any of our factories? Our magnificent warehouses?"

"No!" said Margaret. "I have not seen anything of that description as yet." Then she felt that, by concealing her utter indifference to all such places, she was hardly speaking with truth; so she went on:

"I dare say, papa would have taken me before now if I had cared. But I really do not find much pleasure in going over manufactories."

"They are very curious places," said Mrs. Hale, "but there is so much noise and dirt always. I remember once going in a lilac silk to see candles made, and my gown was utterly ruined."

"Very probably," said Mrs. Thornton, in a short displeased manner. "I merely thought, that as strangers newly come to reside in a town which has risen to eminence in the country, from the character and progress of its peculiar business, you might have cared to visit some of the places where it is carried on; places unique in the kingdom, I am informed. If Miss Hale changes her mind and condescends to be curious as to the manufactures of Milton, I can only say I shall be glad to procure her admission to print-works, or reed-making, or the more simple operations of spinning carried on in my son's mill. Every improvement of machinery is, I believe, to be seen there, in its highest perfection."

"I am so glad you don't like mills and manufactories, and all those kind of things," said Fanny, in a half-whisper, as she rose to accompany her mother, who was taking leave of Mrs. Hale with rustling dignity.

"I think I should like to know all about them, if I were you," replied Margaret quietly.

"Fanny!" said her mother, as they drove away, "we will be civil to these Hales: but don't form one of your hasty friendships with the daughter. She will do you no good, I see. The mother looks very ill, and seems a nice, quiet kind of person."

"I don't want to form any friendship with Miss Hale, mamma," said Fanny, pouting. "I thought I was doing my duty by talking to her, and trying to amuse her."

"Well! At any rate John must be satisfied now."

# CHAPTER XIII—A SOFT BREEZE IN A SULTRY PLACE

"That doubt and trouble, fear and pain,
And anguish, all, are shadows vain,
That death itself shall not remain;
That weary deserts we may tread,
A dreary labyrinth may thread,
Thro' dark ways underground be led;
Yet, if we will one Guide obey,
The dreariest path, the darkest way
Shall issue out in heavenly day;
And we, on divers shores now cast,
Shall meet, our perilous voyage past,
All in our Father's house at last!"
R. C. TRENCH.

Margaret flew upstairs as soon as their visitors were gone, and put on her bonnet and shawl, to run and inquire how Bessy Higgins was, and sit with her as long as she could before dinner. As she went along the crowded narrow streets, she felt how much of interest they had gained by the simple fact of her having learnt to care for a dweller in them.

Mary Higgins, the slatternly younger sister, had endeavoured as well as she could to tidy up the house for the expected visit. There had been rough-stoning done in the middle of the floor, while the flags under the chairs and table and round the walls retained their dark unwashed appearance. Although the day was hot, there burnt a large fire in the grate, making the whole place feel like an oven. Margaret did not understand that the lavishness of coals was a sign of hospitable welcome to her on Mary's part, and thought that perhaps the oppressive heat was necessary for Bessy. Bessy herself lay on a squab, or short sofa, placed under the window. She was very much more feeble than on the previous day, and tired with raising herself at every step to look out and see if it was Margaret coming. And now that Margaret was there, and had taken a chair by her, Bessy lay back silent, and content to look at Margaret's face, and touch her articles of dress, with a childish admiration of their fineness of texture.

"I never knew why folk in the Bible cared for soft raiment afore. But it must be nice to go dressed as yo' do. It's different fro' common. Most fine folk tire my eyes out wi' their colours; but some how yours rest me. Where did ye get this frock?"

"In London," said Margaret, much amused.

"London! Have yo' been in London?"

"Yes! I lived there for some years. But my home was in a forest; in the country."

"Tell me about it," said Bessy. "I like to hear speak of the country and trees, and such like things." She leant back, and shut her eye and crossed her hands over her breast, lying at perfect rest, as if to receive all the ideas Margaret could suggest.

Margaret had never spoken of Helstone since she left it, except just naming the place incidentally. She saw it in dreams more vivid than life, and as she fell away to slumber at nights her memory wandered in all its pleasant places. But her heart was opened to this girl; "Oh, Bessy, I loved the home we have left so dearly! I wish you could see it. I cannot tell you half its beauty. There are great trees standing all about it, with their branches stretching long and level, and making a deep shade of rest even at noonday. And yet, though every leaf may seem still, there is a continual rushing sound of movement all around—not close at hand. Then sometimes the turf is as soft and fine as velvet; and sometimes quite lush with the perpetual moisture of a little, hidden, tinkling brook near at hand. And then in other parts there are billowy ferns—whole stretches of fern; some in the green shadow; some with long streaks of golden sunlight lying on them—just like the sea."

"I have never seen the sea," murmured Bessy. "But go on."

"Then, here and there, there are wide commons, high up as if above the very tops of the trees—"

"I'm glad of that. I felt smothered like down below. When I have gone for an out, I've always wanted to get high up and see far away, and take a deep breath o' fulness in that air. I get smothered enough in Milton, and I think the sound yo' speak of among the trees, going on for ever and ever, would send me dazed; it's that made my head ache so in the mill. Now on these commons I reckon there is but little noise?"

"No," said Margaret; "nothing but here and there a lark high in the air. Sometimes I used to hear a farmer speaking sharp and loud to his servants; but it was so far away that it only reminded me pleasantly that other people were hard at work in some distant place, while I just sat on the heather and did nothing."

"I used to think once that if I could have a day of doing nothing, to rest me—a day in some quiet place like that yo' speak on—it would maybe set me up. But now I've had many days o' idleness, and I'm just as weary o' them as I was o' my work. Sometimes I'm so tired out I think I cannot enjoy heaven without a piece of rest first. I'm rather afeard o' going straight there without getting a good sleep in the grave to set me up."

"Don't be afraid, Bessy," said Margaret, laying her hand on the girl's; "God can give you more perfect rest than even idleness on earth, or the dead sleep of the grave can do."

Bessy moved uneasily; then she said:

"I wish father would not speak as he does. He means well, as I told yo' yesterday, and tell yo' again and again. But yo' see, though I don't believe him a bit by day, yet by night—when I'm in a fever, half-asleep and half-awake—it comes back upon me—oh!

so bad! And I think, if this should be th' end of all, and if all I've been born for is just to work my heart and my life away, and to sicken i' this dree place, wi' them mill-noises in my ears for ever, until I could scream out for them to stop, and let me have a little piece o' quiet—and wi' the fluff filling my lungs, until I thirst to death for one long deep breath o' the clear air yo' speak on—and my mother gone, and I never able to tell her again how I loved her, and o' all my troubles—I think if this life is th' end, and that there's no God to wipe away all tears from all eyes—yo' wench, yo'!" said she, sitting up, and clutching violently, almost fiercely, at Margaret's hand, "I could go mad, and kill yo', I could." She fell back completely worn out with her passion. Margaret knelt down by her.

"Bessy—we have a Father in Heaven."

"I know it! I know it," moaned she, turning her head uneasily from side to side.

"I'm very wicked. I've spoken very wickedly. Oh! Don't be frightened by me and never come again. I would not harm a hair of your head. And," opening her eyes, and looking earnestly at Margaret, "I believe, perhaps, more than yo' do o' what's to come. I read the book o' Revelations until I know it off by heart, and I never doubt when I'm waking, and in my senses, of all the glory I'm to come to."

"Don't let us talk of what fancies come into your head when you are feverish. I would rather hear something about what you used to do when you were well."

"I think I was well when mother died, but I have never been rightly strong sin' somewhere about that time. I began to work in a carding-room soon after, and the fluff got into my lungs and poisoned me."

"Fluff?" said Margaret, inquiringly.

"Fluff," repeated Bessy. "Little bits, as fly off fro' the cotton, when they're carding it, and fill the air till it looks all fine white dust. They say it winds round the lungs, and tightens them up. Anyhow, there's many a one as works in a carding-room, that falls into a waste, coughing and spitting blood, because they're just poisoned by the fluff."

"But can't it be helped?" asked Margaret.

"I dunno. Some folk have a great wheel at one end o' their carding-rooms to make a draught, and carry off th' dust; but that wheel costs a deal o' money—five or six hundred pound, maybe, and brings in no profit; so it's but a few of th' masters as will put 'em up; and I've heard tell o' men who didn't like working places where there was a wheel, because they said as how it mad 'em hungry, at after they'd been long used to swallowing fluff, to go without it, and that their wage ought to be raised if they were to work in such places. So between masters and men th' wheels fall through. I know I wish there'd been a wheel in our place, though."

"Did not your father know about it?" asked Margaret.

"Yes! And he were sorry. But our factory were a good one on the whole; and a steady likely set o' people; and father was afeard of letting me go to a strange place, for though yo' would na think it now, many a one then used to call me a gradely lass enough. And I did na like to be reckoned nesh and soft, and Mary's schooling were to be kept up, mother said, and father he were always liking to buy books, and go to lectures o' one kind or another—all which took money—so I just worked on till I shall ne'er get the whirr out o' my ears, or the fluff out o' my throat i' this world. That's all."

"How old are you?" asked Margaret.

"Nineteen, come July."

"And I too am nineteen." She thought, more sorrowfully than Bessy did, of the contrast between them. She could not speak for a moment or two for the emotion she was trying to keep down.

"About Mary," said Bessy. "I wanted to ask yo' to be a friend to her. She's seventeen, but she's th' last on us. And I don't want her to go to th' mill, and yet I dunno what she's fit for."

"She could not do"—Margaret glanced unconsciously at the uncleaned corners of the room "—she could hardly undertake a servant's place, could she? We have an old faithful servant, almost a friend, who wants help, but who is very particular; and it would not be right to plague her with giving her any assistance that would really be an annoyance and an irritation."

"No, I see. I reckon yo're right. Our Mary's a good wench; but who has she had to teach her what to do about a house? No mother, and me at the mill till I were good for nothing but scolding her for doing badly what I didn't know how to do a bit. But I wish she could ha' lived wi' yo', for all that."

"But even though she may not be exactly fitted to come and live with us as a servant—and I don't know about that—I will always try and be a friend to her for your sake, Bessy. And now I must go. I will come again as soon as I can; but if it should not be to-morrow, or the next day, or even a week or a fortnight hence, don't think I've forgotten you. I may be busy."

"I'll know yo' won't forget me again. I'll not mistrust yo' no more. But remember, in a week or a fortnight I may be dead and buried!"

"I'll come as soon as I can, Bessy," said Margaret, squeezing her hand tight.

"But you'll let me know if you are worse."

"Ay, that will I," said Bessy, returning the pressure.

From that day forwards Mrs. Hale became more and more of a suffering invalid. It was now drawing near to the anniversary of Edith's marriage, and looking back upon the year's accumulated heap of troubles, Margaret wondered how they had been borne. If she could have anticipated them, how she would have shrunk away and hid herself from the coming time! And yet day by day had, of itself, and by itself, been very endurable—small, keen, bright little spots of positive enjoyment having come sparkling into the very middle of sorrows. A year ago, or when she first went to Helstone, and first became silently conscious of the querulousness in her mother's temper, she would have groaned bitterly over the idea of a long illness to be borne in a strange, desolate, noisy, busy place, with diminished comforts on every side of the home life. But with the increase of serious and just ground of complaint, a new kind of patience had sprung up in her mother's mind. She was gentle and quiet in intense bodily suffering, almost in proportion as she had been restless and depressed when there had been no real cause for grief. Mr. Hale was in exactly that stage of apprehension, which, in men of his stamp, takes the shape of wilful blindness. He was more irritated than Margaret had ever known him at his daughter's expressed anxiety.

"Indeed, Margaret, you are growing fanciful! God knows I should be the first to take the alarm if your mother were really ill; we always saw when she had her headaches at Helstone, even without her telling us. She looks quite pale and white when she is ill; and now she has a bright healthy colour in her cheeks, just as she used to have when I first knew her."

"But, papa," said Margaret, with hesitation, "do you know, I think that is the flush of pain."

"Nonsense, Margaret. I tell you, you are too fanciful. You are the person not well, I think. Send for the doctor to-morrow for yourself; and then, if it will make your mind easier, he can see your mother."

"Thank you, dear papa. It will make me happier, indeed." And she went up to him to kiss him. But he pushed her away—gently enough, but still as if she had suggested unpleasant ideas, which he should be glad to get rid of as readily as he could of her presence. He walked uneasily up and down the room.

"Poor Maria!" said he, half soliloquising, "I wish one could do right without sacrificing others. I shall hate this town, and myself too, if she—Pray, Margaret, does your mother often talk to you of the old places of Helstone, I mean?"

"No, papa," said Margaret, sadly.

"Then, you see, she can't be fretting after them, eh? It has always been a comfort to me to think that your mother was so simple and open that I knew every little grievance she had. She never would conceal anything seriously affecting her health from me: would she, eh, Margaret? I am quite sure she would not. So don't let me hear of these foolish morbid ideas. Come, give me a kiss, and run off to bed."

But she heard him pacing about (racooning, as she and Edith used to call it) long after her slow and languid undressing was finished—long after she began to listen, as she lay in bed.

# CHAPTER XIV—THE MUTINY

"I was used
To sleep at nights as sweetly as a child,—
Now if the wind blew rough, it made me start,
And think of my poor boy tossing about
Upon the roaring seas. And then I seemed
To feel that it was hard to take him from me
For such a little fault."
SOUTHEY.

It was a comfort to Margaret about this time, to find that her mother drew more tenderly and intimately towards her than she had ever done since the days of her childhood. She took her to her heart as a confidential friend—the post Margaret had always longed to fill, and had envied Dixon for being preferred to. Margaret took pains to respond to every call made upon her for sympathy—and they were many—even when they bore relation to trifles, which she would no more have noticed or regarded herself than the elephant would perceive the little pin at his feet, which yet he lifts carefully up at the bidding of his keeper. All unconsciously Margaret drew near to a reward.

One evening, Mr. Hale being absent, her mother began to talk to her about her brother Frederick, the very subject on which Margaret had longed to ask questions, and almost the only one on which her timidity overcame her natural openness. The more she wanted to hear about him, the less likely she was to speak.

"Oh, Margaret, it was so windy last night! It came howling down the chimney in our room! I could not sleep. I never can when there is such a terrible wind. I got into a wakeful habit when poor Frederick was at sea; and now, even if I don't waken all at once, I dream of him in some stormy sea, with great, clear, glass-green walls of waves on either side his ship, but far higher than her very masts, curling over her with that cruel, terrible white foam, like some gigantic crested serpent. It is an old dream, but it always comes back on windy nights, till I am thankful to waken, sitting straight and stiff up in bed with my terror. Poor Frederick! He is on land now, so wind can do him no harm. Though I did think it might shake down some of those tall chimneys."

"Where is Frederick now, mamma? Our letters are directed to the care of Messrs. Barbour, at Cadiz, I know; but where is he himself?"

"I can't remember the name of the place, but he is not called Hale; you must remember that, Margaret. Notice the F. D. in every corner of the letters. He has taken the name of Dickenson. I wanted him to have been called Beresford, to which he had a kind of right, but your father thought he had better not. He might be recognised, you know, if he were called by my name."

"Mamma," said Margaret, "I was at Aunt Shaw's when it all happened; and I suppose I was not old enough to be told plainly about it. But I should like to know now, if I may—if it does not give you too much pain to speak about it."

"Pain! No," replied Mrs. Hale, her cheek flushing. "Yet it is pain to think that perhaps I may never see my darling boy again. Or else he did right, Margaret. They may say what they like, but I have his own letters to show, and I'll believe him, though he is my son, sooner than any court-martial on earth. Go to my little japan cabinet, dear, and in the second left-hand drawer you will find a packet of letters."

Margaret went. There were the yellow, sea-stained letters, with the peculiar fragrance which ocean letters have: Margaret carried them back to her mother, who untied the silken string with trembling fingers, and, examining their dates, she gave them to Margaret to read, making her hurried, anxious remarks on their contents, almost before her daughter could have understood what they were.

"You see, Margaret, how from the very first he disliked Captain Reid. He was second lieutenant in the ship—the *Orion*—in which Frederick sailed the very first time. Poor little fellow, how well he looked in his midshipman's dress, with his dirk in his hand, cutting open all the newspapers with it as if it were a paper-knife! But this Mr. Reid, as he was then, seemed to take a dislike to Frederick from the very beginning. And then—stay! These are the letters he wrote on board the *Russell*. When he was appointed to her, and found his old enemy Captain Reid in command, he did mean to bear all his tyranny patiently. Look! This is the letter. Just read it, Margaret. Where is it he says—Stop—'my father may rely upon me, that I will bear with all proper patience everything that one officer and gentleman can take from another. But from my former knowledge of my present captain, I confess I look forward with apprehension to a long course of tyranny on board the *Russell*.' You see, he promises to bear patiently, and I am sure he did, for he was the sweetest-tempered boy, when he was not vexed, that could possibly be. Is that the letter in which he speaks of Captain Reid's impatience with the men, for not going through the ship's manœuvres as quickly as the *Avenger*? You see, he says that they had many new hands on board the *Russell*, while the *Avenger* had been nearly three years on the station, with nothing to do but to keep slavers off, and work her men, till they ran up and down the rigging like rats or monkeys."

Margaret slowly read the letter, half illegible through the fading of the ink. It might be—it probably was—a statement of Captain Reid's imperiousness in trifles, very much exaggerated by the narrator, who had written it while fresh and warm from the scene of altercation. Some sailors being aloft in the main-topsail rigging, the captain had ordered them to race down, threatening the hindmost with the cat-of-nine-tails. He who was the farthest on the spar, feeling the impossibility of passing his companions, and yet passionately dreading the disgrace of the flogging, threw himself desperately down to catch a rope considerably lower, failed, and fell senseless on deck. He only survived for a few hours afterwards, and the indignation of the ship's crew was at boiling point when young Hale wrote.

"But we did not receive this letter till long, long after we heard of the mutiny. Poor Fred! I dare say it was a comfort to him to write it even though he could not have known how to send it, poor fellow! And then we saw a report in the papers—that's to say, long before Fred's letter reached us—of an atrocious mutiny having broken out on board the *Russell*, and that the mutineers had remained in possession of the ship, which had gone off, it was supposed, to be a pirate; and that Captain Reid was sent adrift in a boat with some men—officers or something—whose names were all given, for they were picked up by a West-Indian steamer. Oh, Margaret! how your father and I turned sick over that list, when there was no name of Frederick Hale. We thought it must be some mistake; for poor Fred was such a fine fellow, only perhaps rather too passionate; and we hoped that the name of Carr, which was in the list, was a misprint for that of Hale—newspapers are so careless. And towards post-time the next day, papa set off to walk to Southampton to get the papers; and I could not stop at home, so I went to meet him. He was very late—much later than I thought he would have been; and I sat down under the hedge to wait for him. He came at last, his arms hanging loose down, his head sunk, and walking heavily along, as if every step was a labour and a trouble. Margaret, I see him now."

"Don't go on, mamma. I can understand it all," said Margaret, leaning up caressingly against her mother's side, and kissing her hand.

"No, you can't, Margaret. No one can who did not see him then. I could hardly lift myself up to go and meet him—everything seemed so to reel around me all at once. And when I got to him, he did not speak, or seem surprised to see me there, more than three miles from home, beside the Oldham beech-tree; but he put my arm in his, and kept stroking my hand, as if he wanted to soothe me to be very quiet under some great heavy blow; and when I trembled so all over that I could not speak, he took me in his arms, and stooped down his head on mine, and began to shake and to cry in a strange muffled, groaning voice, till I, for very fright, stood quite still, and only begged him to tell me what he had heard. And then, with his hand jerking, as if some one else moved it against his will, he gave me a wicked newspaper to read, calling our Frederick a 'traitor of the blackest dye,' 'a base, ungrateful disgrace to his profession.' Oh! I cannot tell what bad words they did not use. I took the paper in my hands as soon as I had read it—I tore it up to little bits—I tore it—oh! I believe Margaret, I tore it with my teeth. I did not cry. I could not. My cheeks were as hot as fire, and my very eyes burnt in my head. I saw your father looking grave at me. I said it was a lie, and so it was. Months after, this letter came, and you see what provocation Frederick had. It was not for himself, or his own injuries, he rebelled; but he would speak his mind to Captain Reid, and so it went on from bad to worse; and you see, most of the sailors stuck by Frederick.

"I think, Margaret," she continued, after a pause, in a weak, trembling, exhausted voice, "I am glad of it—I am prouder of Frederick standing up against injustice, than if he had been simply a good officer."

"I am sure I am," said Margaret, in a firm, decided tone. "Loyalty and obedience to wisdom and justice are fine; but it is still finer to defy arbitrary power, unjustly and cruelly used-not on behalf of ourselves, but on behalf of others more helpless."

"For all that, I wish I could see Frederick once more—just once. He was my first baby, Margaret." Mrs. Hale spoke wistfully, and almost as if apologising for the yearning, craving wish, as though it were a depreciation of her remaining child. But such an idea never crossed Margaret's mind. She was thinking how her mother's desire could be fulfilled.

"It is six or seven years ago—would they still prosecute him, mother? If he came and stood his trial, what would be the punishment? Surely, he might bring evidence of his great provocation."

"It would do no good," replied Mrs. Hale. "Some of the sailors who accompanied Frederick were taken, and there was a court-martial held on them on board the Amicia; I believed all they said in their defence, poor fellows, because it just agreed with Frederick's story—but it was of no use,—" and for the first time during the conversation Mrs. Hale began to cry; yet something possessed Margaret to force the information she foresaw, yet dreaded, from her mother.

"What happened to them, mamma?" asked she.

"They were hung at the yard-arm," said Mrs. Hale, solemnly. "And the worst was that the court, in condemning them to death, said they had suffered themselves to be led astray from their duty by their superior officers."

They were silent for a long time.

"And Frederick was in South America for several years, was he not?"

"Yes. And now he is in Spain. At Cadiz, or somewhere near it. If he comes to England he will be hung. I shall never see his face again—for if he comes to England he will be hung."

There was no comfort to be given. Mrs. Hale turned her face to the wall, and lay perfectly still in her mother's despair. Nothing could be said to console her. She took her hand out of Margaret's with a little impatient movement, as if she would fain be left alone with the recollection of her son. When Mr. Hale came in, Margaret went out, oppressed with gloom, and seeing no promise of brightness on any side of the horizon.

# CHAPTER XV—MASTERS AND MEN

"Thought fights with thought;
out springs a spark of truth
From the collision of the sword and shield."
W. S. LANDOR.

"Margaret," said her father, the next day, "we must return Mrs. Thornton's call. Your mother is not very well, and thinks she cannot walk so far; but you and I will go this afternoon."

As they went, Mr. Hale began about his wife's health, with a kind of veiled anxiety, which Margaret was glad to see awakened at last.

"Did you consult the doctor, Margaret? Did you send for him?"

"No, papa, you spoke of his coming to see me. Now I was well. But if I only knew of some good doctor, I would go this afternoon, and ask him to come, for I am sure mamma is seriously indisposed."

She put the truth thus plainly and strongly because her father had so completely shut his mind against the idea, when she had last named her fears. But now the case was changed. He answered in a despondent tone:

"Do you think she has any hidden complaint? Do you think she is really very ill? Has Dixon said anything? Oh, Margaret! I am haunted by the fear that our coming to Milton has killed her. My poor Maria!"

"Oh, papa! Don't imagine such things," said Margaret, shocked. "she is not well, that is all. Many a one is not well for a time; and with good advice gets better and stronger than ever."

"But has Dixon said anything about her?"

"No! You know Dixon enjoys making a mystery out of trifles; and she has been a little mysterious about mamma's health, which has alarmed me rather, that is all. Without any reason, I dare say. You know, papa, you said the other day I was getting fanciful."

"I hope and trust you are. But don't think of what I said then. I like you to be fanciful about your mother's health. Don't be afraid of telling me your fancies. I like to hear them, though, I dare say, I spoke as if I was annoyed. But we will ask Mrs. Thornton if she can tell us of a good doctor. We won't throw away our money on any but some one first-rate. Stay, we turn up this street." The street did not look as if it could contain any house large enough for Mrs. Thornton's habitation. Her son's presence never gave any impression as to the kind of house he lived in; but, unconsciously, Margaret had imagined that tall, massive, handsomely dressed Mrs. Thornton must live in a house of the same character as herself. Now Marlborough Street consisted of long rows of small houses, with a blank wall here and there; at least that was all they could see from the point at which they entered it.

"He told me he lived in Marlborough Street, I'm sure," said Mr. Hale, with a much perplexed air.

"Perhaps it is one of the economies he still practises, to live in a very small house. But here are plenty of people about; let me ask."

She accordingly inquired of a passer-by, and was informed that Mr. Thornton lived close to the mill, and had the factory lodge-door pointed out to her, at the end of the long dead wall they had noticed.

The lodge-door was like a common garden-door; on one side of it were great closed gates for the ingress and egress of lurries and wagons. The lodge-keeper admitted them into a great oblong yard, on one side of which were offices for the transaction of business; on the opposite, an immense many-windowed mill, whence proceeded the continual clank of machinery and the long groaning roar of the steam-engine, enough to deafen those who lived within the enclosure. Opposite to the wall, along which the street ran, on one of the narrow sides of the oblong, was a handsome stone-coped house,—blackened, to be sure, by the smoke, but with paint, windows, and steps kept scrupulously clean. It was evidently a house, which had been built some fifty or sixty years. The stone facings—the long, narrow windows, and the number of them—the flights of steps up to the front door, ascending from either side, and guarded by railing—all witnessed to its age. Margaret only wondered why people who could afford to live in so good a house, and keep it in such perfect order, did not prefer a much smaller dwelling in the country, or even some suburb; not in the continual whirl and din of the factory. Her unaccustomed ears could hardly catch her father's voice, as they stood on the steps awaiting the opening of the door. The yard, too, with the great doors in the dead wall as a boundary, was but a dismal look-out for the sitting-rooms of the house—as Margaret found when they had mounted the old-fashioned stairs, and been ushered into the drawing-room, the three windows of which went over the front door and the room on the right-hand side of the entrance. There was no one in the drawing-room. It seemed as though no one had been in it since the day when the furniture was bagged up with as much care as if the house was to be overwhelmed with lava, and discovered a thousand years hence. The walls were pink and gold; the pattern on the carpet represented bunches of flowers on a light ground, but it was carefully covered up in the centre by a linen drugget, glazed and colourless. The window-curtains were lace; each chair and sofa had its own particular veil of netting, or knitting. Great alabaster groups occupied every flat surface, safe from dust under their glass shades. In the middle of the room, right under the bagged-up chandelier, was a large circular table, with smartly-bound books arranged at regular intervals round the circumference of its polished surface, like gaily-coloured spokes of a wheel. Everything reflected light, nothing absorbed it. The whole room had a painfully spotted, spangled, speckled look about it, which impressed Margaret so unpleasantly that she was hardly conscious of the peculiar cleanliness required to keep everything so white and pure in such an atmosphere, or of the trouble that must be willingly expended to secure that effect of icy, snowy discomfort. Wherever she looked there was evidence of care and labour, but not care and labour to procure ease, to help on habits of tranquil home employment; solely to ornament, and then to preserve ornament from dirt or destruction.

They had leisure to observe, and to speak to each other in low voices, before Mrs. Thornton appeared. They were talking of what all the world might hear; but it is a common effect of such a room as this to make people speak low, as if unwilling to awaken the unused echoes.

At last Mrs. Thornton came in, rustling in handsome black silk, as was her wont; her muslins and laces rivalling, not excelling, the pure whiteness of the muslins and netting of the room. Margaret explained how it was that her mother could not accompany them to return Mrs. Thornton's call; but in her anxiety not to bring back her father's fears too vividly, she gave but a bungling account, and left the impression on Mrs. Thornton's mind that Mrs. Hale's was some temporary or fanciful fine-ladyish indisposition, which might have been put aside had there been a strong enough motive; or that if it was too severe to allow her to come out that day, the call might have been deferred. Remembering, too, the horses to her carriage, hired for her own visit to the Hales, and how Fanny had been ordered to go by Mr. Thornton, in order to pay every respect to them, Mrs. Thornton drew up slightly offended, and gave Margaret no sympathy—indeed, hardly any credit for the statement of her mother's indisposition.

"How is Mr. Thornton?" asked Mr. Hale. "I was afraid he was not well, from his hurried note yesterday."

"My son is rarely ill; and when he is, he never speaks about it, or makes it an excuse for not doing anything. He told me he could not get leisure to read with you last night, sir. He regretted it, I am sure; he values the hours spent with you."

"I am sure they are equally agreeable to me," said Mr. Hale. "It makes me feel young again to see his enjoyment and appreciation of all that is fine in classical literature."

"I have no doubt the classics are very desirable for people who have leisure. But, I confess, it was against my judgment that my son renewed his study of them. The time and place in which he lives, seem to me to require all his energy and attention. Classics may do very well for men who loiter away their lives in the country or in colleges; but Milton men ought to have their thoughts and powers absorbed in the work of to-day. At least, that is my opinion." This last clause she gave out with "the pride that apes humility."

"But, surely, if the mind is too long directed to one object only, it will get stiff and rigid, and unable to take in many interests," said Margaret.

"I do not quite understand what you mean by a mind getting stiff and rigid. Nor do I admire those whirligig characters that are full of this thing to-day, to be utterly forgetful of it in their new interest to-morrow. Having many interests does not suit the life of a Milton manufacturer. It is, or ought to be, enough for him to have one great desire, and to bring all the purposes of his life to bear on the fulfilment of that."

"And that is—?" asked Mr. Hale.

Her sallow cheek flushed, and her eye lightened, as she answered:

"To hold and maintain a high, honourable place among the merchants of his country—the men of his town. Such a place my son has earned for himself. Go where you will—I don't say in England only, but in Europe—the name of John Thornton of Milton is known and respected amongst all men of business. Of course, it is unknown in the fashionable circles," she continued, scornfully.

"Idle gentlemen and ladies are not likely to know much of a Milton manufacturer, unless he gets into parliament, or marries a lord's daughter." Both Mr. Hale and Margaret had an uneasy, ludicrous consciousness that they had never heard of this great name, until Mr. Bell had written them word that Mr. Thornton would be a good friend to have in Milton. The proud mother's world was not their world of Harley Street gentilities on the one hand, or country clergymen and Hampshire squires on the other. Margaret's face, in spite of all her endeavours to keep it simply listening in its expression told the sensitive Mrs. Thornton this feeling of hers.

"You think you never heard of this wonderful son of mine, Miss Hale. You think I'm an old woman whose ideas are bounded by Milton, and whose own crow is the whitest ever seen."

"No," said Margaret, with some spirit. "It may be true, that I was thinking I had hardly heard Mr. Thornton's name before I came to Milton. But since I have come here, I have heard enough to make me respect and admire him, and to feel how much justice and truth there is in what you have said of him."

"Who spoke to you of him?" asked Mrs. Thornton, a little mollified, yet jealous lest any one else's words should not have done him full justice. Margaret hesitated before she replied. She did not like this authoritative questioning. Mr. Hale came in, as he thought, to the rescue.

"It was what Mr. Thornton said himself, that made us know the kind of man he was. Was it not, Margaret?"

Mrs. Thornton drew herself up, and said—

"My son is not the one to tell of his own doings. May I again ask you, Miss Hale, from whose account you formed your favourable opinion of him? A mother is curious and greedy of commendation of her children, you know."

Margaret replied, "It was as much from what Mr. Thornton withheld of that which we had been told of his previous life by Mr. Bell,—it was more that than what he said, that made us all feel what reason you have to be proud of him."

"Mr. Bell! What can he know of John? He, living a lazy life in a drowsy college. But I'm obliged to you, Miss Hale. Many a missy young lady would have shrunk from giving an old woman the pleasure of hearing that her son was well spoken of."

"Why?" asked Margaret, looking straight at Mrs. Thornton, in bewilderment.

"Why! Because I suppose they might have consciences that told them how surely they were making the old mother into an advocate for them, in case they had any plans on the son's heart."

She smiled a grim smile, for she had been pleased by Margaret's frankness; and perhaps she felt that she had been asking questions too much as if she had a right to catechise. Margaret laughed outright at the notion presented to her; laughed so merrily that it grated on Mrs. Thornton's ear, as if the words that called forth that laugh, must have been utterly and entirely ludicrous. Margaret stopped her merriment as soon as she saw Mrs. Thornton's annoyed look.

"I beg your pardon, madam. But I really am very much obliged to you for exonerating me from making any plans on Mr. Thornton's heart."

"Young ladies have, before now," said Mrs. Thornton, stiffly.

"I hope Miss Thornton is well," put in Mr. Hale, desirous of changing the current of the conversation.

"She is as well as she ever is. She is not strong," replied Mrs. Thornton, shortly.

"And Mr. Thornton? I suppose I may hope to see him on Thursday?"

"I cannot answer for my son's engagements. There is some uncomfortable work going on in the town; a threatening of a strike. If so, his experience and judgment will make him much consulted by his friends. But I should think he could come on Thursday. At any rate, I am sure he will let you know if he cannot."

"A strike!" asked Margaret. "What for? What are they going to strike for?"

"For the mastership and ownership of other people's property," said Mrs. Thornton, with a fierce snort. "That is what they always strike for. If my son's work-people strike, I will only say they are a pack of ungrateful hounds. But I have no doubt they will."

"They are wanting higher wages, I suppose?" asked Mr. Hale.

"That is the face of the thing. But the truth is, they want to be masters, and make the masters into slaves on their own ground. They are always trying at it; they always have it in their minds and every five or six years, there comes a struggle between masters and men. They'll find themselves mistaken this time, I fancy,—a little out of their reckoning. If they turn out, they mayn't find it so easy to go in again. I believe, the masters have a thing or two in their heads which will teach the men not to strike again in a hurry, if they try it this time."

"Does it not make the town very rough?" asked Margaret.

"Of course it does. But surely you are not a coward, are you? Milton is not the place for cowards. I have known the time when I have had to thread my way through a crowd of white, angry men, all swearing they would have Makinson's blood as soon as he ventured to show his nose out of his factory; and he, knowing nothing of it, some one had to go and tell him, or he was a dead man, and it needed to be a woman,—so I went. And when I had got in, I could not get out. It was as much as my life was worth. So I went up to the roof, where there were stones piled ready to drop on the heads of the crowd, if they tried to force the factory doors. And I would have lifted those heavy stones, and dropped them with as good an aim as the best man there, but that I fainted with the heat I had gone through. If you live in Milton, you must learn to have a brave heart, Miss Hale."

"I would do my best," said Margaret rather pale. "I do not know whether I am brave or not till I am tried; but I am afraid I should be a coward."

"South country people are often frightened by what our Darkshire men and women only call living and struggling. But when you've been ten years among a people who are always owing their betters a grudge, and only waiting for an opportunity to pay it off, you'll know whether you are a coward or not, take my word for it."

As soon as Jane had given the signal that Mrs. Thornton was in the drawing room with the Hales, Fanny had slipped out the back way. In spite of the heat of the day, she drew up the hood of her cloak and hurried out of the lodge yard. Once on Marlborough Street, she walked away from the gate and waved down a Hansom cab. She climbed inside and called up the address to the driver through the hatch. The cab lurched away with a crack of the driver's whip. Fanny bit her lip as they passed houses and people, and sat back further in the seat in case anyone saw and recognized her. Her heart raced with excitement at the thought of soon meeting her lover. Thank goodness Mr. Hale and Margaret had shown up when they did or she would be home yet, going over details for her mother's dinner party.

For a moment she contemplated Miss Hale. She did not find her interesting at all, but her brother certainly seemed to, for he mentioned her in passing from time to time, and Fanny wondered why. She had an idea Miss Hale liked her brother, though she had pretended otherwise when they had called upon them in Crampton, but she did not think they were lovers. There was something about the way John spoke of her, however, that gave the idea he wanted them to be. Well, she doubted that would happen. Miss Hale had too high an opinion of herself to take a lover, let alone one who was a Milton manufacturer. And really, why would John want to be with a woman who lived in such a small house and who could not even play the piano?

Fanny pushed the disagreeable thought from her head as the cab pulled up at the address she had given. She fumbled in her reticule and passed up a coin to the driver, who came down from his perch and helped her alight. Nodding her thanks to him, she waited until he had driven away, then she walked past the house and turned down another street, toward the livery.

She did not think of the irony, if she was aware of it, that while she complained of living in a dirty, smoky city, that she was going to meet her lover in a place filled with horses and hay. What she thought of, instead, was the stable-hand, Luke, who had brought horses for the carriage last time she and her mother had been out. He had looked at her boldly, as if he knew what she looked like without her chemise and drawers on. That was some weeks ago and she had been seeing him as often as she could get away ever since.

Now she walked quickly into the great building and looked around. It was deserted except for the horses in their stalls. The smell of fresh hay, leather, and manure filled her nostrils and she was just thinking of leaving when behind her she heard the doors close and the bolt slip into place, and an arm caught her around her waist. She was pulled back against a man's lean body and was about to struggle when he spoke.

"You're late."

He released her and she turned around slowly, smiling her most coquettish smile. Luke grinned back and her stomach fluttered. He was quite good looking, with wavy brown hair and dark eyes, and a face perfectly formed with a nice strong chin. He was tall and broad-shouldered, well built in every way.

"Mama kept me busy all morning."

"And I'm going to keep you busy a while myself."

She liked the sound of that, but she demurred. "Not too long. I have to get back before I'm missed."

Luke was already backing her toward the ladder to the loft. He turned her round and nudged her up with a hand on her bottom. Fanny climbed, exaggerating the sway of her hips as she did so. She reached the top and began to move toward the blanket spread upon the soft hay. Luke caught her before she had taken more than two steps. He kissed her roughly, pushing his tongue into her mouth, and she whimpered as lust filled her, making her limbs weak.

He pushed her up against the wall and she held onto the coarse cotton shirt he wore, and gave up, raising her arms round his neck as he pressed himself against her.

"You wear too many clothes," he growled, grinding his crotch against her skirts, his hands cupping her ass and pulling her closer against him.

Fanny closed her eyes as he licked the hollow of her throat. "I'm a lady."

"Ay, that you are. And how would your ladyship like to be fucked today?"

"Any way you want me."

Luke nearly tore her dress, so hasty was he in removing it from her, but he was even more careless with his shirt. Fanny wished she could get out of her corset so she could feel the hard muscles of his chest against her skin. Her breasts swelled, her nipples twin points against the confining garment. Luke's mouth covered hers again as she reached for the closure of Luke's trousers. He gathered her petticoats in his hand and pushed up the material. Fanny spread her legs as wide as she could as he found her sex and caressed her before shoving two fingers into her wet slit. She swayed against him as he moved them in and out of her, his thumb flicking against the sensitive flesh that made her senses reel. Ecstasy washed over her and she clutched at him as his mouth covered hers to quiet her screams.

Luke released her and unfastened his trousers, shoving them down, his dark eyes boring into hers. Fanny's heart pounded wild beats and she ached to be filled again. His calloused hands caught the backs of her thighs and lifted her up against the wall. A moment later Fanny moaned as he pushed his long thick cock up into her.

There was nothing gentle about the way Luke drove into her, but Fanny did not care for gentleness. He made her feel alive and desirable: wanted. She clung to his powerful shoulders as tremors engulfed her body again, moaning in protest as Luke withdrew. Hot liquid splashed onto her thigh as Luke grunted, pressing heavily against her.

After a while she caught her breath and Luke lowered her to the floor, stepping back slightly. She smiled at him, happy and sated, as he helped right her petticoats then moved to pull on his shirt. Fanny struggled back into her dress and began to fasten it. His fingers caught in her hair as he moved to button it up the back and she smiled her thanks. She did her best to straighten her hair, happy that at least her cloak would cover what she could not fix. She said nothing and neither did Luke as he led her downstairs and to the door. He glanced up and down the street and then motioned her to the door. She started out but turned back to him.

"I'll come back soon."

"Until next time, then."

"Until next time."

Mr. Thornton came that evening to Mr. Hale's. He was shown up into the drawing-room, where Mr. Hale was reading aloud to his wife and daughter.

"I am come partly to bring you a note from my mother, and partly to apologise for not keeping to my time yesterday. The note contains the address you asked for; Dr. Donaldson."

"Thank you!" said Margaret, hastily, holding out her hand to take the note, for she did not wish her mother to hear that they had been making any inquiry about a doctor. She was pleased that Mr. Thornton seemed immediately to understand her feeling;

he gave her the note without another word of explanation. Mr. Hale began to talk about the strike. Mr. Thornton's face assumed a likeness to his mother's worst expression, which immediately repelled the watching Margaret.

"Yes; the fools will have a strike. Let them. It suits us well enough. But we gave them a chance. They think trade is flourishing as it was last year. We see the storm on the horizon and draw in our sails. But because we don't explain our reasons, they won't believe we're acting reasonably. We must give them line and letter for the way we choose to spend or save our money. Henderson tried a dodge with his men, out at Ashley, and failed. He rather wanted a strike; it would have suited his book well enough. So when the men came to ask for the five per cent they are claiming, he told 'em he'd think about it, and give them his answer on the pay day; knowing all the while what his answer would be, of course, but thinking he'd strengthen their conceit of their own way. However, they were too deep for him, and heard something about the bad prospects of trade. So in they came on the Friday, and drew back their claim, and now he's obliged to go on working. But we Milton masters have to-day sent in our decision. We won't advance a penny. We tell them we may have to lower wages; but can't afford to raise. So here we stand, waiting for their next attack."

"And what will that be?" asked Mr. Hale.

"I conjecture, a simultaneous strike. You will see Milton without smoke in a few days, I imagine, Miss Hale." He turned his gaze to her as he spoke, and sure enough, little spots of colour formed on her cheeks. He leaned forward in his chair as he awaited her reply.

"But why," asked she, "could you not explain what good reason you have for expecting a bad trade? I don't know whether I use the right words, but you will understand what I mean."

"Do you give your servants reasons for your expenditure, or your economy in the use of your own money? We, the owners of capital, have a right to choose what we will do with it."

"A human right," said Margaret, very low.

"I beg your pardon, I did not hear what you said."

"I would rather not repeat it," said she; "it related to a feeling which I do not think you would share."

"Won't you try me?" pleaded he; his thoughts suddenly bent upon learning what she had said. She was displeased with his pertinacity, but did not choose to affix too much importance to her words.

"I said you had a human right. I meant that there seemed no reason but religious ones, why you should not do what you like with your own."

"I know we differ in our religious opinions; but don't you give me credit for having some, though not the same as yours?"

He was speaking in a subdued voice, as if to her alone. She did not wish to be so exclusively addressed. It lent an intimacy to their conversation, as if they were lovers. His voice brushed over her skin like silk, making her breath catch and her stomach quiver. Warmth sizzled up her spine as if she had caught a fever. Flustered, she did not know how to respond at first, but she managed to regain control after a moment. She replied out in her usual tone:

"I do not think that I have any occasion to consider your special religious opinions in the affair. All I meant to say is, that there is no human law to prevent the employers from utterly wasting or throwing away all their money, if they choose; but that there are passages in the Bible which would rather imply—to me at least—that they neglected their duty as stewards if they did so. However I know so little about strikes, and rate of wages, and capital, and labour, that I had better not talk to a political economist like you."

"Nay, the more reason," said he, eagerly. "I shall only be too glad to explain to you all that may seem anomalous or mysterious to a stranger; especially at a time like this, when our doings are sure to be canvassed by every scribbler who can hold a pen."

"Thank you," she answered, coldly. "Of course, I shall apply to my father in the first instance for any information he can give me, if I get puzzled with living here amongst this strange society."

"You think it strange. Why?"

"I don't know—I suppose because, on the very face of it, I see two classes dependent on each other in every possible way, yet each evidently regarding the interests of the other as opposed to their own; I never lived in a place before where there were two sets of people always running each other down."

"Who have you heard running the masters down? I don't ask who you have heard abusing the men; for I see you persist in misunderstanding what I said the other day. But who have you heard abusing the masters?"

Margaret reddened; then smiled as she said,

"I am not fond of being catechised. I refuse to answer your question. Besides, it has nothing to do with the fact. You must take my word for it, that I have heard some people, or, it may be, only someone of the workpeople, speak as though it were the interest of the employers to keep them from acquiring money—that it would make them too independent if they had a sum in the savings' bank."

"I dare say it was that man Higgins who told you all this," said Mrs Hale. Mr. Thornton did not appear to hear what Margaret evidently did not wish him to know. But he caught it, nevertheless.

"I heard, moreover, that it was considered to the advantage of the masters to have ignorant workmen—not hedge-lawyers, as Captain Lennox used to call those men in his company who questioned and would know the reason for every order." This latter part of her sentence she addressed rather to her father than to Mr. Thornton. Who is Captain Lennox? Asked Mr. Thornton of himself, with a strange kind of displeasure, that prevented him for the moment from replying to her! Her father took up the conversation.

"You never were fond of schools, Margaret, or you would have seen and known before this, how much is being done for education in Milton."

"No!" said she, with sudden meekness. "I know I do not care enough about schools. But the knowledge and the ignorance of which I was speaking, did not relate to reading and writing,—the teaching or information one can give to a child. I am sure, that what was meant was ignorance of the wisdom that shall guide men and women. I hardly know what that is. But he—that is, my informant—spoke as if the masters would like their hands to be merely tall, large children—living in the present moment—with a blind unreasoning kind of obedience."

"In short, Miss Hale, it is very evident that your informant found a pretty ready listener to all the slander he chose to utter against the masters," said Mr. Thornton, in an offended tone, still chafing over who the mysterious Captain Lennox might be.

Margaret did not reply. She was displeased at the personal character Mr. Thornton affixed to what she had said.

Mr. Hale spoke next:

"I must confess that, although I have not become so intimately acquainted with any workmen as Margaret has, I am very much struck by the antagonism between the employer and the employed, on the very surface of things. I even gather this impression from what you yourself have from time to time said."

Mr. Thornton paused awhile before he spoke. Margaret had just left the room, and he was vexed at the state of feeling between himself and her. However, the little annoyance, by making him cooler and more thoughtful, gave a greater dignity to what he said:

"My theory is, that my interests are identical with those of my workpeople and vice-versa. Miss Hale, I know, does not like to hear men called 'hands,' so I won't use that word, though it comes most readily to my lips as the technical term, whose origin, whatever it was, dates before my time. On some future day—in some millennium—in Utopia, this unity may be brought into practice—just as I can fancy a republic the most perfect form of government."

"We will read Plato's Republic as soon as we have finished Homer."

"Well, in the Platonic year, it may fall out that we are all—men women, and children—fit for a republic: but give me a constitutional monarchy in our present state of morals and intelligence. In our infancy we require a wise despotism to govern us. Indeed, long past infancy, children and young people are the happiest under the unfailing laws of a discreet, firm authority. I agree with Miss Hale so far as to consider our people in the condition of children, while I deny that we, the masters, have anything to do with the making or keeping them so. I maintain that despotism is the best kind of government for them; so that in the hours in which I come in contact with them I must necessarily be an autocrat. I will use my best discretion—from no humbug or philanthropic feeling, of which we have had rather too much in the North—to make wise laws and come to just decisions in the conduct of my business—laws and decisions which work for my own good in the first instance—for theirs in the second; but I will neither be forced to give my reasons, nor flinch from what I have once declared to be my resolution. Let them turn out! I shall suffer as well as they: but at the end they will find I have not bated nor altered one jot."

Margaret had re-entered the room and was sitting at her work; but she did not speak. Mr. Hale answered—

"I dare say I am talking in great ignorance; but from the little I know, I should say that the masses were already passing rapidly into the troublesome stage which intervenes between childhood and manhood, in the life of the multitude as well as that of the individual. Now, the error which many parents commit in the treatment of the individual at this time is, insisting on the same unreasoning obedience as when all he had to do in the way of duty was, to obey the simple laws of 'Come when you're called' and 'Do as you're bid!' But a wise parent humours the desire for independent action, so as to become the friend and adviser when his absolute rule shall cease. If I get wrong in my reasoning, recollect, it is you who adopted the analogy."

"Very lately," said Margaret, "I heard a story of what happened in Nuremberg only three or four years ago. A rich man there lived alone in one of the immense mansions which were formerly both dwellings and warehouses. It was reported that he had a child, but no one knew of it for certain. For forty years this rumour kept rising and falling—never utterly dying away. After his death it was found to be true. He had a son—an overgrown man with the unexercised intellect of a child, whom he had kept up in that strange way, in order to save him from temptation and error. But, of course, when this great old child was turned loose into the world, every bad counsellor had power over him. He did not know good from evil. His father had made the blunder of bringing him up in ignorance and taking it for innocence; and after fourteen months of riotous living, the city authorities had to take charge of him, in order to save him from starvation. He could not even use words effectively enough to be a successful beggar."

"I used the comparison (suggested by Miss Hale) of the position of the master to that of a parent; so I ought not to complain of your turning the simile into a weapon against me. But, Mr. Hale, when you were setting up a wise parent as a model for us, you said he humoured his children in their desire for independent action. Now certainly, the time is not come for the hands to have any independent action during business hours; I hardly know what you would mean by it then. And I say, that the masters would be trenching on the independence of their hands, in a way that I, for one, should not feel justified in doing, if we interfered too much with the life they lead out of the mills. Because they labour ten hours a-day for us, I do not see that we have any right to impose leading-strings upon them for the rest of their time. I value my own independence so highly that I can fancy no degradation greater than that of having another man perpetually directing and advising and lecturing me, or even planning too closely in any way about my actions. He might be the wisest of men, or the most powerful—I should equally rebel and resent his interference I imagine this is a stronger feeling in the North of England that in the South."

"I beg your pardon, but is not that because there has been none of the equality of friendship between the adviser and advised classes? Because every man has had to stand in an unchristian and isolated position, apart from and jealous of his brother-man: constantly afraid of his rights being trenched upon?"

"I only state the fact. I am sorry to say, I have an appointment at eight o'clock, and I must just take facts as I find them to-night, without trying to account for them; which, indeed, would make no difference in determining how to act as things stand—the facts must be granted."

"But," said Margaret in a low voice, "it seems to me that it makes all the difference in the world—." Her father made a sign to her to be silent, and allow Mr. Thornton to finish what he had to say. He was already standing up and preparing to go.

"You must grant me this one point. Given a strong feeling of independence in every Darkshire man, have I any right to obtrude my views, of the manner in which he shall act, upon another (hating it as I should do most vehemently myself), merely because he has labour to sell and I capital to buy?"

"Not in the least," said Margaret, determined just to say this one thing; "not in the least because of your labour and capital positions, whatever they are, but because you are a man, dealing with a set of men over whom you have, whether you reject the use of it or not, immense power, just because your lives and your welfare are so constantly and intimately interwoven. God has made us so that we must be mutually dependent. We may ignore our own dependence, or refuse to acknowledge that others depend upon us in more respects than the payment of weekly wages; but the thing must be, nevertheless. Neither you nor any other master can help yourselves. The most proudly independent man depends on those around him for their insensible influence on his character—his life. And the most isolated of all your Darkshire Egos has dependants clinging to him on all sides; he cannot shake them off, any more than the great rock he resembles can shake off—"

"Pray don't go into similes, Margaret; you have led us off once already," said her father, smiling, yet uneasy at the thought that they were detaining Mr. Thornton against his will, which was a mistake; for he rather liked it, as long as Margaret would talk, although what she said only irritated him.

"Just tell me, Miss Hale, are you yourself ever influenced—no, that is not a fair way of putting it;—but if you are ever conscious of being influenced by others, and not by circumstances, have those others been working directly or indirectly? Have they been labouring to exhort, to enjoin, to act rightly for the sake of example, or have they been simple, true men, taking up their duty, and doing it unflinchingly, without a thought of how their actions were to make this man industrious, that man saving? Why, if I were a workman, I should be twenty times more impressed by the knowledge that my master, was honest, punctual, quick, resolute in all his doings (and hands are keener spies even than valets), than by any amount of interference, however kindly meant, with my ways of going on out of work-hours. I do not choose to think too closely on what I am myself; but, I believe, I rely on the straightforward honesty of my hands, and the open nature of their opposition, in contra-distinction to the way in which the turnout will be managed in some mills, just because they know I scorn to take a single dishonourable advantage, or do an underhand thing myself. It goes farther than a whole course of lectures on 'Honesty is the Best Policy'—life diluted into words. No, no! What the master is, that will the men be, without over-much taking thought on his part."

"That is a great admission," said Margaret, laughing. "When I see men violent and obstinate in pursuit of their rights, I may safely infer that the master is the same that he is a little ignorant of that spirit which suffereth long, and is kind, and seeketh not her own."

"You are just like all strangers who don't understand the working of our system, Miss Hale," said he, hastily. "You suppose that our men are puppets of dough, ready to be moulded into any amiable form we please. You forget we have only to do with them for less than a third of their lives; and you seem not to perceive that the duties of a manufacturer are far larger and wider than those merely of an employer of labour: we have a wide commercial character to maintain, which makes us into the great pioneers of civilisation."

"It strikes me," said Mr. Hale, smiling, "that you might pioneer a little at home. They are a rough, heathenish set of fellows, these Milton men of yours."

"They are that," replied Mr. Thornton. "Rosewater surgery won't do for them. Cromwell would have made a capital mill-owner, Miss Hale. I wish we had him to put down this strike for us."

"Cromwell is no hero of mine," said she, coldly. "But I am trying to reconcile your admiration of despotism with your respect for other men's independence of character."

He reddened at her tone. "I choose to be the unquestioned and irresponsible master of my hands, during the hours that they labour for me. But those hours past, our relation ceases; and then comes in the same respect for their independence that I myself exact."

He did not speak again for a minute, he was too much vexed. But he shook it off, and bade Mr. and Mrs. Hale good night. Then, drawing near to Margaret, he said in a lower voice—

"I spoke hastily to you once this evening, and I am afraid, rather rudely. But you know I am but an uncouth Milton manufacturer; will you forgive me?"

"Certainly," said she, smiling up in his face, the expression of which was somewhat anxious and oppressed, and hardly cleared away as he met her sweet sunny countenance, out of which all the north-wind effect of their discussion had entirely vanished. But she did not put out her hand to him, and again he felt the omission, and set it down to pride.

# CHAPTER XVI—THE SHADOW OF DEATH

"Tust in that veiled hand, which leads
None by the path that he would go;
And always be for change prepared,
For the world's law is ebb and flow."
FROM THE ARABIC.

The next afternoon Dr. Donaldson came to pay his first visit to Mrs. Hale. The mystery that Margaret hoped their late habits of intimacy had broken through, was resumed. She was excluded from the room, while Dixon was admitted. Margaret was not a ready lover, but where she loved she loved passionately, and with no small degree of jealousy.

She went into her mother's bed-room, just behind the drawing-room, and paced it up and down, while awaiting the doctor's coming out. Every now and then she stopped to listen; she fancied she heard a moan. She clenched her hands tight, and held her breath. She was sure she heard a moan. Then all was still for a few minutes more; and then there was the moving of chairs, the raised voices, all the little disturbances of leave-taking.

When she heard the door open, she went quickly out of the bed-room.

"My father is from home, Dr. Donaldson; he has to attend a pupil at this hour. May I trouble you to come into his room down stairs?"

She saw, and triumphed over all the obstacles, which Dixon threw in her way; assuming her rightful position as daughter of the house in something of the spirit of the Elder Brother, which quelled the old servant's officiousness very effectually. Margaret's conscious assumption of this unusual dignity of demeanour towards Dixon, gave her an instant's amusement in the midst of her anxiety. She knew, from the surprised expression on Dixon's face, how ridiculously grand she herself must be looking; and the idea carried her down stairs into the room; it gave her that length of oblivion from the keen sharpness of the recollection of the actual business in hand. Now, that came back, and seemed to take away her breath. It was a moment or two before she could utter a word.

But she spoke with an air of command, as she asked:—

"What is the matter with mamma? You will oblige me by telling the simple truth." Then, seeing a slight hesitation on the doctor's part, she added—

"I am the only child she has—here, I mean. My father is not sufficiently alarmed, I fear; and, therefore, if there is any serious apprehension, it must be broken to him gently. I can do this. I can nurse my mother. Pray, speak, sir; to see your face, and not be able to read it, gives me a worse dread than I trust any words of yours will justify."

"My dear young lady, your mother seems to have a most attentive and efficient servant, who is more like her friend—"

"I am her daughter, sir."

"But when I tell you she expressly desired that you might not be told—"

"I am not good or patient enough to submit to the prohibition. Besides, I am sure you are too wise—too experienced to have promised to keep the secret."

"Well," said he, half-smiling, though sadly enough, "there you are right. I did not promise. In fact, I fear, the secret will be known soon enough without my revealing it."

He paused. Margaret went very white, and compressed her lips a little more. Otherwise not a feature moved. With the quick insight into character, without which no medical man can rise to the eminence of Dr. Donaldson, he saw that she would exact the full truth; that she would know if one iota was withheld; and that the withholding would be torture more acute than the knowledge of it. He spoke two short sentences in a low voice, watching her all the time; for the pupils of her eyes dilated into a black horror and the whiteness of her complexion became livid. He ceased speaking. He waited for that look to go off,—for her gasping breath to come. Then she said:—

"I thank you most truly, sir, for your confidence. That dread has haunted me for many weeks. It is a true, real agony. My poor, poor mother!" her lips began to quiver, and he let her have the relief of tears, sure of her power of self-control to check them.

A few tears—those were all she shed, before she recollected the many questions she longed to ask.

"Will there be much suffering?"

He shook his head. "That we cannot tell. It depends on constitution; on a thousand things. But the late discoveries of medical science have given us large power of alleviation."

"My father!" said Margaret, trembling all over.

"I do not know Mr. Hale. I mean, it is difficult to give advice. But I should say, bear on, with the knowledge you have forced me to give you so abruptly, till the fact which I could not withhold has become in some degree familiar to you, so that you may, without too great an effort, be able to give what comfort you can to your father. Before then,—my visits, which, of course, I shall repeat from time to time, although I fear I can do nothing but alleviate,—a thousand little circumstances will have occurred to awaken his alarm, to deepen it—so that he will be all the better prepared.—Nay, my dear young lady—nay, my dear—I saw Mr. Thornton, and I honour your father for the sacrifice he has made, however mistaken I may believe him to be.—Well, this once, if it will please you, my dear. Only remember, when I come again, I come as a friend. And you must learn to look upon me as such, because seeing each other—getting to know each other at such times as these, is worth years of morning calls." Margaret could not speak for crying: but she wrung his hand at parting.

"That's what I call a fine girl!" thought Dr. Donaldson, when he was seated in his carriage, and had time to examine his ringed hand, which had slightly suffered from her pressure. "Who would have thought that little hand could have given such a squeeze? But the bones were well put together, and that gives immense power. What a queen she is! With her head thrown back at first, to force me into speaking the truth; and then bent so eagerly forward to listen. Poor thing! I must see she does not overstrain herself. Though it's astonishing how much those thorough-bred creatures can do and suffer. That girl's game to the back-bone. Another, who had gone that deadly colour, could never have come round without either fainting or hysterics. But she wouldn't do either—not she! And the very force of her will brought her round. Such a girl as that would win my heart, if I were thirty years younger. It's too late now. Ah! Here we are at the Archers'." So out he jumped, with thought, wisdom, experience, sympathy, and ready to attend to the calls made upon them by this family, just as if there were none other in the world.

Meanwhile, Margaret had returned into her father's study for a moment, to recover strength before going upstairs into her mother's presence.

"Oh, my God, my God! But this is terrible. How shall I bear it? Such a deadly disease! No hope! Oh, mamma, mamma, I wish I had never gone to Aunt Shaw's, and been all those precious years away from you! Poor mamma! How much she must have borne! Oh, I pray thee, my God, that her sufferings may not be too acute, too dreadful. How shall I bear to see them? How can I bear papa's agony? He must not be told yet; not all at once. It would kill him. But I won't lose another moment of my own dear, precious mother."

She ran upstairs. Dixon was not in the room. Mrs. Hale lay back in an easy chair, with a soft white shawl wrapped around her, and a becoming cap put on, in expectation of the doctor's visit. Her face had a little faint colour in it, and the very exhaustion after the examination gave it a peaceful look. Margaret was surprised to see her look so calm.

"Why, Margaret, how strange you look! What is the matter?" And then, as the idea stole into her mind of what was indeed the real state of the case, she added, as if a little displeased: "you have not been seeing Dr. Donaldson, and asking him any questions—have you, child?" Margaret did not reply—only looked wistfully towards her. Mrs. Hale became more displeased. "He would not, surely, break his word to me, and"—

"Oh yes, mamma, he did. I made him. It was I—blame me." She knelt down by her mother's side, and caught her hand—she would not let it go, though Mrs. Hale tried to pull it away. She kept kissing it, and the hot tears she shed bathed it.

"Margaret, it was very wrong of you. You knew I did not wish you to know." But, as if tired with the contest, she left her hand in Margaret's clasp, and by-and-by she returned the pressure faintly. That encouraged Margaret to speak.

"Oh, mamma! Let me be your nurse. I will learn anything Dixon can teach me. But you know I am your child, and I do think I have a right to do everything for you."

"You don't know what you are asking," said Mrs. Hale, with a shudder.

"Yes, I do. I know a great deal more than you are aware of. Let me be your nurse. Let me try, at any rate. No one has ever shall ever try so hard as I will do. It will be such a comfort, mamma."

"My poor child! Well, you shall try. Do you know, Margaret, Dixon and I thought you would quite shrink from me if you knew—"

"Dixon thought!" said Margaret, her lip curling. "Dixon could not give me credit for enough true love—for as much as herself! She thought, I suppose, that I was one of those poor sickly women who like to lie on rose leaves, and be fanned all day; Don't let Dixon's fancies come any more between you and me, mamma. Don't, please!" implored she.

"Don't be angry with Dixon," said Mrs. Hale, anxiously. Margaret recovered herself.

"No! I won't. I will try and be humble, and learn her ways, if you will only let me do all I can for you. Let me be in the first place, mother—I am greedy of that. I used to fancy you would forget me while I was away at Aunt Shaw's, and cry myself to sleep at nights with that notion in my head."

"And I used to think, how will Margaret bear our makeshift poverty after the thorough comfort and luxury in Harley Street, till I have many a time been more ashamed of your seeing our contrivances at Helstone than of any stranger finding them out."

"Oh, mamma! And I did so enjoy them. They were so much more amusing than all the jog-trot Harley Street ways. The wardrobe shelf with handles, that served as a supper-tray on grand occasions! And the old tea-chests stuffed and covered for ottomans! I think what you call the makeshift contrivances at dear Helstone were a charming part of the life there."

"I shall never see Helstone again, Margaret," said Mrs. Hale, the tears welling up into her eyes. Margaret could not reply. Mrs. Hale went on. "While I was there, I was for ever wanting to leave it. Every place seemed pleasanter. And now I shall die far away from it. I am rightly punished."

"You must not talk so," said Margaret, impatiently. "He said you might live for years. Oh, mother! we will have you back at Helstone yet."

"No never! That I must take as a just penance. But, Margaret—Frederick!" At the mention of that one word, she suddenly cried out loud, as in some sharp agony. It seemed as if the thought of him upset all her composure, destroyed the calm, overcame the exhaustion. Wild passionate cry succeeded to cry—"Frederick! Frederick! Come to me. I am dying. Little first-born child, come to me once again!"

She was in violent hysterics. Margaret went and called Dixon in terror. Dixon came in a huff, and accused Margaret of having over-excited her mother. Margaret bore all meekly, only trusting that her father might not return. In spite of her alarm, which was even greater than the occasion warranted, she obeyed all Dixon's directions promptly and well, without a word of self-justification. By so doing she mollified her accuser. They put her mother to bed, and Margaret sate by her till she fell asleep, and afterwards till Dixon beckoned her out of the room, and, with a sour face, as if doing something against the grain, she bade her drink a cup of coffee which she had prepared for her in the drawing-room, and stood over her in a commanding attitude as she did so.

"You shouldn't have been so curious, Miss, and then you wouldn't have needed to fret before your time. It would have come soon enough. And now, I suppose, you'll tell master, and a pretty household I shall have of you!"

"No, Dixon," said Margaret, sorrowfully, "I will not tell papa. He could not bear it as I can." And by way of proving how well she bore it, she burst into tears.

"Ay! I knew how it would be. Now you'll waken your mamma, just after she's gone to sleep so quietly. Miss Margaret my dear, I've had to keep it down this many a week; and though I don't pretend I can love her as you do, yet I loved her better than any other man, woman, or child—no one but Master Frederick ever came near her in my mind. Ever since Lady Beresford's maid first took me in to see her dressed out in white crape, and corn-ears, and scarlet poppies, and I ran a needle down into my finger, and broke it in, and she tore up her worked pocket-handkerchief, after they'd cut it out, and came in to wet the bandages again with lotion when she returned from the ball—where she'd been the prettiest young lady of all—I've never loved any one like her. I little thought then that I should live to see her brought so low. I don't mean no reproach to nobody. Many a one calls you pretty and handsome, and what not. Even in this smoky place, enough to blind one's eyes, the owls can see that. But you'll never be like your mother for beauty—never; not if you live to be a hundred."

"Mamma is very pretty still. Poor mamma!"

"Now don't ye set off again, or I shall give way at last" (whimpering). "You'll never stand master's coming home, and questioning, at this rate. Go out and take a walk, and come in something like. Many's the time I've longed to walk it off—the thought of what was the matter with her, and how it must all end."

"Oh, Dixon!" said Margaret, "how often I've been cross with you, not knowing what a terrible secret you had to bear!"

"Bless you, child! I like to see you showing a bit of a spirit. It's the good old Beresford blood. Why, the last Sir John but two shot his steward down, there where he stood, for just telling him that he'd racked the tenants, and he'd racked the tenants till he could get no more money off them than he could get skin off a flint."

"Well, Dixon, I won't shoot you, and I'll try not to be cross again."

"You never have. If I've said it at times, it has always been to myself, just in private, by way of making a little agreeable conversation, for there's no one here fit to talk to. And when you fire up, you're the very image of Master Frederick. I could find in my heart to put you in a passion any day, just to see his stormy look coming like a great cloud over your face. But now you go out, Miss. I'll watch over missus; and as for master, his books are company enough for him, if he should come in."

"I will go," said Margaret. She hung about Dixon for a minute or so, as if afraid and irresolute; then suddenly kissing her, she went quickly out of the room.

"Bless her!" said Dixon. "She's as sweet as a nut. There are three people I love: it's missus, Master Frederick, and her. Just them three. That's all. The rest be hanged, for I don't know what they're in the world for. Master was born, I suppose, for to marry missus. If I thought he loved her properly, I might get to love him in time. But he should ha' made a deal more on her, and not been always reading, reading, thinking, thinking. See what it has brought him to! Many a one who never reads nor thinks either, gets to be Rector, and Dean, and what not; and I dare say master might, if he'd just minded missus, and let the weary reading and thinking alone.—There she goes" (looking out of the window as she heard the front door shut). "Poor young lady! her clothes look shabby to what they did when she came to Helstone a year ago. Then she hadn't so much as a darned stocking or a cleaned pair of gloves in all her wardrobe. And now—!"

# CHAPTER XVII—WHAT IS A STRIKE?

"There are briars besetting every path,
Which call for patient care;
There is a cross in every lot,
And an earnest need for prayer."
ANON.

Margaret went out heavily and unwillingly enough. But the length of a street—yes, the air of a Milton Street—cheered her young blood before she reached her first turning. Her step grew lighter, her lip redder. She began to take notice, instead of having her thoughts turned so exclusively inward. She saw unusual loiterers in the streets: men with their hands in their pockets sauntering along; loud-laughing and loud-spoken girls clustered together, apparently excited to high spirits, and a boisterous independence of temper and behaviour. The more ill-looking of the men—the discreditable minority—hung about on the steps of the beer-houses and gin-shops, smoking, and commenting pretty freely on every passer-by. Margaret disliked the prospect of the long walk through these streets, before she came to the fields which she had planned to reach. Instead, she would go and see Bessy Higgins. It would not be so refreshing as a quiet country walk, but still it would perhaps be doing the kinder thing.

Nicholas Higgins was sitting by the fire smoking, as she went in. Bessy was rocking herself on the other side.

Nicholas took the pipe out of his mouth, and standing up, pushed his chair towards Margaret; he leant against the chimney piece in a lounging attitude, while she asked Bessy how she was.

"Hoo's rather down i' th' mouth in regard to spirits, but hoo's better in health. Hoo doesn't like this strike. Hoo's a deal too much set on peace and quietness at any price."

"This is th' third strike I've seen," said she, sighing, as if that was answer and explanation enough.

"Well, third time pays for all. See if we don't dang th' masters this time. See if they don't come, and beg us to come back at our own price. That's all. We've missed it afore time, I grant yo'; but this time we'n laid our plans desperate deep."

"Why do you strike?" asked Margaret. "Striking is leaving off work till you get your own rate of wages, is it not? You must not wonder at my ignorance; where I come from I never heard of a strike."

"I wish I were there," said Bessy, wearily. "But it's not for me to get sick and tired o' strikes. This is the last I'll see. Before it's ended I shall be in the Great City—the Holy Jerusalem."

"Hoo's so full of th' life to come, hoo cannot think of th' present. Now I, yo' see, am bound to do the best I can here. I think a bird i' th' hand is worth two i' th' bush. So them's the different views we take on th' strike question."

"But," said Margaret, "if the people struck, as you call it, where I come from, as they are mostly all field labourers, the seed would not be sown, the hay got in, the corn reaped."

"Well?" said he. He had resumed his pipe, and put his "well" in the form of an interrogation.

"Why," she went on, "what would become of the farmers."

He puffed away. "I reckon them'd have either to give up their farms, or to give fair rate of wage."

"Suppose they could not, or would not do the last; they could not give up their farms all in a minute, however much they might wish to do so; but they would have no hay, nor corn to sell that year; and where would the money come from to pay the labourers' wages the next?"

Still puffing away. At last he said:

"I know nought of your ways down South. I have heerd they're a pack of spiritless, down-trodden men; welly clemmed to death;

too much dazed wi' clemming to know when they're put upon. Now, it's not so here. We known when we're put upon; and we'en too much blood in us to stand it. We just take our hands fro' our looms, and say, 'Yo' may clem us, but yo'll not put upon us, my masters!' And be danged to 'em, they shan't this time!"

"I wish I lived down South," said Bessy.

"There's a deal to bear there," said Margaret. "There are sorrows to bear everywhere. There is very hard bodily labour to be gone through, with very little food to give strength."

"But it's out of doors," said Bessy. "And away from the endless, endless noise, and sickening heat."

"It's sometimes in heavy rain, and sometimes in bitter cold. A young person can stand it; but an old man gets racked with rheumatism, and bent and withered before his time; yet he must just work on the same, or else go to the workhouse."

"I thought yo' were so taken wi' the ways of the South country."

"So I am," said Margaret, smiling a little, as she found herself thus caught. "I only mean, Bessy, there's good and bad in everything in this world; and as you felt the bad up here, I thought it was but fair you should know the bad down there."

"And yo' say they never strike down there?" asked Nicholas, abruptly.

"No!" said Margaret; "I think they have too much sense."

"An' I think," replied he, dashing the ashes out of his pipe with so much vehemence that it broke, "it's not that they've too much sense, but that they've too little spirit."

"O, father!" said Bessy, "what have ye gained by striking? Think of that first strike when mother died—how we all had to clem— you the worst of all; and yet many a one went in every week at the same wage, till all were gone in that there was work for; and some went beggars all their lives at after."

"Ay," said he. "That there strike was badly managed. Folk got into th' management of it, as were either fools or not true men. Yo'll see, it'll be different this time."

"But all this time you've not told me what you're striking for," said Margaret, again.

"Why, yo' see, there's five or six masters who have set themselves again paying the wages they've been paying these two years past, and flourishing upon, and getting richer upon. And now they come to us, and say we're to take less. And we won't. We'll just clem them to death first; and see who'll work for 'em then. They'll have killed the goose that laid 'em the golden eggs, I reckon."

"And so you plan dying, in order to be revenged upon them!"

"No," said he, "I dunnot. I just look forward to the chance of dying at my post sooner than yield. That's what folk call fine and honourable in a soldier, and why not in a poor weaver-chap?"

"But," said Margaret, "a soldier dies in the cause of the Nation—in the cause of others."

He laughed grimly. "My lass," said he, "yo're but a young wench, but don't yo' think I can keep three people—that's Bessy, and Mary, and me—on sixteen shilling a week? Dun yo' think it's for mysel' I'm striking work at this time? It's just as much in the cause of others as yon soldier—only m'appen, the cause he dies for is just that of somebody he never clapt eyes on, nor heerd on all his born days, while I take up John Boucher's cause, as lives next door but one, wi' a sickly wife, and eight childer, none on 'em factory age; and I don't take up his cause only, though he's a poor good-for-nought, as can only manage two looms at a time, but I take up th' cause o' justice. Why are we to have less wage now, I ask, than two year ago?"

"Don't ask me," said Margaret; "I am very ignorant. Ask some of your masters. Surely they will give you a reason for it. It is not merely an arbitrary decision of theirs, come to without reason."

"Yo're just a foreigner, and nothing more," said he, contemptuously. "Much yo' know about it. Ask th' masters! They'd tell us to mind our own business, and they'd mind theirs. Our business being, yo' understand, to take the bated' wage, and be thankful, and their business to bate us down to clemming point, to swell their profits. That's what it is."

"But," said Margaret, determined not to give way, although she saw she was irritating him, "the state of trade may be such as not to enable them to give you the same remuneration."

"State o' trade! That's just a piece o' masters' humbug. It's rate o' wages I was talking of. Th' masters keep th' state o' trade in their own hands; and just walk it forward like a black bug-a-boo, to frighten naughty children with into being good. I'll tell yo' it's their part,—their cue, as some folks call it,—to beat us down, to swell their fortunes; and it's ours to stand up and fight hard,—not for ourselves alone, but for them round about us—for justice and fair play. We help to make their profits, and we ought to help spend 'em. It's not that we want their brass so much this time, as we've done many a time afore. We'n getten money laid by; and we're resolved to stand and fall together; not a man on us will go in for less wage than th' Union says is our due. So I say, 'hooray for the strike,' and let Thornton, and Slickson, and Hamper, and their set look to it!"

"Thornton!" said Margaret, her heart beating rapidly at the mention of his name, but that was likely due to her annoyance with the man. "Mr. Thornton of Marlborough Street?"

"Aye! Thornton o' Marlborough Mill, as we call him."

"He is one of the masters you are striving with, is he not? What sort of a master is he?"

"Did yo' ever see a bulldog? Set a bulldog on hind legs, and dress him up in coat and breeches, and yo'n just getten John Thornton."

"Nay," said Margaret, laughing, "I deny that. Mr. Thornton is plain enough, but he's not like a bulldog, with its short broad nose, and snarling upper lip."

"No! Not in look, I grant yo'. But let John Thornton get hold on a notion, and he'll stick to it like a bulldog; yo' might pull him away wi' a pitch-fork ere he'd leave go. He's worth fighting wi', is John Thornton. As for Slickson, I take it, some o' these days he'll wheedle his men back wi' fair promises; that they'll just get cheated out of as soon as they're in his power again. He'll work his fines well out on 'em, I'll warrant. He's as slippery as an eel, he is. He's like a cat,—as sleek, and cunning, and fierce. It'll never be an honest up and down fight wi' him, as it will be wi' Thornton. Thornton's as dour as a door-nail; an obstinate chap, every inch on him,—th' oud bulldog!"

"Poor Bessy!" said Margaret, turning round to her. "You sigh over it all. You don't like struggling and fighting as your father does, do you?"

"No!" said she, heavily. "I'm sick on it. I could have wished to have had other talk about me in my latter days, than just the clashing and clanging and clattering that has wearied a' my life long, about work and wages, and masters, and hands, and knobsticks."

"Poor wench! Latter days be farred! Thou'rt looking a sight better already for a little stir and change. Beside, I shall be a deal here to make it more lively for thee."

"Tobacco-smoke chokes me!" said she, querulously.

"Then I'll never smoke no more i' th' house!" he replied, tenderly. "But why didst thou not tell me afore, thou foolish wench?"

She did not speak for a while, and then so low that only Margaret heard her:

"I reckon, he'll want a' the comfort he can get out o' either pipe or drink afore he's done."

Her father went out of doors, evidently to finish his pipe.

Bessy said passionately,

"Now am not I a fool,—am I not, Miss?—there, I knew I ought for to keep father at home, and away fro' the folk that are always ready for to tempt a man, in time o' strike, to go drink,—and there my tongue must needs quarrel with this pipe o' his'n,—and he'll go off, I know he will,—as often as he wants to smoke—and nobody knows where it'll end. I wish I'd letten myself be choked first."

"But does your father drink?" asked Margaret.

"No—not to say drink," replied she, still in the same wild excited tone. "But what win ye have? There are days wi' you, as wi' other folk, I suppose, when yo' get up and go through th' hours, just longing for a bit of a change—a bit of a fillip, as it were. I know I ha' gone and bought a four-pounder out o' another baker's shop to common on such days, just because I sickened at the thought of going on for ever wi' the same sight in my eyes, and the same sound in my ears, and the same taste i' my mouth, and the same thought (or no thought, for that matter) in my head, day after day, for ever. I've longed for to be a man to go spreeing, even it were only a tramp to some new place in search o' work. And father—all men—have it stronger in 'em than me to get tired o' sameness and work forever. And what is 'em to do? It's little blame to them if they do go into th' gin-shop for to make their blood flow quicker, and more lively, and see things they never see at no other time—pictures, and looking-glass, and such like. But father never was a drunkard, though maybe, he's got worse for drink, now and then. Only yo' see," and now her voice took a mournful, pleading tone, "at times o' strike there's much to knock a man down, for all they start so hopefully; and where's the comfort to come fro'? He'll get angry and mad—they all do—and then they get tired out wi' being angry and mad, and maybe ha' done things in their passion they'd be glad to forget. Bless yo'r sweet pitiful face! but yo' dunnot know what a strike is yet."

"Come, Bessy," said Margaret, "I won't say you're exaggerating, because I don't know enough about it: but, perhaps, as you're not well, you're only looking on one side, and there is another and a brighter to be looked to."

"It's all well enough for yo' to say so, who have lived in pleasant green places all your life long, and never known want or care, or wickedness either, for that matter."

"Take care," said Margaret, her cheek flushing, and her eye lightening, "how you judge, Bessy. I shall go home to my mother, who is so ill—so ill, Bessy, that there's no outlet but death for her out of the prison of her great suffering; and yet I must speak cheerfully to my father, who has no notion of her real state, and to whom the knowledge must come gradually. The only person—the only one who could sympathise with me and help me—whose presence could comfort my mother more than any other earthly thing—is falsely accused—would run the risk of death if he came to see his dying mother. This I tell you—only you, Bessy. You must not mention it. No other person in Milton—hardly any other person in England knows. Have I not care? Do I not know anxiety, though I go about well-dressed, and have food enough? Oh, Bessy, God is just, and our lots are well portioned out by Him, although none but He knows the bitterness of our souls."

"I ask your pardon," replied Bessy, humbly. "Sometimes, when I've thought o' my life, and the little pleasure I've had in it, I've believed that, maybe, I was one of those doomed to die by the falling of a star from heaven; 'And the name of the star is called Wormwood; and the third part of the waters became wormwood; and men died of the waters, because they were made bitter.' One can bear pain and sorrow better if one thinks it has been prophesied long before for one: somehow, then it seems as if my pain was needed for the fulfilment; otherways it seems all sent for nothing."

"Nay, Bessy—think!" said Margaret. "God does not willingly afflict. Don't dwell so much on the prophecies, but read the clearer parts of the Bible."

"I dare say it would be wiser; but where would I hear such grand words of promise—hear tell o' anything so far different fro' this dreary world, and this town above a', as in Revelations? Many's the time I've repeated the verses in the seventh chapter to myself, just for the sound. It's as good as an organ, and as different from every day, too. No, I cannot give up Revelations. It gives me more comfort than any other book i' the Bible."

"Let me come and read you some of my favourite chapters."

"Ay," said she, greedily, "come. Father will maybe hear yo'. He's deaved wi' my talking; he says it's all nought to do with the things o' to-day, and that's his business."

"Where is your sister?"

"Gone fustian-cutting. I were loth to let her go; but somehow we must live; and th' Union can't afford us much."

"Now I must go. You have done me good, Bessy."

"I done you good!"

"Yes. I came here very sad, and rather too apt to think my own cause for grief was the only one in the world. And now I hear how you have had to bear for years, and that makes me stronger."

"Bless yo'! I thought a' the good-doing was on the side of gentle folk. I shall get proud if I think I can do good to yo'."

"You won't do it if you think about it. But you'll only puzzle yourself if you do, that's one comfort."

"Yo're not like no one I ever seed. I dunno what to make of yo'."

"Nor I of myself. Good-bye!"

Bessy stilled her rocking to gaze after her.

"I wonder if there are many folk like her down South. She's like a breath of country air, somehow. She freshens me up above a bit. Who'd ha' thought that face—as bright and as strong as the angel I dream of—could have known the sorrow she speaks on? I wonder how she'll sin. All on us must sin. I think a deal on her, for sure. But father does the like, I see. And Mary even. It's not often hoo's stirred up to notice much."

Margaret had indeed gone away in better spirits, but as she walked, her thoughts turned back to her mother, and sadness overtook her again. She was dying, and Margaret must keep the news to herself, pretend all was well when it was not, pretend cheer for her father's sake when she felt worry.

She hardly noticed the rain that had begun to fall, or where her feet led her, and it was with some shock she found herself near the gate to Marlborough Mills. How had she come there? But as her steps faltered, she decided to call on Mrs. Thornton and thank her for the name of the doctor, though the news had been unwelcome. But it was raining hard too, and she was drenched. She could continue home and send a note. No, she was here, and could deliver her thanks in person. And there was no chance of encountering Mr. Thornton, for surely he was somewhere in the mill itself. Before she could change her mind, she rang the bell and the porter let her inside the yard. Margaret hurried over to the house and knocked on the door. It opened and she was unable to contain her surprise at the sight of Mr. Thornton, his coat and cravat nowhere in sight. He seemed as taken aback as she when he greeted her.

"You're soaked through."

"I got caught in the rain. I came to call on your mother. I didn't—I didn't expect you to be here."

"Mother was obliged to be out and I've no idea where Fanny is. I had an ink bottle overturn and stain my shirt, and I have a meeting this evening."

Margaret's tongue darted out to wet her lips as she glanced at the column of skin showing from his open collar. "I don't want to trouble you. Good day, Mr. Thornton."

"Come in, Miss Hale, until the rain stops. You can dry off a little at least, before you catch cold. The servants are downstairs. You've nothing to fear from me."

Margaret drew herself up; of course she was not afraid of him. She followed him as he led her into a small room papered in red, and her gaze widened in approval. A desk and a chair occupied one side of it, and a fireplace another. Two chairs sat before it on a thick rug. It was far more welcoming in here than the drawing room had been.

"You should get out of your clothes," Mr. Thornton said, glancing back at her as he shovelled coal onto the grate and lit a fire.

"I beg your pardon?"

"I'll bring you something to wear."

He walked away before she could refuse, and she realized she was a little cold from the rain. She moved closer to the fire and removed her hat, setting it down close to the hearth and draping her shawl over the back of one chair before warming her hands. Purposeful footsteps sounded behind her and she turned to see Mr. Thornton striding back into the room, a dressing gown of deep blue in his hand. He said nothing about her still being fully dressed as he held the robe open for her, though he smiled slightly, as if mocking her. She raised her chin and turned round. Warm breath ghosted over her neck as she slid her arms into the sleeves. Shivers that had nothing to do with the chill of the rain rushed down her spine and her pulse sped up. She inhaled sharply, and the scents of tobacco, bay rum and soap teased her nostrils. Margaret trembled. It seemed far too intimate to be wearing his clothing in this cosy room, and another tremor rippled through her. She moved away from him and looked up into his face. His expression was unreadable, and she lowered her gaze from his.

"Thank you. Are you not needed at your office? I don't want to keep you. I can see your mother another time."

"I may not have London manners, Miss Hale, but I am not so uncivilized as to leave you alone when you've come to call. Why did you want to see Mother?"

Margaret tried to smile but found she could not. "I wanted to thank her for recommending Dr. Donaldson."

"I hope the news was not bad?"

To her dismay tears sprang to her eyes and she glanced away. "Thank you, Mr. Thornton. It—I..."

Mr. Thornton's hand closed around her forearm and he guided her into a chair. He left again and returned quickly with a glass of amber liquid in hand. He would not accept her quiet refusal, so she took it.

"Brandy," he said. "It will help, I promise."

She took a sip. It was sweeter than her aunt's favoured wines, and Margaret handed it back to him after another. Already it warmed her insides and when she looked at him again she felt a bit more composed. "Thank you. I'll be all right now."

He nodded and rose, placing the glass on the desk before moving back to watch her. She lowered her gaze, hoping he would not pry.

"Would you tell your father I can't make it tonight? As I said I have a meeting with some of the other owners."

Margaret looked up at him, gratified at the change of topic. "I'm sure papa will understand."

"I'm glad of it. I hate to disappoint him."

"Surely if you explained to your workers—."

"Miss Hale, this is between my employees and me. I'll thank you to remember that."

Incensed, she rose and removed the dressing gown, thrusting it toward him. "I had better go. Thank you, Mr. Thornton."

He stood as well. "It's still raining."

"I'll be fine."

"Then I wish you good day, Miss Hale."

But she made no move to gather her hat and shawl as she looked up at him. Instead, she found herself wanting to smooth the frown from his brow, and she tore her gaze away, unable to understand the feeling. She cleared her throat and glanced back at him. He was suddenly closer, and his expression had grown more intent, his eyes darting from hers to her lips and back again. Her pulse began to race again and heat flared in her stomach. "Mr. Thornton."

"John," he said, his voice a little deeper and more rough than usual. "My name is John."

Before Margaret could reply, his hands cupped her face, and his lips brushed hers. Her eyes, which had drifted closed, opened wide and she stared at him, her tongue darting out to taste where he had kissed. Mr. Thornton released a harsh breath and his lips covered hers again, moving over them with slow, lingering caresses. Margaret was too astonished to push him away. She was further stunned to realise she did not want to. She liked this kiss: from the light tingling pressure of his mouth on hers, to the soft scrape of his stubble against her face. She liked it very much! Heady excitement rushed through her veins, warming her as it spread through her limbs, her body. She began to kiss him back, answering each ardent stroke of Mr. Thornton's lips with one of her own as she sought more of the wonderful feelings.

His voice broke through the haze. "Open your lips."

She did, and his tongue slipped into her mouth as little jolts of pleasure played on her skin, beneath it. And when his tongue found hers she jumped as the unexpected sensation echoed in her nipples and between her thighs. She raised her hands to his shoulders for support, clutching at his waistcoat. "Oh," she said, when at last he raised his head slightly.

His eyes searched hers, his hands slid into the coil of hair at the back of her head and the pins fell away. His mouth captured hers again and her lips parted, eager now. The tremors in her limbs and stomach intensified and an ache began to build inside her. Margaret's fingers tightened on his shoulders when his tongue slipped from her mouth and he took her bottom lip between his, sucking gently while his hands sifted through her hair. He pushed her abruptly away, and she tilted her head back to find him gazing at her—face flushed and taut, lips compressed and eyes darker. She did not know what it meant, only that it made her pulse race faster and that she wanted to kiss him again, but when she rose up to do so he stopped her.

"You should go."

"Why?"

A sound, half growl, half groan escaped him. "Because I want to make love to you, that's why."

Margaret's heart pounded harder and she felt moisture slick her curls below. She stepped closer, placed her palm against his chest. The feel of his heart beating fast vibrated through her, echoed her own. "But we don't like each other."

"No, we don't." But he drew her close and kissed her again, this time his lips running down her throat before moving back up toward her left ear. "Margaret, tell me to stop."

It was wrong to make love with him when she disliked the way he treated his workers. When she disliked him. She knew it. But nothing had ever felt as right as being in his arms, and she wanted the same thing he wanted. She wanted him. She wanted to feel something besides the dread of coming loss, and the tight edge of grief waiting to be expelled.

"Margaret."

"I don't want to stop," she whispered. "I..."

Mr. Thornton groaned again. He unfastened her gown and pulled it over her head. A moment later he spread his dressing gown on the floor, urging Margaret back upon it as he shed his waistcoat and shirt and lowered his trousers. Margaret's eyes widened as she took in the sight of his muscular form. She lowered her gaze, but not before she had seen his penis, swollen and flushed darker than the rest. But then he was above her, between her legs, nudging them apart.

"Don't be afraid."

"I'm not."

He did not enter her right away, as she had expected, but covered her lips with his while one hand drew her skirts up and his fingers found her wetness. One eased inside her. She jumped and turned startled eyes to his as he stroked her, in and out again. He smiled back, his lips tight.

"I can't wait any more," he said, placing himself between her thighs. He entered her, his eyes meeting hers as she gasped and clutched at him, her short nails digging into his shoulders.

The look of mingled contrition and pleasure on his face made her heart catch before beating as rapidly as before. She had not expected such tenderness, and she raised a hand to his face in imitation of his earlier caress. He lowered his head and touched his lips to hers again as he withdrew a little then pushed himself back into her. His movements were slow and careful and Margaret began to relax, to enjoy. The slight pain at his entrance began to fade and be replaced by a pleasant warmth and friction. She caressed his back, marvelling at his strength as he braced himself above her, his muscles bunching beneath her hands as he thrust in and out of her.

The heat inside her built until overflowing, a tight coil of euphoria that exploded outward, washing her in pleasure. She shuddered and clung to him, now afraid and enraptured. She had barely recovered when a moment later he withdrew from her, his teeth gritted and his eyes closed. He grunted something that sounded like her name, but his voice was so low she could not be sure. Hot liquid fell onto her skin.

He moved, fumbled in his clothing and found a handkerchief. He wiped her clean and then himself, and stood, pulling his trousers back up. Margaret rose slowly to her feet before he could offer a hand, wincing as she stood.

"I'm sorry," he murmured, kissing her, a whisper of lips against hers, her cheek, and finally her brow. "I should not have."

"It's all right." She looked everywhere but at him as she drew a little away and pulled her skirt and blouse back on with shaky hands. Finger-combing her hair was even more difficult, but she managed well enough and tucked the pins back into place. She caught up her hat and secured it and her shawl and was halfway to the door when he spoke again.

"Margaret."

There was a question in his voice, and in his eyes when she turned to face him again. She had no idea what to say to him. "It's all right," she said again at last. "Good day, Mr. Thorn—Good day."

She rushed from the house and across the yard. The rain still poured down and she was grateful for the cooling it gave her still heated body and her burning face. But the rain could not wash away what had happened. She was not engaged, yet she had made love—with Mr. Thornton! A man she could not like. She was ruined. Oh! She must hurry home and pray. It would not happen again, she vowed. She had been overwrought, but her good sense had returned. It would not happen again.

# CHAPTER XVIII—LIKES AND DISLIKES

"My heart revolts within me, and two voices
Make themselves audible within my bosom."
WALLENSTEIN.

On Margaret's return home she found two letters on the table: one was a note for her mother,—the other, which had come by the post, was evidently from her Aunt Shaw—covered with foreign post-marks—thin, silvery, and rustling. She took up the other, and was examining it, when her father came in suddenly:

"So your mother is tired, and gone to bed early! I'm afraid, such a thundery day was not the best in the world for the doctor to see her. What did he say? Dixon tells me he spoke to you about her."

Margaret hesitated. Her father's looks became more grave and anxious:

"He does not think her seriously ill?"

"Not at present; she needs care, he says; he was very kind, and said he would call again, and see how his medicines worked."

"Only care—he did not recommend change of air?—he did not say this smoky town was doing her any harm, did he, Margaret?"

"No! Not a word," she replied, gravely. "He was anxious, I think."

"Doctors have that anxious manner; it's professional," said he.

Margaret saw, in her father's nervous ways, that the first impression of possible danger was made upon his mind, in spite of all his making light of what she told him. He could not forget the subject,—could not pass from it to other things; he kept recurring to it through the evening, with an unwillingness to receive even the slightest unfavourable idea, which made Margaret inexpressibly sad.

"This letter is from Aunt Shaw, papa. She has got to Naples, and finds it too hot, so she has taken apartments at Sorrento. But I don't think she likes Italy."

"He did not say anything about diet, did he?"

"It was to be nourishing, and digestible. Mamma's appetite is pretty good, I think."

"Yes! and that makes it all the more strange he should have thought of speaking about diet."

"I asked him, papa." Another pause. Then Margaret went on: "Aunt Shaw says she has sent me some coral ornaments, papa; but," added Margaret, half smiling, "she's afraid the Milton Dissenters won't appreciate them. She has got all her ideas of Dissenters from the Quakers, has not she?"

"If ever you hear or notice that your mother wishes for anything, be sure you let me know. I am so afraid she does not tell me always what she would like. Pray, see after that girl Mrs. Thornton named. If we had a good, efficient house-servant, Dixon could be constantly with her, and I'd answer for it we'd soon set her up amongst us, if care will do it. She's been very much tired of late, with the hot weather, and the difficulty of getting a servant. A little rest will put her quite to rights—eh, Margaret?"

"I hope so," said Margaret,—but so sadly, that her father took notice of it. He pinched her cheek.

"Come; if you look so pale as this, I must rouge you up a little. Take care of yourself, child, or you'll be wanting the doctor next."

But he could not settle to anything that evening. He was continually going backwards and forwards, on laborious tiptoe, to see if his wife was still asleep. Margaret's heart ached at his restlessness—his trying to stifle and strangle the hideous fear that was looming out of the dark places of his heart. He came back at last, somewhat comforted.

"She's awake now, Margaret. She quite smiled as she saw me standing by her. Just her old smile. And she says she feels refreshed, and ready for tea. Where's the note for her? She wants to see it. I'll read it to her while you make tea."

The note proved to be a formal invitation from Mrs. Thornton, to Mr., Mrs., and Miss Hale to dinner, on the twenty-first instant. Margaret was surprised to find an acceptance contemplated, after all she had learnt of sad probabilities during the day. But so it was. The idea of her husband's and daughter's going to this dinner had quite captivated Mrs. Hale's fancy, even before Margaret had heard the contents of the note. It was an event to diversify the monotony of the invalid's life; and she clung to the idea of their going, with even fretful pertinacity when Margaret objected.

"Nay, Margaret? If she wishes it, I'm sure we'll both go willingly. She never would wish it unless she felt herself really stronger— really better than we thought she was, eh, Margaret?" said Mr. Hale, anxiously, as she prepared to write the note of acceptance, the next day.

"Eh! Margaret?" questioned he, with a nervous motion of his hands. It seemed cruel to refuse him the comfort he craved for. And besides, his passionate refusal to admit the existence of fear, almost inspired Margaret herself with hope.

"I do think she is better since last night," said she. "Her eyes look brighter, and her complexion clearer."

"God bless you," said her father, earnestly. "But is it true? Yesterday was so sultry every one felt ill. It was a most unlucky day for Mr. Donaldson to see her on."

So he went away to his day's duties, now increased by the preparation of some lectures he had promised to deliver to the working people at a neighbouring Lyceum. He had chosen Ecclesiastical Architecture as his subject, rather more in accordance with his own taste and knowledge than as falling in with the character of the place or the desire for particular kinds of information among those to whom he was to lecture. And the institution itself, being in debt, was only too glad to get a gratis course from an educated and accomplished man like Mr. Hale, let the subject be what it might.

After he had gone, Margaret again attempted to write the note, but each time she dipped the pen into the ink and put it to paper, her hand faltered. To see Mr. Thornton again, and so soon! How could she face him after what they had done? After what she had allowed him to do? He must think her a wanton. She closed her eyes, but the memory played in her mind, every vivid detail, until she was warm all over and filled with shame. She could not face him, yet she knew she must, either here or at his own home. Would it not be better to have it over with rather than wait and dread the event? Trembling, she scribbled the note and hastily posted it.

"Well, mother," asked Mr. Thornton that night, "who have accepted your invitations for the twenty-first?"

"Fanny, where are the notes? The Slicksons accept, Collingbrooks accept, Stephenses accept, Browns decline. Hales—father and daughter come,—mother too great an invalid—Macphersons come, and Mr. Horsfall, and Mr. Young. I was thinking of asking the Porters, as the Browns can't come."

"Very good. Do you know, I'm really afraid Mrs. Hale is very far from well, from what Dr. Donaldson says."

"It's strange of them to accept a dinner-invitation if she's very ill," said Fanny.

"I didn't say very ill," said her brother, rather sharply. "I only said very far from well. They may not know it either." And then he suddenly remembered that, from what Dr. Donaldson had told him, Margaret, at any rate, must be aware of the exact state of the case.

"Very probably they are quite aware of what you said yesterday, John—of the great advantage it would be to them—to Mr. Hale, I mean, to be introduced to such people as the Stephenses and the Collingbrooks."

"I'm sure that motive would not influence them. No! I think I understand how it is."

"John!" said Fanny, laughing in her little, weak, nervous way. "How you profess to understand these Hales, and how you never will allow that we can know anything about them. Are they really so very different to most people one meets with?"

She did not mean to vex him; but if she had intended it, she could not have done it more thoroughly. He chafed in silence, however, not deigning to reply to her question.

"They do not seem to me out of the common way," said Mrs. Thornton. "He appears a worthy kind of man enough; rather too simple for trade—so it's perhaps as well he should have been a clergyman first, and now a teacher. She's a bit of a fine lady, with her invalidism; and as for the girl—she's the only one who puzzles me when I think about her,—which I don't often do. She seems to have a great notion of giving herself airs; and I can't make out why. I could almost fancy she thinks herself too good for her company at times. And yet they're not rich, from all I can hear they never have been."

"And she's not accomplished, mamma. She can't play."

"Go on, Fanny. What else does she want to bring her up to your standard?"

"Nay! John," said his mother, "That speech of Fanny's did no harm. I myself heard Miss Hale say she could not play. If you would let us alone, we could perhaps like her, and see her merits."

"I'm sure I never could!" murmured Fanny, protected by her mother. Mr. Thornton heard, but did not care to reply. He was walking up and down the dining-room, wishing that his mother would order candles, and allow him to set to work at either reading or writing, and so put a stop to the conversation. But he never thought of interfering in any of the small domestic regulations that Mrs. Thornton observed, in habitual remembrance of her old economies.

"Mother," said he, stopping, and bravely speaking out the truth, "I wish you would like Miss Hale."

"Why?" asked she, startled by his earnest, yet tender manner. "You're never thinking of marrying her?—a girl without a penny."

"She would never have me," said he, with a short laugh.

"No, I don't think she would," answered his mother. "She laughed in my face, when I praised her for speaking out something Mr. Bell had said in your favour. I liked the girl for doing it so frankly, for it made me sure she had no thought of you; and the next minute she vexed me so by seeming to think——Well, never mind! Only you're right in saying she's too good an opinion of herself to think of you. The saucy jade! I should like to know where she'd find a better!" If these words hurt her son, the dusky light prevented him from betraying any emotion. In a minute he came up quite cheerfully to his mother, and putting one hand lightly on her shoulder, said:

"Well, as I'm just as much convinced of the truth of what you have been saying as you can be; and as I have no thought or expectation of ever asking her to be my wife, you'll believe me for the future that I'm quite disinterested in speaking about her. I foresee trouble for that girl—perhaps want of motherly care—and I only wish you to be ready to be a friend to her, in case she needs one. Now, Fanny," said he, "I trust you have delicacy enough to understand, that it is as great an injury to Miss Hale as to me—in fact, she would think it a greater—to suppose that I have any reason, more than I now give, for begging you and my mother to show her every kindly attention."

"I cannot forgive her her pride," said his mother; "I will befriend her, if there is need, for your asking, John. I would befriend Jezebel herself if you asked me. But this girl, who turns up her nose at us all—who turns up her nose at you——"

"Nay, mother; I have never yet put myself, and I mean never to put myself, within reach of her contempt."

"Contempt, indeed!"—(One of Mrs. Thornton's expressive snorts.)—"Don't go on speaking of Miss Hale, John, if I've to be kind to her. When I'm with her, I don't know if I like or dislike her most; but when I think of her, and hear you talk of her, I hate her. I can see she's given herself airs to you as well as if you'd told me out."

"And if she has," said he—and then he paused for a moment—then went on: "I'm not a lad, to be cowed by a proud look from a woman, or to care for her misunderstanding me and my position. I can laugh at it!"

He said the words bravely, goaded by guilt over taking where he had no right to take, and feeling that Margaret's opinion of him was now, if possible, lower than before. But he felt himself stir and begin to harden, thinking of her beneath him, her tight, wet heat clasping him. He ground his teeth, willing his body to behave.

"To be sure! And at her too, with her fine notions and haughty tosses!"

"I only wonder why you talk so much about her, then," said Fanny. "I'm sure, I'm tired enough of the subject."

"Well!" said her brother, with a shade of bitterness. "Suppose we find some more agreeable subject. What do you say to a strike, by way of something pleasant to talk about?"

"Have the hands actually turned out?" asked Mrs. Thornton, with vivid interest.

"Hamper's men are actually out. Mine are working out their week, through fear of being prosecuted for breach of contract. I'd have had every one of them up and punished for it, that left his work before his time was out."

"The law expenses would have been more than the hands them selves were worth—a set of ungrateful naughts!" said his mother.

"To be sure. But I'd have shown them how I keep my word, and how I mean them to keep theirs. They know me by this time. Slickson's men are off—pretty certain he won't spend money in getting them punished. We're in for a turn-out, mother."

"I hope there are not many orders in hand?"

"Of course there are. They know that well enough. But they don't quite understand all, though they think they do."

"What do you mean, John?"

Candles had been brought, and Fanny had taken up her interminable piece of worsted-work, over which she was yawning; throwing herself back in her chair, from time to time, to gaze at vacancy, and think of nothing at her ease.

"Why," said he, "the Americans are getting their yarns so into the general market, that our only chance is producing them at a lower rate. If we can't, we may shut up shop at once, and hands and masters go alike on tramp. Yet these fools go back to the prices paid three years ago—nay, some of their leaders quote Dickinson's prices now—though they know as well as we do that, what with fines pressed out of their wages as no honourable man would extort them, and other ways which I for one would scorn to use, the real rate of wage paid at Dickinson's is less than at ours. Upon my word, mother, I wish the old combination-laws were in force. It is too bad to find out that fools—ignorant wayward men like these—just by uniting their weak silly heads, are to rule over the fortunes of those who bring all the wisdom that knowledge and experience, and often painful thought and anxiety, can give. The next thing will be—indeed, we're all but come to it now—that we shall have to go and ask—stand hat in hand—and humbly ask the secretary of the Spinner' Union to be so kind as to furnish us with labour at their own price. That's what they want—they, who haven't the sense to see that, if we don't get a fair share of the profits to compensate us for our wear and tear here in England, we can move off to some other country; and that, what with home and foreign competition, we are none of us likely to make above a fair share, and may be thankful enough if we can get that, in an average number of years."

"Can't you get hands from Ireland? I wouldn't keep these fellows a day. I'd teach them that I was master, and could employ what servants I liked."

"Yes! To be sure, I can; and I will, too, if they go on long. It will be trouble and expense, and I fear there will be some danger; but I will do it, rather than give in."

"If there is to be all this extra expense, I'm sorry we're giving a dinner just now."

"So am I,—not because of the expense, but because I shall have much to think about, and many unexpected calls on my time. But we must have had Mr. Horsfall, and he does not stay in Milton long. And as for the others, we owe them dinners, and it's all one trouble."

He kept on with his restless walk—not speaking any more, but drawing a deep breath from time to time, as if endeavouring to throw off some annoying thought. Fanny asked her mother numerous small questions, all having nothing to do with the subject, which a wiser person would have perceived was occupying her attention. Consequently, she received many short answers. She was not sorry when, at ten o'clock, the servants filed in to prayers. These her mother always read,—first reading a chapter. They were now working steadily through the Old Testament. When prayers were ended, and his mother had wished him goodnight, with that long steady look of hers which conveyed no expression of the tenderness that was in her heart, but yet had the intensity of a blessing, Mr. Thornton continued his walk. All his business plans had received a check, a sudden pull-up, from this approaching turn-out. The forethought of many anxious hours was thrown away, utterly wasted by their insane folly, which would injure themselves even more than him, though no one could set any limit to the mischief they were doing. And these were the men who thought themselves fitted to direct the masters in the disposal of their capital! Hamper had said, only this very day, that if he were ruined by the strike, he would start life again, comforted by the conviction that those who brought it on were in a worse predicament than he himself,—for he had head as well as hands, while they had only hands; and if they drove away their market, they could not follow it, nor turn to anything else. But this thought was no consolation to Mr. Thornton. It might be that revenge gave him no pleasure; it might be that he valued the position he had earned with the sweat of his brow, so much that he keenly felt its being endangered by the ignorance or folly of others,—so keenly that he had no thoughts to spare for what would be the consequences of their conduct to themselves. He paced up and down, setting his teeth a little now and then. At last it struck two. The candles were flickering in their sockets. He lighted his own, muttering to himself:

"Once for all, they shall know whom they have got to deal with. I can give them a fortnight,—no more. If they don't see their madness before the end of that time, I must have hands from Ireland. I believe it's Slickson's doing,—confound him and his dodges! He thought he was overstocked; so he seemed to yield at first, when the deputation came to him,—and of course, he only confirmed them in their folly, as he meant to do. That's where it spread from."

# About the Author

Brenna Chase grew up in Florida, but has since lived in several states and the former West Germany. She holds a bachelor's degree in history and a minor in English from Cameron University in Oklahoma. An avid reader of romance novels, she finally decided to try writing them. When she isn't daydreaming about dashing heroes, she enjoys traveling, watching classic movies, curling up with a good book, and knitting. Brenna currently lives in the Midwest with her husband and two daughters.

She can be found on the web at *brennachase.com*.

# A Sneak Peek from Crimson Romance
## (From *Mansfield Park: The Wild and Wanton Edition, Volume 1* by Nina Mitchell and Jane Austen)

Portsmouth, 18___

It had been presumed by many that Mrs. Franny Price, formerly Miss Frances Ward, would find scarce comfort in the three sparsely furnished rooms she found herself occupying and sharing with Lieutenant Mr. Price following a hasty marriage about which it could be said the union was less cause for celebration than evidence of retribution of the sort that endures one's lifetime; the lifetime of the former Miss Frances Ward in particular. But while the dwelling was absent of adequate light and lacking the sort of comforts to which Mrs. Price had grown accustomed in her upbringing, it contained a warm and well-tended hearth—considered by many to be the true heart of a home—attended to solely by Mrs. Price, who had not only learnt to keep it burning; but to procure, without the sort of human assistance she had once depended upon in her youth, the source of its heat as well. It was customary for Mrs. Price to be found seated quite comfortably before the hearth, her firstborn swaddled at her breast, herself in contemplation of the life she had chosen for herself—a life she might have never imagined a mere twelvemonth prior—whilst her handsome husband snored softly under the bedcovers a few short paces away.

Mrs. Price found perhaps the majority of her comfort in watching her husband sleep, for it was in the quiet hours of the night that he held exceeding appeal. During daylight she found him to be like the hearth, in constant need of tending with tea to be made or toast or a wash, and it was during his daily demands that she found herself most doubtful of the decision that was beyond her abilities to change. It was during the moments of the day when Mr. Price demanded his boots polished that her thoughts would wander to her sister Maria's favourable match to Sir Thomas Bertram with a man of his own to polish his gentleman's boots. It was when Mr. Price's chamber pot needed a wash that even her sister Mrs. Norris's union with the stodgy Rev. Mr. Norris and his meager annual allowance, was imagined to be quite blissful. It was in the solitude of the darkness that Mrs. Price remembered her youthful conviction that her match would be one of the heart; and it was this memory that softened her feelings towards Mr. Price as she set the babe in his cradle and moved quietly under the bed covers to settle herself in the warmth of her husband's embrace.

Mr. Price's chest charmed her in every manner by which a lady could find herself charmed. Though she may also have admired his form in his tight breeches, it was his wide expanse of chest that she found herself dreaming of before she had known him as a wife knows a husband. It was his chest that she had first pressed her bosom against, his heart beating wildly beneath it, as she held tightly to his strong shoulders, her face buried in his neck, in stolen moments spent in the darkened corners of the library before she became Mrs. Price, moments when she delighted in the insistent prodding of his arousal against her belly and looked forward without question to the delicious mystery of finally feeling his manhood inside her after matrimony.

She delicately traced her fingertips across his chest as he breathed softly in slumber, and found herself once more aroused by the ripple of muscle beneath her touch. She reached for him under the bed linens and smiled at his quick attentiveness to her nearness even as he slept. She considered taking him in her mouth as he'd shewn her after returning from a sea excursion. A man of the sea is known to arrive home with many treasures to bequeath! The realisation that she had come to fancy bestowing such an act nearly as much as he took joy in being its recipient had surprized her and she had become a most eager pupil. But this night she had set her mind that she was ready to take pleasure in him as her husband once again. The skin of her belly had begun to tighten since birthing young William and the soreness between her legs had ceased, yearning once again to feel the heat and thrust of him inside her depths. She lifted her night-dress and slowly straddled him.

"Mrs. Price!" exclaimed he, now fully awake, his grey eyes gazing appreciatively at her form hovering above him.

"Quiet, Mr. Price! If the babe wakes you will soon find yourself alone under these quilts."

"It looks to me as though you are wanting to make another babe."

She imagined him winking in the darkness and smiled as he lifted her night-dress over her head; and a soft moan escaped her as his strong, calloused hands held her hips and guided her over the length of his arousal. She gasped when he held her there, slowly rubbing her most sensitive area with the tip of his manhood. She had to bite her bottom lip to stop from calling out his given name when he finally entered her—tenderly at first—before filling her fully.

"You have made me a happy man, Mrs. Price, and I do love you so," he said as he raised himself onto his elbows to better reach her hardened nipples with his tongue. The movement drove him farther into her depths and the friction against her sensitive parts increased and drove her deeper into their passion as she awaited her release. She ran her fingers through his golden curls and pulled him towards her.

His mouth found hers and his tongue brushed gently against her bottom lip. He pushed himself up to meet her as she rocked over him with more force, both of them surrendering at the same time, joyous tears of release streaming down her cheeks. She collapsed onto his exquisite chest. He stroked her back gently as she lay over him, not wanting yet to release him from inside her.

"Do you think we made another child?" whispered she as she felt his breathing slow and thought him to be asleep. She was not certain it was a question she wanted answered.

Her husband's hand brushed the hair from her cheek. "Perhaps a girl this time," said he.

She shook her head and sat up to look at him. "Only sons, Mr. Price. As my husband, I ask that you give me only sons." She did not offer more and felt him begin to harden again inside her as he gently pulled her beneath him so that he could rise above her, always willing to tend to her wishes in the darkness.

In the mood for more Crimson Romance?
Check out *Room with a View: The Wild and Wanton Edition* by
Coco Rousseau and E.M. Forster at *CrimsonRomance.com.*

Printed in Great Britain
by Amazon.co.uk, Ltd.,
Marston Gate.